THE TASTE OF TEMPTATION

"You are a very tempting woman, Rachel Hammond," Clint told her, putting her from him.

She was puzzled. She didn't know why he'd stopped kissing her. She wanted to go back into his arms and stay there, but his next words stopped her.

"But you are the preacher's daughter."

His words jarred her back to reality.

"Oh—"

A mixture of conflicting emotions assailed Rachel as she stood there, momentarily lost in the confusion of the battle between her emotions and logic.

Clint knew they both needed a distraction, so he went to his saddlebags and rifled through them.

"Since we're going to be stuck here a while longer, you want to have a little fun?" he asked her as he finally found what he'd been looking for.

"I thought we were having fun—" she said, feeling a little wild as she said it.

Clint bit back a groan at her remark. In her innocence, she was the perfect seductress. He could only imagine what she would have been like if she'd known what she was doing and the effect she had on him.

BOBBI SMITH

DEFIANT

LEISURE BOOKS NEW YORK CITY

A LEISURE BOOK®

April 2006

Published by

Dorchester Publishing Co., Inc.
200 Madison Avenue
New York, NY 10016

ISBN 0-8439-5664-X

The name "Leisure Books" and the stylized "L" with design are trademarks of Dorchester Publishing Co., Inc.

Printed in the United States of America.

Chapter One

It was getting late as twenty-five-year-old Clint Williams walked out on the front porch of his family's ranch house to find his father sitting alone on the top step, staring off into the night.

"I thought I might find you here," Clint said as he sat down next to him. He'd noticed how quiet his father had been during dinner and wondered what was troubling him.

"I needed some time to think," Frank Williams answered, his tone worried.

"What's wrong?"

"This Tucker Gang I've been tracking is trouble—bad trouble," he told him.

"I've seen the wanted posters. How close are you to catching them?"

"I've been on their trail for several months now, and I think I'm finally closing in."

1

"Good." Clint knew what a fine Texas Ranger his father was. Frank Williams was the reason Clint had become a Ranger, too. Clint knew that if anyone could catch this gang, it would be his father.

Frank went on, "These men are the most cold-blooded killers I've ever seen. There's got to be more going on here than just robbery. Glen Tucker and Ax Hansen seem to be the leaders, but I'm beginning to think they're not really running things. I've got a few ideas, but nothing I can prove—yet."

"You'll do it. You'll stop them."

Frank looked over at his eldest son. "I have to. Too many innocent people have died."

They shared a look of understanding.

"Well, I'm just glad we both happened to show up here at the ranch at the same time." Clint said. "It's good to have this time together. How long can you stay on?"

"One more day, unless I get word that something new has happened. What about you?"

"I have to ride out first thing in the morning," Clint answered.

"It's always good to get home, even if only for a short while." Frank loved his family and their ranch, the Lazy W. He planned to retire there eventually, but not yet—not while evil men like the Tucker Gang were still on the loose. "Your brother's keeping things running smooth around here."

"Yes, he is," Clint agreed, proud of Jason.

"What are you two doing, sitting out here in the dark?" Kate asked as she came outside to find her husband and son deep in conversation.

"Just relaxing in the peace and quiet," Frank told her. "Come on and join us." She was the love of his life, and he missed her when he was away.

Kate sat down between them. She loved having her whole family together. It didn't happen often, so she treasured every minute. It was always hard for her to watch Frank ride off on his assignments, for she never knew if he'd come home again, and since Clint had followed in his father's footsteps and joined the Rangers, she had him to worry about, too.

Kate looked over at her handsome eldest son with a mother's love shining in her eyes. Many times, she'd wanted to try to stop her husband and son from leaving, knowing the danger they faced, but they were Williams men, and once they were determined to do something, they did it. She prayed a lot while they were gone and always gave thanks when they made it home safely.

"Are you sure you have to leave tomorrow?" she asked Clint.

"Yes, I have to report to Captain Meyers by Wednesday," he told her.

"Well, let's hope your captain gives you an easy assignment this time."

"I'll tell him you said so," Clint chuckled, "but I don't think he's got many 'easy' assignments."

Jason returned from the stable then to join

them, and they spent the next hour enjoying each other's company before calling it a night.

It was a few hours before sunup, and the outlaw gang was ready to take action.

The boss had sent word to Tuck that Frank Williams was back home at the Lazy W. Williams was the Ranger who'd been tracking the gang so relentlessly, and the boss believed he was getting too close to them. That was why he wanted him taken care of—now.

The gang had ridden hard to get to the ranch while Williams was still there. They'd reached the Lazy W late that night and had hidden out to plan their strategy.

And now it was time.

They were going to strike with lethal force and take care of Ranger Williams once and for all.

It didn't matter that the Ranger's family was there with him. The boss wanted Williams dead, and what the boss wanted, the boss got. If any of Williams' family happened to get in the way, they'd be killed, too.

"Tuck—when do we make our move?" Ax Hansen asked Glen Tucker in a quiet voice as they crouched with the other men in the brush on the hillside overlooking the house and outbuildings.

"Now." Tuck knew the men were anxious to set their plan in motion. "His wife and son should be the only ones in the main house with him. There are a few ranch hands in the bunkhouse."

"Isn't one of his sons a Ranger, too?"

"Yeah, but I don't think he's around, and even if he is, it won't matter. They're not expecting us. We're in control here. We'll set the fires and be waiting for them. Just make sure you shoot straight and fast when they come running out."

Tuck knew what a formidable foe Frank Williams was. Williams's reputation among the Rangers was almost legendary, and if Tuck had his way, Williams really was going to be a legend after this night. A dead one.

Tuck turned his attention back down to the buildings, studying the lay of the land. He told the other gunmen, "Ax, you and Rick take the bunkhouse. Walt, you and John come with me. We'll take the main house."

"What about the stable? Do you want us to burn it down, too?" Ax asked.

"Don't worry about the stable. Nobody's out there," he said. "Now go. I'll signal you when we're in position."

The killers started down toward the buildings with only one thing on their minds: murder.

When they were ready, Tuck gave the signal. They set fire to the main house and the bunkhouse, then ran to position themselves so they would have full coverage of all the doors and windows. The moment people ran from the burning buildings, they would be easily gunned down.

It didn't take long for the killing to begin.

Tuck and the others were set when they heard the shouts of horror coming from those trapped inside. They watched as the doors were thrown open and the Williams family and their hired hands came rushing out of the buildings.

Tuck noticed that a few of the men had been smart enough to grab their guns as they'd fled, but that didn't matter. Silhouetted against the blaze as they were, they made easy targets.

And the gang took full advantage.

Tuck recognized Frank Williams and took careful aim. His shots rang out with deadly accuracy, killing the Ranger instantly. Not even the screams of the horrified woman running to her fallen husband's side deterred the gunmen. They all kept firing, and the woman was shot down in cold blood, too.

Tuck was surprised when two more men came running out of the main house and tried to go to her aid. He'd expected only one son to be there, but that didn't matter. If this was Frank Williams's other son, that meant they would be killing two Rangers tonight instead of just one.

The thought made Tuck smile.

The gang kept firing, driving the two men away from the woman's body with their unending barrage. The two made a run for the stable. They had their guns and tried to return fire as they ran, but Tuck and Ax took careful aim and brought them both down.

The gunmen continued to shoot at the emerging ranch hands until they all lay unmoving on the ground.

Then the gunfire ceased.

The scene before Tuck and Ax was eerily quiet.

The only sounds in the night were the deadly roars of the fires.

Tuck and Ax carefully made their way down to the front of the burning house to check on Frank Williams. They had to make sure the Ranger wouldn't be causing them any more trouble. The other gunmen followed.

Ax knelt down and turned Frank Williams over to get a look at him. "Tuck, he's dead."

"Good shooting, boys," Tuck complimented them. "The boss is gonna be real proud of us, Ax."

"Too bad he couldn't be here to see it." Ax smiled at Tuck as he stood up.

They took one last look at the deadly havoc they'd wreaked and felt satisfied with their work. The flames cast a hellish red glow on everything and everyone.

"We'd better get out of here. It's almost day-light," Tuck told the men.

"Do you want to split up? The Rangers are going to be tracking us." Ax didn't want to take any chances.

"Yeah, you stay with me. Walt, Rick, and John, you ride out together. We'll arrange to meet up later." They had ways of staying in touch, so he wasn't worried about getting the word out when the time was right.

"Sounds good. Let's go."

The outlaw gang returned to where they'd left their horses and mounted up.

It was over.

They rode quickly away, wanting to put distance between themselves and the ranch as fast as they could.

Tony Villigram and Paul Taylor, two of the Lazy W's ranch hands, had been working the herd and had camped out overnight. They'd been sleeping soundly until their horses began to stir and the herd grew restless in the predawn hours. Tony got up to take a look around. It was then that he saw the strange glow in the night sky in the direction of the house.

"Paul! Wake up! We got trouble!"

They broke camp and rode as quickly as they could back to the ranch house. With every mile they covered, they realized more and more the seriousness of what they were about to face. It was light when they finally topped the low rise that overlooked the buildings and discovered the death and devastation below. The large ranch house and bunkhouse were smoldering ruins, and many bodies lay motionless scattered on the ground. Tony and Paul raced down to the scene.

"Who could have done this?" Tony was horrified by the carnage.

"It wasn't Comanche."

They knew the signs of an Indian raid, and this definitely hadn't been one.

Tony and Paul had worked for the Williams family for many years and considered them friends. It was a gruesome and heartbreaking task to search for survivors. They found Frank and Kate both dead, and all the ranch hands, too. Then they spotted Clint and Jason by the stable, which was still intact, and they ran to check on them.

"Jason's dead," Paul called out to Tony.

"Oh, my God! Clint's alive!" Tony shouted when he discovered Clint was still breathing.

Paul rushed to Clint's side and saw how badly he'd been injured. It was a miracle he'd survived. He'd been shot several times and had lost a lot of blood.

"We gotta get him over to the Anderson's place. It's closer than trying to take him into town," Paul said. "As bad as he is, I don't think he could make it to town."

They quickly did what they could to bind Clint's wounds, then rushed to hitch up the buckboard. With great care, they lifted Clint into the back and cushioned him there with horse blankets.

"What should we do about the others?" Paul worried.

"You go ahead and take Clint to the Circle A," Tony told Paul. "I'll stay here and bury them."

"What should I tell the Andersons about what happened?"

"I don't know." Tony paused and looked around at the carnage again. "Whoever did this wanted everybody dead."

"Do you think it was somebody who was after Frank?"

"Clint will know. He'll tell us—"

"If he makes it."

They shared a sad, knowing look as Paul

climbed up on the driver's bench and took up the reins.

"Keep what happened quiet until we have a chance to talk to the sheriff. We don't know who did this, and the killers might still be around and try to come after Clint again if they learn he's alive."

"All right. As soon as I get Clint over to the Circle A, I'll ride for town and get the doc and Sheriff Nelson."

"I'll meet you at the ranch."

Tony stood unmoving, watching Paul drive away until he had disappeared from sight. Then, slowly and with a heavy heart, he turned back to the task that awaited him.

Chapter Two

Three Days Later

Clint's consciousness returned slowly, and with it came deep and vicious pain. It tore at him with savage intensity, and a primal groan escaped him.

Doc Martin had been dozing in the chair across the room. At the sound of Clint's moan, he came awake instantly. He'd been keeping vigil at his patient's side since coming out to the Anderson ranch, and he was relieved to find him stirring. Until this moment, he'd held little hope Clint was going to make it. His wounds were very serious, and he'd lost a lot of blood.

Clint groaned again and struggled to open his eyes.

"Easy, Clint," Doc Martin said, trying to calm him.

At the sound of the vaguely familiar voice, Clint quieted for a moment. In his pain-wracked confusion, he tried to remember to whom the voice belonged, but he was lost. He had no concept of where he was or why he was there.

A sudden sense of panic threatened, and Clint opened his eyes in terror as visions of violence and death came to him. He fought to sit up, but found that someone was pressing him down. He struggled against the restraint, wanting to break free. He needed to escape. He had to get away—

"Lie back, Clint." Doc Martin was surprised by his patient's surge of strength. After what Clint had been through, he'd expected him to be too weak to move.

"No! I have to—"

"It's over, Clint."

"It's over—?" Clint finally looked up and saw that it was Doc Martin holding him down. Then the images of the burning house and the unceasing gunfire returned to torture him. "No!"

"There's nothing you can do."

What little strength he had failed him, and Clint collapsed back on the bed. He closed his eyes again and locked his jaw against the pain and weakness that overwhelmed him. "Where am I—?"

"You're at the Circle A. Two of your men found you and brought you here," Doc Martin explained.

"My family—where's my family?" Clint looked up at the doctor, frowning as the horrifying memory of watching his father and mother being gunned down played in his mind.

"Clint, I . . ." Doc Martin heard the desperation

in his patient's agonized question and wished there were some way he could ease his pain, but he knew there wasn't.

"Tell me!" Clint ground out, frantic to know what had happened to his family. He grasped the physician's forearm with what strength he could muster and demanded, "Tell me now!"

Their gazes met, and before Doc Martin could respond, Clint knew the answer.

"They're dead, aren't they?" he asked, remembering even more of what had happened that hellish night.

Doc Martin was filled with sorrow as he told him, "You were the only one who made it."

"When did it happen? How long ago?"

"This is the third day."

"Did Sheriff Nelson go after the killers? Did he catch them?" Clint struggled to sit up, wanting to take action, *needing* to take action.

"Sheriff Nelson got a posse together, and they started tracking them that same day. We sent word to the Texas Rangers, too. Captain Meyers showed up here late yesterday. After checking to see how you were, he headed out after the posse. We haven't heard back from either of them yet."

Clint collapsed back on the bed and stared sightlessly at the ceiling. His breathing was ragged as he struggled for control. He was glad Sheriff Nelson and Captain Meyers were tracking the killers, but he wished he were the one who was leading the hunt. Savage emotional pain stabbed at him, and he knew he needed to be left alone.

"Get out," he told the doctor in a voice completely devoid of emotion.

Doc Martin knew those two words were more powerful than any rage Clint might have expressed. He got up and quietly left the bedroom, closing the door behind him to give his patient the privacy he needed. He made his way downstairs to let the Andersons know Clint had finally regained consciousness.

Mary Anderson heard the doctor coming down the steps and hurried over to the foot of the staircase. These last few days had been tense, and she feared the worst as she saw Doc Martin's strange expression.

"How is he?" Mary asked cautiously, fearful of what he was about to tell her. "Is he—?"

For the first time since he'd come out to the ranch to take care of Clint, Doc Martin managed to smile at her. "Clint's regained consciousness."

"What?" She was shocked.

"He's awake, and he's even talking a little."

"Oh, thank God." Relief flooded through her. She and her husband, Joe, were longtime friends of the Williams family, and they'd been horrified by what had taken place. "Clint's going to make it?"

"I don't know yet. As weak as he is, it's too soon to tell," the doctor answered honestly. "He did have three bullets in him, so just keep praying no fever sets in."

"We will," Mary promised. "Is there anything I can do to help, now that he's awake?"

"We can try to get some broth in him."

14

"I'll heat some up right away. You're going to stay on for a while longer, aren't you?"

"I'll stay for at least another day," he answered. As grievous as Clint's wounds were, he knew it wasn't safe to leave him just yet. If any kind of medical emergency came up in town, his wife knew where to find him.

"Good. I'm worried about him."

"We all are. I just hope Sheriff Nelson and the posse can track down the killers who did this. These were all good people—the Williams family and their hired hands. They didn't deserve to be slaughtered this way."

"Do you think we did the right thing, telling everybody that Clint had been killed, too?" she asked, worried about the deception they'd created.

"Yes. Other than the two hands from the Lazy W and your people, only Sheriff Nelson and Captain Meyers know the truth about Clint. They both agreed that letting everybody else think he was dead was the best way to keep him safe for now."

"And we're going to make sure Clint stays safe while he recovers."

"It's not going to be easy for him."

"No. It's not. Things will never be the same again."

They both looked up the staircase at the closed bedroom door and understood the torment Clint was facing.

Clint lay unmoving in the bed, staring at the ceiling, his thoughts dark and troubled.

Guilt filled him.

Why had his entire family been killed along with the ranch hands, yet he alone had survived?

Who had done this to them—and why?

Had his father had enemies who hated him so much that they would kill anyone and everyone at the Lazy W just to get even with him?

Clint remembered the conversation he'd had with his father about the outlaws he'd been tracking. His father had said Glen Tucker and Ax Hansen were involved, and possibly an unknown leader. He'd told him they were the most cold-blooded killers he'd ever seen, and Clint wondered if they were the ones who'd done this.

As he thought of the killers, he had a vague memory of hearing two men talking after he'd been shot. He'd been slipping in and out of consciousness, so he couldn't be sure if he'd dreamed it or not, but he thought he'd heard them use the names "Ax" and "Tuck."

Bitterness and hatred grew within Clint.

Could it have been the Tucker Gang?

And then Clint recalled hearing one of them say, "The boss is gonna be real proud"—and he knew his memories were real.

The murderous Tucker Gang had been the ones who'd attacked the ranch.

Had they known his father was about to come after them, so they'd decided to strike first?

A fierce and undying determination grew within him. He didn't have all the answers right

16

then, but as soon as he was able, he was going to find out. If Captain Meyers and the posse from town didn't find the killers, he would.

There would be no place for them to hide once he was on their trail.

Whoever had done this was going to pay.

A week passed. Clint slowly regained some strength. Being incapacitated frustrated him. He was used to being in control and active, and it was difficult for him to deal with his weakness. The wound in his right shoulder seemed to be healing, but he worried the injury might have affected his ability to use his gun. As soon as he was able, he was going to get outside and start practicing his draw. As a Ranger, he had to be accurate with his gun.

Late one afternoon, Clint finally managed to move from the bed to sit in a chair in the bedroom. The effort had been exhausting, but he'd been determined to prove to himself that he could do it. He was just settling in when he heard the sound of horses riding up to the house.

"Who is it?" he asked Mary.

She looked out the window and recognized Captain Meyers and Sheriff Nelson leading the group.

"It's the posse," she told him excitedly.

"Are they bringing anybody in?"

"I don't know," she answered, for she had no idea how many men had ridden out with the sheriff in the first place. "I'll go down and get them, so you can find out."

Clint waited tensely as she left the room. A few moments later he heard footsteps coming down the hall. He looked up as Captain Meyers walked in.

"Clint—" Captain Meyers was relieved to find him sitting up. He hadn't been sure what he was going to learn about Clint's condition when they returned from the futile search for the killers. "You're better."

"Yeah, if you can call it that," Clint answered coldly. He didn't want to talk about himself. He was interested in only one thing. "What happened? Did you get them?"

"No," the captain answered in disgust. He'd badly wanted to find the outlaws. Frank had been his friend, and so was Clint. "They split up after they rode out. We went after both gangs, but they headed over rocky terrain, and we lost their trails."

Clint was furious. "Where were they headed?"

"The three I tracked headed north. Sheriff Nelson and his men followed the other two toward Rim Rock."

"As soon as I'm able, I'm going after them," Clint told him angrily.

"I know." The captain recognized the power of Clint's resolve.

The two men shared a look of understanding.

"Do you have any idea how long you'll be laid

18

up here?" Captain Meyers could tell Clint was still weak despite his fierce determination.

"The doc said it was going to take weeks for me to recover fully," he answered.

"Let me know when you're up and about."

"Don't worry. I will."

"What are you going to do about your ranch?"

"The Andersons are going to take care of things for me."

"Good. If I learn anything about the killers, I'll let you know. Do you have any idea who they were?"

"I'm pretty sure it was the Tucker Gang. The night of the attack, my father told me he was closing in on them. If he was that close, they would have wanted him out of the way."

"Yes, they would have. The Tucker Gang is as deadly as they come."

"That's what my father said, and I do think I remember hearing the killers say the names Ax and Tuck."

The captain's expression grew even more grim. "It was them all right. I'll stay on it, and I'll send word to you here if I make any progress. Did your father have any other known enemies you can think of?"

"None that he'd mentioned lately."

The captain was thoughtful, wanting to consider every possible angle. "What about you? Is there anyone in your past who might have wanted you dead?"

"A few, but I think they're still locked up." Clint told him the names of several gunmen who'd vowed revenge when he'd brought them in.

"I'll check to make sure they're still in prison. Do you remember anything else that happened that might give us a lead?"

"No. It was the middle of the night, and we were just running for our lives, trying to escape the fire. Whoever set this up knew exactly what they were doing. We didn't have a chance. They wanted us all dead."

"Yes, they did"—the captain paused as his gaze met Clint's—"but you're alive."

Clint nodded. "Yes. I am."

They understood each other.

"I'm sorry about your family, Clint." His words were heartfelt. "Your father was a good man and a fine Ranger."

"I know."

"I'll be in touch."

"I want to ride out with you," Clint ground out in frustration.

"I wish you could, but right now the most important thing is for you to heal. I'll keep you informed of what's happening."

"I'll be waiting."

Six Weeks Later

Clint was tense as he stood ready to shoot. In an instant, he drew his gun and fired. He hit the target dead on. His long hours of practice these past two weeks had paid off.

Satisfied that he had his accuracy and fast draw back, Clint turned to face Captain Meyers. He'd arranged to meet with the Ranger captain at the ruins of the Lazy W so he could tell him what he planned to do.

"You were a fast draw before, but I think you may be even quicker now."

"Good. I need to be."

"What's your plan?"

Clint was grim as he explained. "Except for a few people here in the area, everyone believes I was killed during the attack on the ranch. I want it to stay that way. Clint Williams is dead. From now on, I'm Kane McCullough."

"You want to take on a new identity?" Meyers was surprised.

"Yes, and this is where I need your help—because Kane McCullough is a gunfighter, and he needs a reputation. I want you to get the word out."

Captain Meyers realized Clint was right. Clint's going undercover this way just might work. No one would suspect who he really was, since everyone believed he was dead. As a deadly gunman, he could move in the same circles as the killers, and either attempt to join up with them or just bring them down by some trick. One way or the other, the gang's reign of terror was going to end.

"I can do that," Meyers said.

"Thanks."

Captain Meyers reached in his pocket and took out two sheets of folded paper. He handed them over to Clint. "Here are the wanted posters."

Clint unfolded them and stared down at the rough sketches of Glen Tucker and Ax Hansen.

"Are there any new leads?"

"They've been laying low, but I just got word from one of my men that he caught up with one of the gang members in San Miguel, a fellow named Rick. He was ready to bring him in. He wanted to get information out of him, but Rick drew on him and was killed."

"Did he find out anything about where Tuck or Ax were hiding out?"

"In his saddlebags he found a telegram from John Sanders, another member of the gang, telling him he was holing up in Black Canyon waiting to hear from Tuck."

"I'm riding to Black Canyon." Clint's mood was grim.

"Good luck." Captain Meyers knew if anyone could bring down this gang, it would be Clint. He was his father's son.

The two men shook hands.

"Captain—" Clint paused. He'd thought long and hard about this, but he knew what he had to do. He took his Ranger badge out of his pocket and handed it to Meyers. "I'm on my own on this one."

"There's no need for you to—" Meyers protested.

"Yes." Clint looked him straight in the eye. "There is."

The captain saw the fierceness in his expression and realized there was no point in arguing. "Keep in touch."

"I will."

Captain Meyers mounted up. He started to ride away, then reined in and looked back. "Clint—"

Clint looked up at him.

"I'll be keeping this for you," Meyers told him as he put the badge in his saddlebag.

Clint only nodded.

The captain rode away, leaving him alone.

There was only one more thing Clint had to do before he headed out.

He made his way to the place where Tony had buried his family. He stood over their graves, staring down at the markers that bore their names.

And then his gaze fell on the marker over the grave that had been dug for him.

Clint Williams
Born February 16, 1852
Died March 23, 1877

Clint realized as he stared at his own marker that he really was dead.

He was dead inside. The man he had once been no longer existed.

Clint turned away and went back to mount up.

He was ready. It was time to start hunting for the killers.

Clint Williams was dead.

Kane McCullough was riding out.

Chapter Three

Black Canyon

"Missy—who's that?" Clint heard a dance hall girl ask her friend as he strode into the saloon.

"I don't know, Lily, but I intend to find out," Missy said brazenly, giving him a sensuous smile. She started toward him.

"Oh, no. I saw him first. He's mine."

With that, the one named Lily pushed past her friend, her eyes never leaving him.

"Evenin', cowboy," she purred as she joined Clint at the bar. It was obvious she wanted him and she wanted his money. She stood sideways next to him. So he could get a clear view of her low-cut bodice and ample cleavage. "You're new here, aren't you?"

"Just passing through," Clint answered, giving her only a quick glance before telling the barkeep, "Whiskey."

"You gonna buy me a drink, too, big guy?" She looked up at him and smiled.

"Give the lady whatever she wants," he directed the bartender, pushing enough money across the bar to pay for both drinks.

"Thanks—I'll take my usual." Lily moved a little closer. "You want to go sit at a table?"

"All right." Clint picked up their drinks and followed her to a quiet table in the back corner. He was after information, and he had a feeling she knew everything that went on in this town.

"Are you going to be in Black Canyon for very long?" she asked hopefully.

"I'll be here for as long as it takes," Clint answered cryptically.

Lily gave him a knowing, inviting smile. Playing off his reply, she responded, "We can make it take as long as you want."

Clint looked up at her more seriously. She was pretty, and he didn't doubt she was talented enough to live up to her promise, but he wasn't interested in what she was selling. He had more important things on his mind.

"Fast is what I'm after," he told her. "I'm looking for someone—maybe you can help me."

"Who are you looking for?"

"A man who goes by the name of John Sanders. Have you heard of him around town?"

Lily's eyes widened a bit at the mention of the name. "Yeah, I know of him."

Clint heard the disgust in her tone and wondered at it. "Is he here in town?"

"Give me twenty dollars and I'll take you right to the bastard," Lily offered. "He beat up one of the girls in a drunken rage the other night, and now we all dread it whenever he walks into the saloon."

Clint handed Lily the money.

She tucked it safely down the bodice of her dress.

"Do you want to finish our drinks first?" she asked.

Clint picked up his glass and drained it in one long swallow. "I'm done."

Lily pushed her glass aside and stood up. "Mine can wait. Come on."

"Where is he?" Clint asked as he followed her to the saloon's swinging front doors.

"Over there," she told him, pointing to the hotel up the street. "He's got a room on the second floor."

"Thanks."

"If he's not there, take a look in the other saloons in town. All he does is drink and gamble."

And kill, Clint thought as he started from the saloon. He had to get to Tucker as quickly as possible. The longer he took, the more innocent people would die.

"I'm looking for John Sanders," Clint told the clerk at the hotel's front desk.

"He's upstairs right now," the man answered. "Third room on the left."

Clint mounted the steps slowly, cautiously. Sanders was a cold-blooded killer, so he had to be ready for anything. The best way to take him was to catch him by surprise, and that was exactly what Clint planned to do.

He stopped before the door to Sanders's room and drew his gun. He paused to listen for a moment, then made his move. With one violent kick, he broke in the door and stormed inside to find the half-naked man scrambling to get out of bed and grab his gun.

"Hold it, Sanders," Clint ground out. He had him dead in his sights.

The outlaw was smart enough to know he had no chance. He looked up at the gunman who stood over him and knew he was facing death. He made no further effort to get out of bed.

"Who are you?" John Sanders asked, quaking visibly. There was something strangely familiar about this gunman, but he couldn't place him.

"My name's McCullough. Kane McCullough."

"What do you want?"

"I want answers," Clint ground out coldly.

"What kind of answers?"

"Where's the rest of your gang?"

"What gang?" Sanders hedged. "I don't know anything about any gang."

"Oh, I think you know plenty," Clint threatened, and he took a step closer to intimidate the man. "Like who's really behind the Tucker Gang, and where the rest of them have been hiding out since the attack on the Williams ranch."

The outlaw was suddenly filled with pure terror as he realized whom he was facing. "Your name's not McCullough! You're Frank Williams's son!"

"That's right."

"We thought you were dead!" Sanders couldn't believe this man had survived. They'd shot him at least twice that night.

"You thought wrong." Clint gave him a cold smile. "Now start talking."

"No! They'll kill me if I talk!"

"And I'll kill you if you don't." Clint cocked his gun.

Sanders swallowed nervously.

"Who's the boss? Who runs the gang?"

From the look in his eyes, Sanders didn't doubt for a minute that Williams would do exactly what he said he would do. "I don't know who the boss is."

"What do you mean, you don't know?" Clint had no time to listen to lies. He took a threatening step toward the outlaw.

"I haven't been riding with them that long. I've never seen the boss or talked to him!" Sanders said, panicked. "He sends the orders about when and where we should make our moves, and then Tuck and Ax make sure we do it."

Clint heard hurried footsteps coming down the hall. He shifted his position so his back was to the wall just as the clerk appeared in the doorway.

"What's going on here?" the clerk demanded, then stopped when he saw that the stranger was standing there with his gun aimed at the hotel guest.

"Go take care of the front desk," Clint ordered

in a deadly tone that unnerved the clerk even more.

"But you can't—"

"I can, and I just did," Clint answered. "Get out of here—now! This is private."

The clerk realized there was nothing he could do, so he turned tail and ran. He had to get the sheriff.

"Where are Tuck and Ax?"

"Last I heard, they were heading to Dry Springs."

"Why Dry Springs?"

"I don't know."

"Sanders—" Clint took a threatening step forward.

"I tell you, I don't know!" He cowered before Clint. "I was supposed to meet up with them at the Last Chance Saloon there sometime after the first of the month."

"Looks like you're going to miss your meeting," Clint told him coldly.

"*No!*" Sanders stared down the barrel of Clint's gun, believing he was about to shoot.

"Get up," Clint directed, gesturing with the gun for him to get out of bed. "We're going to take a little walk."

Sanders didn't hesitate. He jumped out of the bed and made a grab for his pants.

"No," Clint ordered. "I like you dressed just the way you are. Let's go. I'm sure the clerk's had time to go after the sheriff by now, so start moving."

30

Sanders got up and stumbled through the door and out into the hallway half naked. Clint followed, keeping his gun trained on him. He didn't trust the gunman and thought he might try to make a break for it.

They had just started down the steps when the clerk rushed in, followed by the sheriff.

Sanders stopped and looked around, hoping for a chance to escape.

"What's going on?" the lawman demanded, drawing his gun as he kept a careful watch on the two men on the stairs.

"This is John Sanders. He's one of the Tucker Gang." Clint nudged the outlaw in the back with his gun to get him to move down the steps.

The sheriff was surprised by the news. He'd heard of the savage Tucker Gang. "You sure about that?"

"I'm sure," Clint answered.

Sanders knew he had no choice. If this sheriff took him to jail, he'd hang. He had to try to get away.

"You're under arrest—" the lawman began.

"Like hell I am!" Sanders shouted.

Sanders knocked the clerk down and launched himself at the sheriff. His surprise attack caught the lawman off guard. Sanders managed to grab the sheriff's gun from him, and he spun around ready to take aim at Clint.

But Clint had been expecting trouble and was ready when the gunman made his move. As

Sanders turned and got off a shot, Clint fired. Clint watched emotionlessly as the killer collapsed to the floor, dead.

Shaken, the sheriff and the clerk got to their feet. The sheriff hurried to get his handgun back from the dead outlaw.

"Thanks." He looked up at the stranger still standing on the staircase, his gun in hand.

Clint nodded and holstered his own sidearm.

The lawman eyed him uneasily. The stranger had been so fast with a gun, the sheriff wondered if he was a wanted man, too. "How did you know about Sanders?"

"I have my ways," Clint answered cryptically.

"What's your connection to all this?"

"Let's just say I want to see justice done." Clint continued down the steps. After one last look at Sanders lying dead on the floor, he walked out of the hotel and never looked back.

Clint knew where he was headed next.

Tuck and Ax were holed up near Dry Springs.

He was on his way.

It took the sheriff a moment before he realized he hadn't learned the stranger's name, and he found himself wondering about him. The man hadn't even stayed around to find out if there was a reward posted for Sanders. He'd just disappeared. The sheriff shrugged. The good news was, the town was now a safer place. A killer was off the streets.

Clint stopped back at the saloon. He wanted to buy Lily another drink before he rode out.

"Thanks for your help," he told her as they stood at the bar together. "Sanders won't be bothering anybody anymore."

"What happened?"

"Let's just say the sheriff has him." He knew the news of what had happened would reach her soon.

"Thank you." The bar girl smiled up at him with genuine delight. "Are you sure you won't stick around for a while and have some fun with us?"

"I appreciate your offer, but I've got to move on." Clint tipped his hat to her and walked out of the saloon.

"You be careful," she called out to him, sighing as she watched him go.

Chapter Four

Dry Springs

Dressed in his dark suit and tie and holding his Bible, Reverend Martin Hammond stood on the front steps of God's Grace Christian Church, looking out over the crowd of almost twenty people gathered before him. They had just completed their evening prayer service and were ready to put their faith into action.

"Are you strong enough to join me tonight? Are you ready to save souls?"

"Yes!" they shouted in reply.

"Then let's go spread the Lord's word!"

Carrying his Bible, Reverend Hammond led the way toward the bad part of town—toward the place where sin ran rampant, where liquor flowed freely, where women sold themselves for money and men wagered their very souls.

Rachel Hammond, the reverend's nineteen-year-old daughter, was nervous. She stayed close by her mother's side as they joined the others following her father through the darkened streets. Ever since her father had found himself struck by the desire to gamble, he'd been praying for salvation and working hard to save others from what he believed was the devil's own temptation.

"Are you sure we should be doing this again?" Rachel asked her mother a little nervously. "The sheriff wasn't very happy with us the last time."

"Your father believes he's been called to do this, so we have to support him. We're not alone, you know. Look at all the folks who are with us. It will be fine."

"I hope you're right."

Rachel thought about the first time they'd gone crusading several weeks earlier when her father had led them into the Gold Rush Saloon. It was a small establishment, and they'd been able to disrupt business for quite a while before Sheriff Reynolds had shown up and forced them to leave.

Tonight, however, her father had decided to go to the Last Chance, the most decadent saloon in the town. Raucous music was blaring from inside, and she could hear the sounds of drunken laughter and women shrieking.

"What's going on in there?" she whispered to her mother when she heard the women's shouts.

"It's best you don't know, darling," Anne Hammond answered as she prepared to follow her husband into the den of iniquity.

Reverend Hammond faced his followers as he

stopped them in front of the saloon for a moment. He led them in a short prayer, then said, "Let us bring the Lord's word to those who have fallen by the wayside."

"Amen!" the crowd responded.

The preacher turned and fearlessly mounted the steps, then threw wide the swinging doors to the Last Chance Saloon to lead the way inside.

Clint had arrived in Dry Springs earlier that afternoon; taken his time looking over the town, then rented a room at the only hotel. After settling in, he'd made his way to the Last Chance Saloon. According to what Sanders had told him, this was to be the meeting place, so he was going to sit tight and keep a sharp lookout for Tuck and Ax. He'd had a drink at the bar, then joined in a poker game. He was going to be here for at least a few days, so he needed to get the feel of the place.

"How many?" Ed, the dealer, asked him.

Clint looked down at his cards. It wasn't a pretty hand, but he wasn't ready to fold just yet. He threw down the two worst and answered, "Give me two."

Ed dealt him two cards and went on to the next player.

Clint picked up the new cards and stared down at the lowly pair of fours. He knew he wasn't going to win any big pots with luck like that tonight. He was about to throw his hand down when a loud disturbance coming from the front of the saloon interrupted the game.

"Praise the Lord! Repent while there's time!"

Clint heard the shout and glanced up to see the saloon being invaded by what looked like a Bible-toting minister and his entire congregation—ladies included. The people who'd been standing at the bar scattered as the minister approached.

"Get out of here, preacher man!" Trey, the bartender, ordered angrily. He'd heard what Reverend Hammond had done at the other saloon a few weeks ago, and he didn't want the same kind of trouble here. Business was good and he wanted to keep it that way.

"I can't walk away, knowing these poor souls may be condemned to eternal fire! I must work to save their souls. I must do all I can to protect them from the calling of the devil!"

"The only devil in here is you!" Trey countered.

The church people gasped at his cruel words.

"But we've come to help you . . . to save you!" one of the ladies insisted.

"If we wanted to be saved, we'd be in church. Now get out of here or I'll send for Sheriff Reynolds!"

"In good conscience, I can't leave any of you this way." Reverend Hammond looked around at the crowd in the smoke-filled room and gestured at them. "Give up your vices and turn to God's love," he extolled them.

The ladies who'd come with him broke into song, a longtime favorite hymn.

Trey signaled the piano player to start playing another tune, to drown them out. The man looked decidedly uncomfortable at this order, but did as he was directed. Trey was his boss. He began banging out a loud song.

Reverend Hammond was not about to be deterred. He joined his followers in singing as he strode through the room, looking at the lost souls and praying for their redemption. The rest of the church folk branched out and encircled all the tables where the gambling was taking place.

Clint looked over at the other men at his table. He'd expected trouble in Dry Springs, but not this kind of trouble. "Do you always have this kind of excitement here in town?"

"No. Somebody should do something about that crazy old man," Ed snarled. "He went into the Gold Rush not too long ago and got everybody stirred up."

"And look at all the women he brought with him! They shouldn't be in a place like this," another man at their table added in outrage. "Some of them are grandmothers!"

"Yeah, but not that one." Ed grinned and nodded toward the pretty, dark-haired young woman in the sedate gown. Though she was the complete opposite in character and morals of the women who worked in the saloon, he thought she was more sexy than they were. "That one's the preacher's daughter. She's a real looker."

Clint looked up at Ed's comment and caught sight of the young woman for the first time. He immediately understood Ed's sentiments.

"Yes, she is," he agreed.

The preacher's daughter was pretty, there was no question about that. Tall and slender, she moved with elegance through the chaos her father had created. For some reason, the thought that she was pure and innocent troubled Clint, and he was angry that her father had subjected her to this seamy side of life. Women like her were meant to be protected and cherished.

Clint frowned at the thought. He told himself to mind his own business. He had come to the Last Chance for one reason and one reason only, and it had nothing to do with any preacher's daughter. He looked away from the graceful beauty.

When the invaders broke into "Amazing Grace," Trey had had enough. He came out from behind the bar to confront Reverend Hammond.

"I want you out of here, preacher man!" he ordered, angry that his business was being disrupted.

"I have to save souls," Reverend Hammond announced calmly, looking him confidently in the eye.

"You're not saving any souls in my saloon! Take your followers and get out—now!"

"No, we must pray for your salvation." He opened his Bible, ready to quote Scripture.

"There's lots of praying going on in here, Reverend," one of the drunken gamblers called out to him, chuckling. "We always pray when we're playing poker."

"Gambling is a sin!"

"But sin is fun!" another drunk yelled back.

The crowd in the saloon hooted in raucous laughter at his remark, but Reverend Hammond and his followers were shocked by the gamblers' decadence and their refusal to listen to the Word.

Though the people in the saloon were laughing, Rachel sensed the growing tension and knew it was time for the church group to leave. God gave mankind free will, and these men and women were making their own choices about how to live their lives. Even so, she knew how determined her father was to try to preach to them. She inched closer to her mother's side, wishing the night were over and they were back home safe and sound.

"Go on, preacher man. Get out of here now, while you still can," Trey told him, taking another threatening step toward him.

Reverend Hammond looked up at the bartender, his expression serene. "God loves you."

"Reverend—" Trey ground out, not above physically removing him from the saloon.

"I think I need some redemption," Ed said loudly with a sly grin. He shifted in his chair and was able to reach out and snare Rachel around the waist. He pulled her forcefully down on his lap. "Come here, girlie. I want you to save me."

Rachel was caught unawares. Shocked by his actions; she struggled to break away from him as he planted a wet, slobbery kiss on her neck.

"Rachel! You let my daughter go!" Anne erupted in fury at the sight of her daughter being so manhandled. She charged toward the gambler to try to free Rachel, but another drunk grabbed her and held her back.

"Why do you want me to let her go? She's saving me," Ed sneered, enjoying having Rachel on his lap. The more she fought him, the better he liked it. "Aren't you saving me, honey?"

"Stop!" Rachel cried out, fighting off his hands as he tried to grope her.

The reverend saw what was happening.

"Unhand my daughter!" Reverend Hammond demanded. He rushed toward the gambler in a father's fury, but two of the other drunks in the saloon blocked his way.

"Go away, old man." Ed ignored her father's shouts as he tried to force Rachel to kiss him. "Come on, you little angel—give me some salvation and I'll make a *big* donation to your church—"

"Why, you!" Rachel slapped him, disgusted by his vile behavior.

Ed was a mean drunk, and a woman rejecting him right there in front of God and everybody infuriated him.

"Why, you little—!" He drew back, ready to hit her. He was all set to drag her upstairs and teach her a lesson.

Clint knew what Ed was about to do, and he'd had enough. He'd tried to stay quiet and let the situation work itself out, but there was no way he could sit by and let an innocent fall into the hands of a man like Ed.

"Let her go," Clint commanded quietly.

"Hell, no!" Ed answered, mindless now with anger and arousal.

Clint stood up, ready to confront him. "I said, let her go."

"Mind your own damned business."

Clint drew his gun. "She is my business. Get your hands off of her—now."

Ed froze at the sight of the gun pointed straight at him. "What are you getting so riled up about? She's just a whore like the rest of them."

"No. She's not," Clint said in a voice that was so calm it was deadly. He reached over and took Rachel by the arm, drawing her off the other man's lap.

"What are you doing? Do you want some of that, too?" Ed asked Clint, still leering at Rachel.

Clint ignored his remark as he glanced down at the young woman to make sure she was all right. She was trembling, and he could see she was close to tears. He understood her fear.

"Leave now, while you can," Clint directed in a low voice, releasing her arm.

Rachel was stunned. She looked up at the tall, broad-shouldered, dark-haired stranger who'd just rescued her. She had no idea who he was, but she was thankful for his help. Too upset to speak, she only nodded in response and hurried toward her father.

Clint still had his gun drawn as he watched her cross the room, so everyone else in the saloon eased off.

Rachel's mother and father rushed to embrace her. Her father cast one last condemning look around the room, then led his shaken daughter and wife from the den of iniquity. The rest of his flock followed him.

Clint remained standing with his gun drawn until they were all safely out of the saloon. Only then did he holster his gun and sit back down at the table. He looked over at Ed, who was glaring at him in obvious fury.

"A pair of fours," Clint said, picking up his hand and laying it out on the table for the rest of the players to see. His easy tone hid the tension that filled him as he awaited the dealer's response. He wasn't sure what Ed might do.

The others in the game folded.

Ed finally relaxed a bit and managed a smile. He spread out his cards.

"Three jacks," he announced.

Ed was raking in his winnings as Sheriff Pete Reynolds entered the saloon.

"I heard there was trouble down here," the lawman stated, his hand resting on his holstered sidearm as he looked around the room. "What happened?"

Trey quickly told him what had gone on. "Ed was just funning around with the preacher's daughter. He didn't mean her no harm." Trey had decided to make light of Ed's part in the confrontation. After all, Ed was a regular customer. Then he pointed at Clint. "He was the one who drew his gun."

The sheriff turned and eyed both men at the table with open interest. He walked slowly over to them.

"I understand you haven't been behaving yourself, Ed." Sheriff Reynolds came to stand beside him.

"The preacher was here trying to save souls, so I just thought I'd give him something to pray about." Ed was feeling confident that he was in no trouble with the law.

"Stand up," the lawman ordered.

"What? Why?" Suddenly leery, Ed did as he was ordered. He didn't want to be on Sheriff Reynolds's bad side.

Without warning, the sheriff drew his gun and violently pistol-whipped him. The force of the blows knocked Ed backward into his chair, and the chair crashed over onto the floor.

Ed was bloodied and battered by the lawman's unexpected assault. He wasn't about to fight back, though. He'd seen Sheriff Reynolds in action before and knew better than to try anything. This sheriff was one violent man.

Clint was shocked by the sheriff's assault on Ed, and he understood now why the whole town feared the man.

Sheriff Reynolds turned his attention to the stranger, his gun in hand. "You're new here in town, aren't you?"

"I just rode in this morning," Clint answered, wondering why Reynolds was still holding his gun.

"Well, know this: I don't put up with any gun-play here in Dry Springs."

"I'll remember that," Clint answered, meeting the lawman's cold-eyed regard straight on.

"You planning to stay around awhile or are you just passing through?"

"I haven't decided yet."

"Dry Springs is a nice, quiet town, and we like it that way. What's your name, friend?"

Clint wondered about the lawman's belief that Dry Springs was nice and quiet. From what he'd seen, it was no wonder the Tucker Gang wanted to meet up there. Clint wondered, too, if word of his "new" reputation had reached the sheriff yet. "My name's McCullough. Kane McCullough."

He noticed no change in Sheriff Reynolds's expression.

"Well, welcome to our town, Mr. McCullough. Enjoy your stay."

"Thanks. I intend to do just that."

The lawman turned and walked away.

"Sheriff, you need to go talk with that damned preacher man !" Trey shouted at him angrily as he was leaving the saloon. "I don't want him coming back in here again causing more trouble."

"I'll go pay him a visit right now, Trey," Sheriff Reynolds assured him.

"You'd better. It could get real ugly if he keeps this up!"

Clint watched the lawman leave the saloon, then turned his attention back to the poker game.

Bleeding from the sheriff's assault, Ed got up

and left the Last Chance. Another man took over dealing for him, and the other players stayed on to finish the game. This wasn't the first time there had been trouble in the Last Chance, and it certainly wouldn't be the last.

Clint anted up and hoped he'd be dealt a better hand this time. As he continued to play cards, the young woman named Rachel slipped into his thoughts. He hoped she was all right, and he hoped her father had learned from his experience tonight. The preacher could keep praying all he wanted, but some men in the world were beyond redemption.

Sheriff Pete Reynolds was angry as he made his way through the streets of Dry Springs. The thought that Reverend Hammond had put Rachel at risk infuriated him. The preacher was a fool. No man in his right mind would want his innocent daughter exposed to the ugliness that was life in the saloons.

Pete thought of the lovely young woman he'd been trying to woo and smiled to himself. Rachel was a real looker. He understood why Ed had grabbed her, but Rachel wasn't that kind of girl. He was glad the other man had broken things up before she'd gotten hurt in any way, but he still didn't like the stranger being so fast to use his gun.

The name McCullough sounded vaguely familiar, and he wondered where he'd heard it before. There weren't any new wanted posters around, so he wasn't an outlaw on the run, but something about that name bothered him and he knew he'd have to keep an eye on the man if he decided to stay around.

Pete headed toward the Hammond house to speak with the minister. He didn't care that it was late. He was going to set him straight on a few things—and check on Rachel.

Chapter Five

Reverend Hammond gathered his followers together in front of their church. He blessed them and led them in a concluding prayer.

Anne Hammond clung to her daughter as they prayed with him. In her heart she was truly frightened by what had happened that night. She knew her husband believed sinners could be redeemed, but the man who had accosted Rachel seemed beyond redemption to her.

"Let's go home," Martin told his family as everyone began to move off.

"Let's," Anne agreed, her fear turning to anger.

Rachel was nineteen and a young woman now, but to Anne she was still her precious daughter—a gift from God—and she was going to make sure Rachel was never caught in a situation like that again. She knew her husband would object to what she was going to do, but she didn't care. Her daughter had to be protected. That was all that mattered.

Anne was ready to take Rachel aside when they reached the house, but when they finally did get home, they found Eve Carson, a longtime family friend and member of the congregation, waiting anxiously for them on their front porch. Anne and Martin knew something had to be terribly wrong for the frail, elderly widow to have come out to see them at this time of the evening.

"Reverend Hammond, thank heaven you've finally come home," Eve said desperately as they came up the steps to the porch. "I have to speak with you."

"Come inside," he invited, ushering her into the house. He lit the lamp in the parlor and directed her to a chair. "What is it, Eve? How can I help you?"

Martin was deeply concerned now that they were in a lighted room, for he could see her more clearly and realized she'd been crying.

"This came for me today." Eve held out a telegram for him to read.

Martin took the missive from her and read it quickly. Sorrow filled him at the tragic news she'd received from the doctor in San Ramon. Her son and daughter-in-law had died of a terrible fever, and now her seven-year-old grandson, Jacob, was orphaned and alone.

"I'm so sorry." Martin reached out and took her hand, offering what comfort he could.

Anne and Rachel had followed them into the parlor, and Martin handed them the wire so they would understand what had happened.

"Jacob needs me. I have to go to him. I have to bring him here to live with me," Eve sobbed.

"From the sound of the telegram, the doctor will take care of him until you can get there. How soon did you want to leave?"

"I'll have to go tomorrow. I'll take the morning stage," she answered. "I can't leave poor Jacob there in San Ramon all alone. Not after this."

"You really should have someone travel with you," Anne suggested, concerned about Eve's delicate health. She knew the widow wasn't a strong woman.

"They were my only family. There is no one to travel with me, but that doesn't matter. All that matters is that I get to Jacob as quickly as I can," Eve said fiercely.

"I'll go with you," Rachel said, glancing toward her parents for their approval. She had always been fond of the elderly lady and wanted to help her.

"You will?" Eve looked up hopefully toward Rachel and her parents. "Are you sure?"

"That will be fine," her father said.

"Oh, thank you, Reverend—Anne. Thank you." The depth of her emotion was obvious.

"Have you checked on when the stage heads out?"

"It leaves at nine o'clock."

"I'll come by your house and pick you up at eight-thirty," Martin promised her.

"I'll be ready." Eve was still numb from the devastation of her loss, but she felt as if a great weight had been lifted from her, just knowing Rachel would be accompanying her.

"Now, let me walk you home. It's too late for you to be out alone," the reverend said.

Anne and Rachel both hugged Eve before she left.

Rachel was ready to go up to her room to pack for the trip. She knew they would be gone at least three days. She was just starting up the steps when someone knocked on the front door.

Anne answered it to find Sheriff Reynolds standing there.

"Evenin', Mrs. Hammond." Pete looked inside and caught sight of Rachel standing on the stairs. His gaze lingered on her. "Rachel—it's good to see you're all right. I was just down at the Last Chance and heard what happened."

"Please come in, Sheriff Reynolds," Anne invited.

"Thank you, and you know you can call me Pete," he said.

"All right, Pete, come in."

Rachel went back down the steps to speak with him.

"So you're really all right?" he asked, looking at her with concern. It angered him to think of Ed's filthy hands upon her.

"Yes, I'm fine," she told him, touched that he was worried about her. She liked Pete, and they did see each other socially on occasion.

"Good. That whole scene down at the saloon

could have turned real ugly real fast. I'm glad nothing too bad happened."

"So are we," Anne agreed.

Pete turned to the preacher's wife. "I need to speak with your husband."

"I'm sorry, but he's not here right now. He had some church business he had to attend to," Anne answered. "He probably won't be back for a while."

"I see." Pete was not happy with the news. He'd been ready to give the old fool a piece of his mind about disrupting business at the saloons and putting Rachel in danger, and now he had to bide his time. "Let him know I came by, and tell him I'll try to meet up with him tomorrow."

"I will," Anne assured him.

"Good night." Pete looked at Rachel and gave her a warm smile as he started from the house.

"Good night," they bade him.

When he had gone, Rachel once again started to go upstairs.

"Rachel—"

Her mother's call stopped her.

"What?"

"Are you really sure you're feeling all right? I was so frightened when we were at the Last Chance."

Rachel went to embrace her mother. "I was, too, but it's over. Everything turned out fine, thanks to that stranger." An image of the mysterious man who'd rescued her played in her mind.

"I wonder who he was."

"I don't know. Do you think we'll ever see him again?"

"I hope so. I'd like to thank him for helping you."

Rachel noticed that her mother still looked troubled. "Is something wrong?"

"Yes." Anne nodded. "I'm worried about you taking this trip with Eve."

"It should be safe."

"We can hope, but—come with me a moment." Anne drew Rachel into the study with her.

Rachel was puzzled by her mother's demeanor.

"I know your father doesn't approve, but after what happened tonight, I don't ever want you to be caught in a situation like that again."

Anne went to a locked chest, opened it, and took out a gun case. Opening the case, she took the revolver out and handed it to her daughter along with some extra bullets.

"I didn't know you still had this," Rachel said, staring down at the weapon.

Several years before, they had both learned how to load and fire the revolver. They weren't proud of the ability and rarely spoke of it, but they knew there were times in life when no matter how peace-loving you were, bad things could happen and you had to be able to defend yourself.

Tonight had been a perfect example. They knew the sheriff had done his best to bring law and order to Dry Springs, but men with low moral values did frequent the bad side of town. That was why her father had led the church group down to the Last Chance to pray. They would never know what kind of impact they'd made on the lives of the people in the saloon, but if they'd changed any hearts, they believed the effort was worth it.

"Oh, yes. I've kept it safely stowed here just in case there came a time when I needed it, and I think this is that time. I want you to carry it with you on this trip. You never know what might happen. I'll be praying for your safety, but it never hurts to be prepared as well—just in case."

"It's a shame I have to do this," Rachel said sadly, staring down at the gun she held. She wished life could be different. She wished life could be about peace and love.

"If having that gun with you keeps you safe, that's all that matters." Anne kissed her cheek.

"You're right. There won't always be someone around like the handsome stranger at the saloon tonight to help out."

"I sure am glad he was there."

"I think he might have been my guardian angel," Rachel said with a smile, her first in quite a while.

"He certainly was the answer to my prayer," her mother agreed. "I'm just thankful nothing more terrible happened."

"It was scary for a minute or two, that's for sure."

Rachel gave her mother another hug, glad they were back safe in the haven of their home, then she escaped to her room.

Rachel had planned to pack for the trip, but she could not forget the memory of Ed's disgusting hands upon her. Desperate to bathe, she stripped off her clothes and scrubbed herself clean. Only when she'd finished bathing was she able to put the ugly memory of what had happened at the Last Chance from her. She donned her nightgown and started to pack.

Later, when she'd finally stowed the gun and ammunition in her satchel, Rachel went to bed. She found as she lay there that she was anxious about making the trip. It was going to be difficult for Eve, and Rachel knew the elderly woman was going to need all the emotional support she could get. She was facing the loss of her only son and his wife, and taking responsibility for her young grandson. Rachel would do whatever she could to help her.

Firm in her resolve, Rachel finally relaxed. As she started to drift off to sleep, her last conscious thought was of the mysterious stranger who'd rescued her. She wondered again what his name was and if they would ever meet again.

Clint was tired. He wanted to rest. He needed to rest, but now that he was in Dry Springs, he was on edge. He expected Tuck, Ax, and the others in the gang to show up any day now, and he had to be ready.

56

Clint had planned to lie low and just hang around the saloon, listening to all the talk. He hadn't wanted to draw attention to himself, but his unexpected encounter with the preacher and his daughter tonight had changed all that.

As much as he'd wanted to stick to his original plan, Clint knew he could never have stood by and watched the innocent young beauty be abused that way. His mother had raised him better than that.

The thought of his mother stirred deep, troubling emotions within him and left him feeling even more angry because he had been unable to save her. When sleep finally did come to him, it was not restful but filled with torturous dreams of that terrible night at the ranch.

Rachel was packed and ready to go right on time the next morning. She and her mother left the house together to meet Eve and Martin at the stage depot. The reverend had already gone to the widow's house to help her get to the station.

"I need to stop and see Michelle for a minute. Since I'm making this trip with Eve, I won't be able to attend the social with her tomorrow," Rachel told her mother.

Michelle's family owned and ran the only hotel in town, and her friend worked there in the small dining room.

"All right. Give me your suitcase, and I'll go on to the depot and buy your ticket."

"I won't be long," Rachel promised. She hurried off to find her friend.

Michelle had just finished cleaning off one of the tables when she saw Rachel come in. There was no one else in the dining room at that moment, so Rachel had time to chat with her for a few minutes.

"Are you all set for tomorrow?" Michelle was eagerly looking forward to the social.

"That's why I had to come and see you. I'm not going to be able to go." Rachel went on to explain all that had happened.

"Tell Eve we'll be praying for her and her grandson," Michelle said with heartfelt emotion. She was very fond of the elderly woman, too.

"I will."

"I'll see you when you get back. I'm sorry about missing the social, but we've still got the Festival to look forward to."

"Yes, we do."

Rachel started from the hotel, anxious to get to the stage depot. She'd just walked out the door when she stopped. There before her on his way into the hotel was her mystery man.

"It's you—" she breathed, smiling up at him. She'd thought he was attractive the night before, but in the light of day, he was even more so. Lean and darkly handsome, he had an aura about him that commanded attention, and he had hers—all of it.

"I could say the same thing, Miss—?" Clint was surprised to run into her again, and he was glad to see that she'd suffered no lasting harm from her ugly encounter with the drunk. She was even more lovely than he remembered, especially when she smiled.

"I'm Rachel Hammond," she said, a bit flustered by her racing heart. "And you're—?"

"Kane McCullough," he answered.

"It's nice to finally meet you, Mr. McCullough." She was still smiling.

"Kane."

"Kane," she repeated, loving the sound of his name.

"You, too, Miss Hammond."

"Rachel." She laughed. "I realized after we left the saloon last night that I didn't even know your name, and I wanted to thank you for your help."

"You're welcome."

"So what are you doing in Dry Springs?"

"I'm just passing through," he answered noncommittally.

"Are you going to stay around long?"

"I haven't decided."

"Oh. Well, I hope to see you when I get back."

"Where are you off to?"

"I have to go to San Ramon for a few days."

"Have a safe trip."

"Thanks." Rachel moved off down the street.

For a moment, Clint stood there watching her go. His gaze lingered on the graceful way she moved, the feminine sway of her hips. When he realized the direction of his thoughts, he forced himself to look away.

No matter how attractive or alluring she was,

he had no time for any involvement with an innocent like her.

Rachel Hammond was a distraction he couldn't afford.

Chapter Six

Three Days Later

Tuck, Ax, and a new man who'd joined up with them, Holt Richards, hid out in some rocks overlooking the main road into Dry Springs. They were smiling as they watched the stagecoach draw ever nearer to their position.

"It won't be long now," Tuck said.

"I'm ready. What about you, Holt?" Ax asked as he checked his gun.

Holt had only been riding with them for a few weeks now, and this would be his first stage robbery.

"Yeah. I'm set. You and Tuck take care of the driver and the shotgun, and I'll take care of the passengers," he answered.

"It should go real smooth. As quiet as it's been around here for a while, they won't be expecting anything," Ax said.

"It's time," Tuck alerted them.

They went to mount up, ready to leave their hiding place and head down to the main road.

"Thank you so much for making the trip with me," Eve told Rachel with heartfelt sincerity as she sat across from her in the stagecoach bound for Dry Springs. "I don't know what I would have done without you."

"Everything worked out well," Rachel assured her.

They shared a sad and knowing smile as they glanced at Eve's grandson Jacob, who was sitting quietly next to her and staring out the window. He was having a hard time dealing with his terrible loss.

Rachel fully understood how difficult this had been for Eve, and she could only imagine how devastated young Jacob was. They were almost home now, though, and it was time for Eve and Jacob to begin thinking about the new life they would have together. They had each other. They weren't alone anymore. Rachel believed the worst was behind them.

And then she heard gunfire erupt outside the stagecoach.

"What's that?" Eve gasped in horror.

"Somebody's shooting at us!" Jacob exclaimed, scrambling to get a better look out the window.

"Get down!" Rachel warned.

She reacted quickly. She grabbed the boy and pulled him back inside so he'd be safe, just as Joe, the stage driver, whipped the team to a breakneck speed to try to outrun the would-be robbers. They could hear Hank, the man who was riding shotgun, returning the outlaws' gunfire.

Inside the stage, Rachel, Eve, and Jacob were thrown around as the stage raced wildly on.

"God, help us!" Eve prayed frantically.

Rachel was silently praying, too, as she realized what she had to do.

"Both of you get down on the floor and stay there! Eve, hold on to Jacob!" she directed.

Eve did as she was told and watched as Rachel opened the satchel she'd been carrying and started to dig through it.

"What are you doing? You should get down here on the floor with us where it's safe!"

"I'm getting this," Rachel answered with fierce determination as she pulled the handgun out of her bag.

"You've been carrying a gun all this time?" Eve exclaimed in a shocked tone.

"My mother insisted I take it with me on this trip, and right now I think that was some of the best motherly advice she's ever given me," Rachel answered, cringing as another blast of gunfire blazed around them.

"Do you know how to use it?" young Jacob asked, watching her in wide-eyed wonder. Lady that Miss Rachel was, he never would have guessed she could use a sidearm.

"Yes," Rachel answered as she carefully positioned herself at the window.

She peeked out and saw a masked outlaw riding at full speed, closing in on the stage. He was firing wildly at them, and she knew what she had to do. She took careful aim, which wasn't easy with the jolting of the stagecoach, and managed to get off several shots.

Rachel was stunned when the man let out a yell and was thrown from his horse. Since she knew Hank was firing at him, too, she wasn't sure if one of her shots had hit him or if it had been Hank's, and it didn't matter. All that mattered was there was one less outlaw to threaten them.

Even as she had the thought, though, another outlaw with the same deadly intent replaced the man who'd been gunned down. This gunman pursued them just as relentlessly, shooting continuously as he came charging toward the stagecoach.

Joe and Hank had been shocked when someone inside the stage started returning the outlaws' gunfire. They had no idea which one of the ladies was armed, but they were more than thankful for the help.

Joe stayed hunkered down and tried to concentrate on his driving. He had to keep the team under control.

Hank kept firing at their assailants, but he took a bullet in his upper arm. It slowed him down, but it was only a flesh wound, so he was able to keep blasting away. He knew all their lives depended on his holding off the outlaws.

When Tuck, Ax, and Holt had first gone after the stagecoach, they had been confident it would be easy pickings and the robbery would be over in no time. They'd expected the driver to give up after the first couple of shots were fired. Sure, there had been a man riding shotgun, but there were three of them and only one of him. They'd been shocked when one of the passengers had started firing out the side of the stagecoach.

Still, Tuck and Ax weren't about to give up. Even when they'd seen Holt take a bullet, they had refused to quit. They rode even harder, wanting to stop the stage as quickly as they could. But when Ax was wounded in his shooting arm, Tuck knew it was over.

"Give it up!" Tuck yelled to Ax, who was still trying to keep up the pursuit in spite of his wound.

Both men were furious at their failure as they turned their horses away and rode off. There was nothing they could do about it, though, for Tuck was the only one who could still handle a gun. In frustration, they headed back to check on Holt.

"They're quitting! They're riding away!" Rachel cried out as she watched the outlaws give up their pursuit.

"Thank God!" Eve rejoiced. "Rachel—you were wonderful! You helped save us!"

"Yeah," young Jacob agreed, still looking at Rachel in amazement and awe. He'd never known a lady like her before. "You can shoot real good."

"Thanks." Rachel sat back, trembling. She

smiled weakly at them from across the width of the stage. The gun battle had been frightening, but at least they were safe. When she realized she was still clutching the gun in a viselike grip, she quickly stowed it in her bag.

"You all right in there?" the driver shouted down to them.

Jacob leaned out the window and called out, "We're fine. Miss Rachel helped save us!"

"Yes, she did, sonny. Now hold on tight 'cause we ain't gonna stop 'til we're in town! And tell Miss Rachel thanks. We sure appreciated her help."

The boy sat back and grinned at Rachel. He was no longer terrified, but excited now that everything had turned out all right. "The driver said thanks."

"I heard him." She felt a little calmer.

"What does your father think about you using a gun?" Eve asked, still shaken by all that had happened. "He always preaches about loving one another and turning the other cheek."

"It troubled him at first, but then he realized that there are times in life when you have to be able to defend yourself."

"Like today," Jacob put in.

"Like today," Eve agreed, thinking once again how blessed they were that Rachel had been armed. She could only imagine what horrible things might have happened to them if the outlaws had managed to stop the stage. "I can't wait until we get to town so we can tell Sheriff

Reynolds. The faster he gets a posse together and goes after those men, the better."

"At least one of them was wounded, so that'll slow them down a little and give him a better chance of catching up with them," Rachel agreed.

"Let's just hope he does. Men like those shouldn't be on the loose."

"Grandma? Do bad things like this happen a lot around here?" Jacob asked, worrying about the new town he was going to be calling home.

"No, darling—and we can be thankful about that."

They all managed a little laughter as they eagerly anticipated reaching Dry Springs

Tuck was furious.

He'd thought it would be easy to rob the stage, but he'd been wrong.

And Tuck didn't like being wrong.

"What the hell happened out there?" he snarled as he tied a makeshift bandage around the wound in Holt's chest.

Holt was bleeding heavily, and Tuck wasn't sure he would make it. They'd retreated to the place where they'd camped the night before, to regroup and try to figure out what to do next.

"I wish I knew," Ax said in disgust as he tended to his own wounded arm. "It was almost like they knew we were coming and were ready for us."

"If Rick and Walt had been along, things would have turned out different," Tuck said, missing their two cohorts. "Or even if we'd had John with us."

Ax didn't respond. There was nothing he could say. They'd gotten word that John had been killed, and they were due to meet up with Rick and Walt in Dry Springs in a few more days. They'd taken on Holt to replace John, but he'd proved useless in the holdup attempt today, and now he was wounded, so he wouldn't be doing them any good for a long while—if ever.

"Rick and Walt should be showing up soon." Tuck said. "Once they do, we can get something going for the boss."

"We'd better. He ain't gonna be happy when he hears what happened today."

"You're right. A posse will be after us real soon, so we'd better make some tracks." Tuck looked at Holt. "You able to ride?"

"I'll make it," the wounded outlaw answered.

Tuck had his doubts, but a short time later, they were on the move.

The stagecoach didn't slow down as it reached Dry Springs. It raced straight on down Main Street right past the stage depot and didn't stop until it reached the sheriff's office.

"Sheriff Reynolds!" the driver yelled as he reined in.

People from town had seen the racing stage and had immediately known something was wrong. They came running out of their homes and businesses to see what had happened.

"Somebody get the doc!" Joe ordered as he helped Hank down from the driver's bench.

Sheriff Reynolds rushed out of his office. "What's going on here?"

"A gang of outlaws tried to rob us!" Hank told him, grimacing in pain as he came to stand before the sheriff, holding his still bleeding upper arm.

"How bad's your arm?" he asked.

"It's just a flesh wound, but it could have been worse—a lot worse."

"You'd better have the doc take a look at it. Nick—help Hank over to the doc's," the sheriff ordered his deputy. Then he looked back at the driver. "What happened out there?"

"Three of them came after us about five miles out of town," Joe explained. He went on to relate everything he could remember about the attempted ambush.

"I'll get a posse together, and we'll ride out after them right away. How much did they get away with? What did they steal? What were you carrying?"

"That's the amazing part," Joe told him as he opened the stagecoach door to let his passengers out. "They didn't get anything. We held them off—thanks to some help from our sharpshooting passenger."

"Are you serious?" the lawman asked, surprise in his voice.

"Yes. Thanks to Miss Hammond, we were able to get away. I know she winged one of them for sure."

"Rachel?" Pete repeated. He was shocked to find out that she was onboard and that she had been carrying a gun and knew how to use it.

"Yes, I'm here," she called out to Pete from inside the stagecoach.

"You were all lucky," Pete told them.

"I'll say," Joe said. "Without Rachel's straight shooting, this would have been a whole different story. We might have all been killed. Hank was doing his best to hold them off, but there were three of them."

Joe helped his elderly female passenger down first, then waited for the young boy to climb out on his own.

When Rachel appeared in the doorway, Pete moved past Joe to take her hand and help her descend. She smiled at him, finally feeling safe now that they were back in town.

"You were carrying a gun with you today?" he asked.

"After the other night at the Last Chance, my mother wanted me to carry it with me to make sure I was safe," she told him. "And it's a good thing she did."

Pete looked down at Rachel and managed to smile. "I'm glad you're all right."

"Thank you, Rachel." Joe interrupted Pete's moment with her to speak with great sincerity. "We owe you a lot. I don't think we would have gotten away from them without your help."

"Miss Rachel was great," Jacob chimed in, grinning proudly up at his new friend. "Maybe she should start riding shotgun on your stagecoach all the time!"

"I don't know about that, but you were wonderful," Eve agreed, giving her a hug.

Rachel was embarrassed by all the praise. "I'm just glad we were able to get away." She noticed Hank walking off with Nick and asked, "Is Hank going to be all right?"

"He should be. His wound didn't look too serious. I think the outlaws are in a lot worse shape than we are," the stage driver answered.

"It's just good that you made it back safely," Pete said. "Now, where did you say they tried to ambush you?"

Once Joe told him the exact location, Pete was ready to get his posse together.

"I'll see you later, Rachel," Pete said.

"Good luck finding them," she told him.

Pete hurried off. He wanted to get on the trail as quickly as he could while the outlaws' tracks were still fresh. If some of the gunmen had been wounded as the driver had said, there was a good chance he could catch up with them and bring them in. He wouldn't stand for any outlaws terrorizing his town. He was going to see that justice was done.

The news of the stagecoach's return and the attempted robbery reached Rachel's parents quickly. They rushed over to the stage to check on Rachel, Eve, and Jacob.

"You're all right!" Anne embraced her daughter. "I was so terrified when I heard the news!"

"We're all fine," Rachel assured her, wanting to calm her parents' fears. As soon as her mother released her, she went to hug her father, too.

"Thank God," Martin offered up.

"Thank God, indeed," Eve repeated. "If you hadn't suggested that Rachel accompany me to bring Jacob home, we might not be alive right now."

"We're glad you're all here, safe and sound."

"So are we," Rachel agreed.

Martin looked over at young Jacob. "Welcome to Dry Springs, Jacob."

"Jacob, this is Reverend Hammond. Miss Rachel's father," Eve quickly made the introduction.

"Is it always this exciting in Dry Springs?" Jacob asked him, looking around at the crowd of people who'd turned out.

"Thankfully, no," Martin told him. "But now that you're here with us, things just might get livelier around town."

Jacob smiled at him.

"Are you ready to go home, Jacob?" Eve asked her grandson.

He looked up at her with a look of pure love in his eyes. "Yes, Gramma. Let's go home."

"I'll send your bags over later," Joe told Eve and Rachel as they started to leave.

"Thanks, Joe, and let me know how Hank is doing."

"I will."

"Rachel, thank you for everything," Eve said.

They were surprised when Jacob impulsively threw his arms around Rachel and hugged her tight.

"Thanks!"

Rachel hugged him back, then watched as they started off, hand in hand, toward Eve's home—the elderly widow and her orphaned grandson, ready to begin their new life together.

"What about you?" Martin asked his daughter. "Are you ready to go home?"

"Oh, yes," she answered as she and her parents turned toward home.

Chapter Seven

The first week of the month was almost over, and Clint's frustration had grown during the three days he'd been in town. He'd been keeping a constant lookout for anyone or anything suspicious, but had found nothing. He was beginning to wonder if the gang's plans had changed.

Clint realized he had to be patient and wait it out, but it wasn't easy for him.

He wanted revenge.

Clint was sitting at a table in the back of the Last Chance when older man ran into the saloon.

"Have you heard the news?" the man shouted to anyone who'd listen.

"What news, Ira?" Trey demanded. He knew it had to be serious from the way Ira was acting. It wasn't often he got this excited about anything.

"The stage was robbed! Hank was shot! He and Joe just pulled into town. They're down by the sheriff's office!"

"How's Hank? Is he dead?" Trey asked, worried.

"No. From what I could see, it looked like he just got hit in the arm," Ira answered.

Clint was instantly alert. He wondered if this was the work of the Tucker Gang—if this was the way they were going to announce their arrival in the area. As casually as he could, Clint got up from his table and went outside to see what was going on. He joined the crowd in front of the sheriff's office and listened to the talk around him to see if he could learn any details about the robbery.

"You mean there was all this shooting and the robbers didn't get away with anything?" one man repeated in astonishment.

"That's right! They didn't get a cent!" another announced proudly. "That preacher's daughter was on the stage, and she was carrying a gun!"

"Rachel had a gun?" someone else asked, shocked.

"That's right, and from what I heard, she was damned good at using it, too! She helped run them off. Without her, this would have been a whole different story. As it is, Hank got winged, but he still managed to hold his own."

Clint tensed as he listened to the conversation. It had troubled him to learn Rachel had been on the stage, but when he found out she'd been carrying a weapon, he was torn. Logically, he told himself all that mattered was that Rachel was back home safe, but knowing the threat she'd faced during the robbery attempt disturbed him. If it had been the Tucker Gang and they'd known she was armed, they wouldn't have hesitated to kill her if they had managed to stop the stage.

The thought of Rachel being harmed by the bloodthirsty outlaws tore at Clint. He tried to deny his feelings. He fought against the rage that threatened to overwhelm him. He reminded himself over and over that he had no time for any emotional involvement with anyone.

He must not care about Rachel.

He must not care about anybody.

He had to be cold and calculating.

Clint kept his tone easy as he asked, "Where did it happen?"

"About five or six miles out of town," the man answered. "Sheriff Reynolds is getting a posse together to go after them. Joe, the stage driver, said at least one of the outlaws was wounded—maybe two of them. With any luck, Sheriff Reynolds will be able to track them down and bring them in."

"So none of the passengers were hurt?"

"That's right. They all made it just fine—Eve and her little grandson and Rachel."

Moving away from the crowd, Clint went to the stable. He could lose no time before riding out to start tracking the would-be stage robbers. He had to find out if this was the Tucker Gang. This aborted robbery didn't sound like the work of the deadly gang, but he had to be sure. He rather hoped it was them, for then he would know he wasn't wasting his time and that he was on the right track.

Clint got his horse, then returned to the hotel to gather up his things. When he rode out of town a short time later, he was surprised to find that Sheriff Reynolds still hadn't gotten his posse organized. In a way, he was glad. The longer the lawman took, the more time he had to check things out on his own.

Clint rode to the site of the attack and found the outlaws' trail much more easily than he'd expected. It was getting late as he started after them. He made sure to cover his own tracks, for he didn't want anyone to know what he was doing. He was puzzled, though, by the fact that he still hadn't seen any sign of the posse. He wondered why it was taking the sheriff so long to get organized.

When darkness finally claimed the land, Clint made camp reluctantly. He slept little. The prospect of possibly being so close to the killers left him restless and anxious for the new day to dawn.

At first light, Clint was on the trail again. He believed he was making good progress, and then at noon he made a gruesome discovery. Wrapped in a blanket, lying in the brush, was the body of one of the gunmen.

Clint didn't recognize the man. He wasn't anyone he'd seen on the wanted posters. He checked the body for some kind of identification, but found nothing. He considered burying him, but decided against it. He left the body where he'd found it, knowing the sheriff was in pursuit and would want a look at the dead man, too.

The previous day, Clint had thought he'd had a chance of closing in on the outlaws, but now, unburdened by their wounded, dying partner, the two remaining outlaws were able to travel much faster. Still, Clint didn't give up.

As the day aged, Clint noticed threatening clouds beginning to gather on the horizon. He concentrated on his tracking, trying to cover as much ground as he could and hoping the bad weather would pass over him. But just at dusk, a heavy downpour started up. Before long it was scouring the land.

Clint sought what shelter he could find in a rocky outcropping and passed a miserable night. He feared the trail would be lost because of the rain, and the following morning he discovered that it had, indeed, been washed away. Disgusted, he went over the area carefully, searching for some clue to the direction in which they'd ridden. His search proved useless.

Disappointed, but knowing there was no point in trying to find something that wasn't there, Clint decided to ride for town. He took a different, more circuitous route, for he didn't want to risk running into the posse.

It was late in the day when word of the posse's unexpected early return spread through the town. A crowd began to gather in front of the sheriff's office, anxious to learn what had happened. Since the posse had returned so quickly, the townsfolk expected to find that Sheriff Reynolds had caught the outlaws and brought them in.

Eve was at the general store with Jacob when they heard someone outside shouting the news.

"Gramma! We gotta go see what happened! We gotta go find out if they got them!" Jacob insisted, grabbing her hand to draw her from the store.

"We'll be back," Eve called out to the shopkeeper as she left with Jacob.

They were hurrying down the street to join the others when Jacob saw Rachel and her mother come out of another shop.

"Miss Rachel!" Jacob hollered. He let go of his grandmother's hand to run over to speak with her. "They're back!"

"Hi, Jacob," Rachel said warmly, then asked, "Who's back?"

She looked up at Eve, who'd finally caught up with him.

"The sheriff and the posse!" Jacob explained.

"Already?" Rachel's eyes widened at the news. She was impressed that Pete had caught up with and arrested the outlaws so quickly. "That was fast work."

"I know. I couldn't believe it either," Eve said. "That's why we're going over to the jail. I want to find out what happened."

"We'll go, too," Anne said. She wanted to know

for sure that the gunmen were under arrest and wouldn't be a threat to the community anymore.

They joined the crowd waiting in front of the jail for Sheriff Reynolds to come outside and let them know what had happened. It wasn't long before he appeared.

"I see you heard we were back," Pete began.

"How did it go? Did you get them all, Sheriff?" someone called out.

"We tracked the outlaws for almost a full day, and then we found a body on the trail. The man had been shot several times."

At the sheriff's announcement, Jacob looked up at Rachel, his eyes wide. "Do you think he's the one you shot, Miss Rachel?"

At Jacob's question, almost everyone in the crowd turned to look at Rachel.

"I—I don't know." She was horrified to think she might actually have killed someone.

Anne reached out to her daughter and took her hand supportively. She could well imagine what Rachel was going through.

"What about the rest of the gang?" another man asked.

Pete looked out at the townsfolk and told them, "They got away."

"What do you mean, they got away!" the man demanded. "Why didn't you stay after them?"

Pete turned a cold-eyed glare on the man who'd dared to criticize his decision to call off his pursuit of the outlaws. "Whoever these gunmen were, they hadn't succeeded in robbing the stage and they'd lost one of their men."

"But they shot Hank!"

"Yes, they did, but it was only a flesh wound, and he's going to make a full recovery."

"You should have kept after them!"

"You should have brought them in!"

Pete was getting angry with their demands. "I didn't want to put the posse at risk, chasing down a couple of worthless outlaws. And besides, a storm was brewing. I figured it would wash the trail out on us even if we did stay after them."

"But who's to say they won't come back? Who's to say they won't try again?" someone asked, frightened that the gunmen were still on the loose.

"They're long gone," Pete told them.

"How can you be sure?" another challenged him.

"I'm sure. Things are back to normal now. You can go on about your business. Everything will be fine."

Summarily dismissed, the uneasy crowd disbanded. They weren't happy with the lawman's decision not to try to bring in the gunmen, but there was nothing they could do about it.

"What's he gonna do, Gramma? Is the sheriff going back out after them again?" Jacob asked, confused.

"No, darling. Sheriff Reynolds thinks the bad men are gone and they won't be back."

"Good. I'm glad," he replied, sighing in relief

as he followed his grandmother back to the General Store.

Anne could tell Rachel was upset, so they went straight home. They didn't speak until they were inside the house. Only then did Anne embrace her daughter.

Rachel had tried to be strong on the walk home, but now, wrapped in the safety of her mother's arms, she gave in to the torment that filled her soul.

"What if I did shoot him?" she asked tearfully. "What if I was the one who killed him?"

Anne kissed Rachel's cheek and hugged her even tighter. "We will never know whose bullet killed the outlaw, and it doesn't matter. He was trying to kill you."

"I know, but—"

"What matters is you're safe. Think what would have happened if you hadn't been able to defend yourself."

"But Papa always says—"

"Rachel." Anne's voice grew stern as she drew back to look her daughter straight in the eye. She knew her husband always preached love, not hate. Peace, not violence. But Rachel's very life had been at stake. "What you did was very brave. You acted in self-defense, and in doing so, you not only saved your own life but you helped to save Eve and Jacob and Joe and Hank, too. I'm proud of you, darling. Never doubt that for a moment."

"You are?"

"Yes. I am."

Anne gave her another hug, and then Rachel went upstairs to her bedroom to be alone for a while. It had been one thing to know she'd fired the gun at someone. It was another to learn that that person had died from gunshot wounds.

Rachel lay on her bed and buried her face in her pillow as memories of that horrifying day threatened to overwhelm her. She remembered the danger they'd faced as the would-be robbers fired on them, and how terrified she'd been that young Jacob or Eve might be shot.

Rachel drew a shuddering breath as she fought to control her runaway emotions. It was a terrible truth, but she finally accepted that her mother had been right. If she hadn't taken the gun with her on that fateful trip and been brave enough to use it, they might all have been killed.

It took a while, but Rachel finally managed to find some peace deep within herself. She prayed she would never find herself in a situation like that again.

Chapter Eight

As Clint rode slowly back into Dry Springs, he noticed some kind of activity going on at the far end of town. It looked like a fair or picnic of some kind, but other than that, nothing seemed to have changed during his absence. Riding to the stable, he left his horse there, then went to the hotel.

"Nice to have you back, Mr. McCullough," Mr. Lofton said as he gave him a room key. "Will you be staying with us long?"

"I'll be here for at least a few more days," Clint answered.

"Good. Make sure you visit the Festival," he encouraged. "We have it every year, and it's going on right now. There's a dance later on tonight, too."

"So that's what all the excitement is about. I saw the crowd and wondered what the attraction was."

"Folks come from miles around."

"So why aren't you down there?" Clint asked with a grin.

"Somebody's got to take care of business."

"I guess that's right."

He went up to his room and dropped off his things before heading over to the Last Chance. He was surprised to find that the saloon was quiet. Since it was late Saturday afternoon and the Festival was going on, he'd expected it to be busy.

"Where is everybody?" Clint asked Trey as he walked up to the bar.

"At the picnic. Business will pick up later once the dancing starts. It always does," Trey told him. "Where've you been these last few days?"

"I had some business I had to take care of. How've you been? Has the preacher man been back to give you any more trouble?" he asked with an easy smile, wanting to direct their conversation away from himself.

"No, it's been nice and peaceful around here, just the way I like it."

"Some days are better than others."

"What'll it be?"

"Whiskey."

Trey poured him a healthy drink in a tumbler and slid it across the bar to him.

"Have you heard anything new on the attempted stage robbery? Has there been any word back from the posse?" Clint asked as he paid the bartender and picked up the glass to take a drink.

"Sheriff Reynolds and the posse rode back in yesterday," Trey said.

"They're back already?" Clint was honestly surprised by the news, but he was careful to hide his reaction. Even taking the longer return route that he had used, he'd expected to beat the posse back to town. Since the storm hadn't moved in their direction and they still had a trail to follow, he wondered why they'd called off their pursuit of the gunmen so soon.

"Yeah, they're back, and they brought one of the 'good' outlaws with them."

"I didn't know there were any 'good' outlaws." Clint frowned, wondering what the other man meant.

"There are. They're the dead ones."

"Oh. What about the rest of the gang? Did the sheriff have any luck finding them?"

"No. They got clean away."

"Does anyone know who the dead outlaw was?"

"Not right off. Sheriff Reynolds said he was going to do some checking to see if he could find out."

"What's he saying about the gunmen? Does he think they'll be back?"

"The sheriff seems to think they're long gone." Trey shrugged. "And I hope he's right. We don't need their kind around here causing trouble."

"I'm with you on that," Clint agreed.

Picking up his drink, he made his way to a table in the back of the saloon. He settled in to relax for a few minutes and try to figure out what to do next.

It didn't take him long to make up his mind. He decided to sit tight and wait a few more days to see if Tucker would show up. In the meantime, he was going to find the people who'd been on the stage and talk to them. He hoped to find out if they'd noticed anything unusual about the outlaws. He figured the stage driver was probably off on another run by now, so he decided to go to the Festival and look for the man named Hank who'd been riding shotgun—and Rachel.

Something stirred deep within Clint at the thought of seeing the innocent beauty again.

He forced the feeling from him.

He was going after information on the would-be robbers.

That was all.

Finishing his drink, Clint left the saloon and returned to the hotel. After three days of hard riding, he needed to get cleaned up before going to the Festival.

The Dry Springs Annual Festival was in full swing. There were booths and games and refreshments. Folks had come from all over to enjoy themselves.

"Who are you looking for?" Michelle asked Rachel as they stopped at one of the game booths. She'd noticed how her friend had been searching the crowd ever since they'd arrived.

"Oh, nobody."

"I know you better than that. Who are you hoping to see?"

Rachel knew there was no way she could keep anything from her best friend. Michelle knew her too well. "I was looking for Kane McCullough. I haven't seen him since I went to San Ramon with Eve, and I thought he might be here today. Have you talked to him at the hotel lately?"

Michelle hated to be the bearer of bad news, but she had to tell the truth. "No. In fact, he checked out a few days ago and left town."

"He did?" Rachel was surprised at how disappointed she was to learn that Kane was gone. "I guess he really was just passing through."

"There's still Pete," Michelle encouraged, knowing the sheriff was interested in her friend. "And—speak of the devil, he's coming our way right now."

"Afternoon, ladies." Pete smiled at both of them, but it was clear his interest was in Rachel alone. "How are you doing, Rachel?" he asked solicitously.

"I'm fine," she said a bit stiffly. A part of her wanted to ask him if he'd heard anything more about the gunmen who'd gotten away or if he'd learned the identity of the man who'd been shot, but she didn't want to bring up an uncomfortable subject. She just wanted to relax and enjoy herself today.

"Are you having a good time?" Pete asked.

"Oh, yes. The Festival is always fun," Michelle replied.

"What about you, Rachel?" Pete asked. His gaze was warm upon her.

"Of course," she said, managing a smile.

"You ladies will be at the dance tonight, won't you?"

"We're looking forward to it," Rachel told him.

"I'm counting on having a dance with each one of you," he told them.

"We'll be watching for you," they promised.

"I'll see you later," Pete said, casting a lingering look back at Rachel as he walked away.

"He is so sweet on you, Rachel," Michelle sighed.

"Pete's nice enough," she hedged.

" 'Nice enough'? You think he's just 'nice'?"

"Yes. Why? Do you like him?" Rachel turned the tables on her friend who, she knew, was trying to play Cupid.

"Pete's all right." Michelle told her.

Rachel was intrigued by her evasive answer. She'd thought she knew her friend through and through, but now she was discovering Michelle was hiding something from her. "I get the feeling there's something you're not telling me."

"Well . . ." Michelle looked around to make sure no one was near enough to overhear their conversation. "There's someone I'm hoping I'll get a chance to dance with tonight.

"Who is it?"

"It's Nick—Nick Evans," Michelle sighed dreamily.

"Really?" Rachel was surprised. Nick was Pete's new deputy. He was very handsome and had a reputation around town as being quite a ladies' man.

"He is so cute," Michelle gushed.

Nick had been in town for several years. He'd worked at the stable as a horse trainer for a while, then took the job as deputy sheriff a few months before, when longtime deputy Ben Taggart quit. No one had ever heard why Ben had moved on. Everyone thought he'd been happy as deputy, but one day he'd just up and left. Nick was doing a good job in his place, so nobody seemed to miss the older man too much.

"Nick will ask you to dance tonight. You just wait and see." Rachel sounded positive, wanting to encourage her friend. If she couldn't be with Kane, she wanted Michelle to be happy with the deputy.

"But so many other girls in town are after him, too," Michelle said.

"They may be, but you're the one who's going to get him," Rachel told her confidently.

"Do you really think so?" Michelle looked brighter at the thought.

"Of course. You're pretty and smart, and your father owns the only hotel in town, so you're rich. That's a great combination! A man would be crazy not to want you."

"Sure. That's why Nick's been courting me so wildly all these weeks," Michelle said sarcastically.

"He hasn't come courting because he probably doesn't know you like him. We'll figure something out tonight at the dance. You just wait and see."

"Well, what about you? Since Kane's left town . . ."

The moment of intrigue and excitement Rachel had felt for her friend faded. "I don't know. I just wonder if I'll ever get to see him again."

"You could always go looking for him. You could find out where he was heading and go after him," Michelle suggested daringly.

Both girls shared a look as Rachel actually considered doing just that, and then they both started laughing. They could well imagine what would happen to Rachel's reputation if she cast her fate to the wind and boldly chased after a man.

"I think that just might raise a few eyebrows around town," Rachel remarked wryly.

"I think you're right."

"And then there is the matter of my father. You know, I don't think he'd approve."

Michelle was beginning to realize just how much Rachel really did care about the stranger.

"What was there about Kane that attracted you so?" Michelle asked.

"I don't know. He was handsome—there's no doubt about that. But I've been around handsome men before, and never felt this way about any of them. It's strange, because I really didn't spend much time with him. I don't know him at all. But there's just something about him."

"Maybe it was love at first sight for you. Why don't you start praying that he comes back to town?" Michelle encouraged her. "Your father's the minister, so you've got special connections."

"I may just do that," Rachel said, her mood lightening. Then, wanting to have some fun, she changed the topic. "Come on, let's go see if we can win a quilt down at the quilting booth."

"There are some pretty ones. Eilleen and Cyrilla have been working on them for months," Michelle agreed.

They started off to visit the quilters. There were a lot of activities going on that day, and the girls wanted to enjoy them all.

It was much later that afternoon when Rachel and Michelle approached the lemonade stand. They'd been having such a good time that they were tired and ready to sit down with a cool drink at one of the picnic tables.

They were waiting in line when Rachel caught sight of Nick Evans walking by. Michelle was standing with her back to him, so she didn't know he was there. Brazenly, Rachel decided to make the first move for her friend.

Smiling sweetly, she called out, "Deputy Evans—would you like to join us for some lemonade?"

Michelle was shocked by her friend's bold action. She froze for a moment, but then realized she had no choice but to go along with her. She turned quickly around to smile at her dream man.

Rachel's invitation had taken Nick by surprise. He saw Rachel at church on Sundays and around town, but had never socialized with her or with Michelle Lofton, the hotel owner's daughter, who was standing beside her at the lemonade stand. But just because they hadn't socialized in the past, that didn't mean they couldn't start today.

Rachel and Michelle were two of the prettiest women in town, and he wasn't about to miss the opportunity to spend some time with them. He smiled as he walked over to join them.

"Thank you for the invitation, Miss Hammond. I'd be glad to join you, but only if you let me buy," he offered.

"Well, first of all, please call me Rachel, and you know Michelle, don't you?"

"Of course—we've met."

Nick smiled down at Michelle.

Michelle felt her heartbeat quicken as she returned his smile.

"And," Rachel went on, "*we* invited *you*, so your lemonade is on us."

"It's not Sadie Hawkins Day," he insisted. "It's my treat."

Rachel knew when to back down and let a man be a man. "Thank you."

"My pleasure."

Michelle couldn't believe what was happening. She was embarrassed that Rachel had invited him to join them, but she was also delighted that Nick had said yes. He was actually going to have lemonade with them! Her spirits soared.

"Why don't you find a table for us while I get the drinks?" Nick suggested.

Rachel and Michelle looked around the crowded seating area and spotted an empty table on the far side. They went to claim it for their own.

"What am I going to do with you?" Michelle said to her friend in mock indignation.

"Thank me?" Rachel cast her an impish grin.

"You're right! Thanks!"

They were both laughing as they settled in to wait for Nick to join them.

It was only a few minutes later when he sought them out.

"Here we are," Nick said as he set the sweet, cool drinks down on the table and then sat opposite Rachel and Michelle.

"You're a true gentleman," Rachel teased.

"I don't know about that. There might be a few around town who'd disagree with you."

"I don't know who they could be," Michelle put in.

"Good. Let's keep it that way."

They were all laughing.

Michelle took a deep drink of her lemonade and sighed, "We have the best lemonade ever."

"You're right about that," Nick agreed, and then, looking at Rachel, he added with a wink, "And the best part is, we can drink all we want and we don't have to worry about your father showing up in protest."

"You're right!" Rachel started laughing. "But knowing how much he loves this lemonade, I'll bet he'd start protesting if they ran out."

They all joined in laughter at that thought.

"Will you be at the dance tonight, Nick?" Rachel asked boldly.

"Yes. What about you?"

"We will, too."

"Then I'll see you both this evening," he told

them as he finished his drink and stood up to go. "I'd better get back to work now, though."

"Thanks again for the lemonade," Michelle said, smiling up at him.

Nick tipped his hat and moved off.

Rachel noticed how Michelle watched him walk away. "See how easy that was!"

Michelle's face wore an excited expression as she looked at her friend. "I can't believe you did that, but I'm so glad you did. How much longer until the dance starts? How many hours do I have to wait? This is so exciting! Nick's going to dance with me!"

"We've got an hour or so yet," Rachel told her, happy that things had gone so well with the deputy.

"Now all we have to do is find Kane for you, and this will turn out to be the best Festival ever!"

"I don't think that's going to happen. I think he really has moved on."

"Have you been praying on it, like I told you to?" Michelle looked at her.

"Yes."

"Then never give up! Prayers *are* answered. You're a preacher's daughter. You should know that."

They finished their drinks, then took the time to enjoy a few more booths and games before going home to change clothes and get ready for the dance.

Chapter Nine

"You look lovely, darling," Martin told Rachel as he watched her descend the staircase in the front foyer of their home. In her demure, lace-trimmed blue ball gown with her hair done up in a cascade of curls, she was the picture of elegant feminine beauty.

"Thank you," Rachel said with a smile. When she reached the bottom of the stairs, she went to kiss him on the cheek. "Are we all ready to go?"

"We're still waiting for your mother."

"Here I am," Anne declared as she appeared at the top of the steps in her fancy dress.

"I am going to be the envy of all the men in Dry Springs tonight," Martin said proudly as she came down the steps to join them. He offered them each an arm to escort them to the dance. "The two prettiest ladies in town are with me."

"You are such a charmer, Reverend Hammond!" Anne teased.

"I only speak the truth."

His wife and daughter both kissed him, one on each cheek. They were all laughing as they started from the house, intent on having a wonderful time that evening.

The dance was being held outside in the park-like area near the courthouse. A dance floor had been set up, and decorative lanterns had been hung all around it. The musicians were playing on a small stage that had been built just for this night. Tables and chairs were available, so the onlookers could relax and enjoy themselves.

"I have a very serious problem here," Martin said, frowning as they stood at the side of the dance floor, watching the couples who were already dancing.

"What's that, dear?" Anne asked.

He looked between his wife and his daughter. "Whom do I dance with first?"

"You and Mother, go ahead," Rachel encouraged. "I just saw Michelle with her family, and I think I'll go visit with them for a while."

"All right, young lady, but you owe me a dance," her father told her with a smile.

"No, you owe me one," she countered.

Martin led Anne out to join the other dancers while Rachel started off to speak with Michelle. Rachel hadn't gotten very far when she heard someone call her name. She turned to find Pete coming toward her.

"Good evening, Rachel," he said, his gaze warm upon her.

"Hello, Pete."

"You look stunning."

"Thank you."

"Would you like to dance?"

"Yes."

They moved together out onto the dance floor.

Clint's mood was dark as he watched the people smiling and laughing and enjoying the evening's activities. He found that their lightheartedness only emphasized the emptiness of his life.

There was no joy in his existence.

There was only his unending quest for justice and revenge.

Clint moved through the crowd, watching and listening. He glanced out at the dancing couples, and saw Rachel in the arms of Sheriff Reynolds. He stopped to watch them dance, his gaze only on Rachel. She was a vision of loveliness, moving with grace and elegance. He'd seen no sign of Hank yet, so he stayed back, waiting for the right moment to approach Rachel and ask her about the attempted robbery.

When the song ended, Pete escorted her to where Michelle was standing.

"This next dance is mine," Pete told Michelle.

"I saved it just for you," she agreed with a smile, but as he drew her out onto the dance floor, she couldn't help wondering what had happened to Nick. She hadn't seen him around all evening.

Rachel watched Michelle dance with Pete for a moment, then decided it was time to get a drink from the refreshment table. She turned away from the dance floor and came face to face with the man she'd thought she would never see again—

Kane.

"You're back," Rachel breathed, gazing up at him in amazement. He looked as handsome as ever, and a shiver of delight coursed through her when he smiled down at her.

"I heard tonight was special," Clint told her. He hadn't thought she could be more beautiful than before, but she was. In the modest but enticing pale blue gown she was wearing, and with her hair done up, she was stunning.

"It is special—now that you're here," she breathed.

"Would you like to dance?"

She nodded, unable to speak in her excitement.

Clint reached out to take her hand and lead her onto the dance floor.

At that one simple touch, Rachel's heartbeat quickened, and when Kane took her in his arms, her breath caught in her throat. It was pure ecstasy being so close to him. She lifted her gaze to study the hard, lean line of his jaw and to admire his rugged good looks, then she closed her eyes and gave herself over to the sensuality of the moment as they began to move together to the melody.

"Have you been enjoying yourself tonight?" Clint asked, wanting to start a conversation and distract himself from his all-too-intense physical awareness of her. She was far too tempting for his peace of mind.

"It's been fun," Rachel said. "And I needed some fun after everything that's happened to me this week. Between the incident at the saloon when you had to rescue me, and the robbery attempt on the stage, it's been a scary week."

"I'm just glad you're safe. I heard the talk about the attack on the stagecoach."

"After what had happened at the Last Chance, my mother insisted I carry a gun when I had to make the unexpected trip to San Ramon."

"Your mother's a wise woman."

"I was thinking the same thing that afternoon when the gunmen started shooting at us. But it was terrible when the posse brought in the dead outlaw, and I realized that I might have been the one who killed him."

Clint understood her emotional torment. "You are a brave woman, Rachel. You did what you had to do to save not only yourself but the others, too."

She lifted her gaze to his, and he could see the depth of her pain and uncertainty reflected there.

"I keep telling myself that."

"I heard down at the saloon that the posse didn't have much luck tracking the outlaws."

"I know. I couldn't believe Pete came back so quickly. I thought the posse would keep after them for a while."

Clint found it interesting that Rachel felt the same way he did about the posse's efforts. "Sheriff Reynolds must have had his reasons."

"I guess. I just hope I never see those outlaws again."

"Would you recognize them if you did?"

Rachel was thoughtful. "I honestly don't know. I don't remember much of anything about that day, except thinking how hard it was to get off a shot when we were being bounced around so much. It all happened so fast, yet at the time, their attack seemed to go on forever."

Rachel frowned, deep in thought. "But, you know, now that you mention it, there was something. The second gunman . . ."

"What about him?"

"His horse was a roan, and it had an unusual marking on its chest."

"Would you recognize the horse if you saw it again?"

"I think so. The marking sort of looked like a star, I guess. Yeah, now that I think about it, it did look like a star. Funny that I didn't remember that sooner."

"Our minds work in mysterious ways." Clint was glad she'd remembered that much. It was something for him to go on.

They fell silent as they continued to move about the dance floor, allowing themselves to just enjoy the moment.

Rachel's spirits were soaring. Kane was actually there dancing with her.

"When Michelle told me you'd checked out of the hotel the other day, I thought you'd left town for good."

"I had to take care of some business, but I'm back now."

"Will you be staying around long this time?" Rachel asked hopefully.

"For a while yet."

"I'm glad."

Clint looked down at Rachel, and their gazes met and locked. For a moment, all time and reality seemed suspended. There were no other couples dancing near them, no hubbub of voices and music surrounding them. There were only the two of them, moving to the subtle rhythm of the dance.

And then the music stopped.

And they were forced to move apart.

"Thank you," she breathed, deeply regretting that the dance was over.

"We're not done yet," Clint said, unwilling to part company with her just yet. He took her hand again as the musicians began another tune.

She laughed in delight. "Are you sure?"

"I'm sure."

Clint drew her back into his arms. They hadn't been dancing long when someone tapped him on the shoulder.

"Mind if I cut in, McCullough?" Pete asked. He was smiling at them, but it was a cold smile.

Clint did mind. He wanted to keep dancing with Rachel and never let her go, but he knew he had no choice in this social setting.

"Rachel, thank you."

He handed Rachel over to the lawman, nodding to her as he strode away.

Rachel watched Kane go as she pretended to enjoy dancing with Pete. She regretted the lawman's interference. Being in Kane's arms had been heavenly, but she knew there had been no way to refuse the sheriff's invitation without making a scene, and that would never do. She managed to smile at Pete as he squired her about.

Pete didn't know what a gunman like Kane McCullough was doing in Dry Springs, but one thing he did know: McCullough had no business being with Rachel. Pete had had his eye on the preacher's daughter for quite a while now, and if he had his way, ultimately she was going to be his. Pushing all thoughts of McCullough aside, Pete relaxed and concentrated on wooing the lovely woman in his arms.

Clint lost himself in the crowd of onlookers. He stood quietly watching Rachel and the lawman dance together. There was something about Sheriff Reynolds that left him on edge, but he couldn't figure out what it was.

Clint tried to tell himself he was only reacting this way because of Rachel, and, in part, he knew that was true, but the fact was, it troubled him that the lawman had given up so quickly on tracking down the outlaws. The trail had been there for the posse to follow. The storm he'd encountered had been far ahead of the posse and it had been moving off in the opposite direction. If the sheriff and his men had been serious about hunting the gunmen down, they would have stayed on their trail for at least another half day until they'd discovered it had been washed out. Only then would they have turned back.

Clint was frowning when he finally made up his mind what he was going to do. Captain Meyers could help him with his concerns about the sheriff. Clint would ride to the next town and send the captain a wire from there, requesting any information he had on Pete Reynolds. He wanted to find out everything he could about the sheriff of Dry Springs. He had seen how violent the lawman could be in the way he'd pistol-whipped Ed, and he'd noticed how the townsfolk were a bit uneasy around him. Clint knew it didn't bode well for his efforts to locate the Tucker Gang if Reynolds proved to be as bad a lawman as he was beginning to believe.

It was getting late when Nick finally made it to the dance. He had been looking forward to attending the dance all day, for he was eager to be with the ladies, but Sheriff Reynolds had had other plans for him. Just as the evening's activities were all set to begin, the sheriff had sought him out and ordered him to stay on the streets and keep watch, just in case anything happened around town.

Nick realized there was always the possibility of trouble occurring when there were this many people in town, and with the recently attempted stage robbery, everybody was still a little on edge. But even so, the sheriff's ordering him to work on the night of the big dance had annoyed him.

But it was his job.

Nick had just hoped as he walked the deserted streets of Dry Springs that if he was ever relieved of his duties, it wouldn't be too late to have a little fun.

It was after eleven when Pete finally sought Nick out and told him he'd take over for him.

Nick didn't waste any time getting to the dance. He was anxious to see which girls were still in attendance, and he was pleased when he spotted Michelle and Rachel right away.

"Evening, ladies," he greeted them. They were both pretty, but he knew better than to pursue Rachel. Pete had made that perfectly clear to him several times.

"We were wondering what happened to you," Rachel told the handsome deputy.

"I was keeping an eye on things around town. Sheriff Reynolds and I wanted to make sure everything was peaceful tonight."

"You did a fine job. It's been a wonderful evening, and now that you're here, it's even better," Michelle said, giving him an inviting smile.

"Would you like to dance, Michelle?" he invited.

"I would love to dance with you," she answered quickly, not worried about seeming too eager. He had finally come! That was all that mattered.

Michelle slipped her hand into Nick's and followed along as he drew her out to join the other couples.

Rachel was smiling as she watched her friend dancing with the man of her dreams. She understood how it felt, for she had felt the same way while dancing with Kane.

Rachel glanced around, looking for Kane, but saw no sign of him. She wondered where he'd gone. She kept up her spirits by reminding herself that he had told her he was going to be in town for a while and they would be seeing each other again.

Equally gratifying was the memory of a very handsome young man asking her to dance right after Kane had released her. She grinned, remembering young Jacob's invitation. Eve had brought him to the festivities, and he'd told his grandmother that he had to dance with Miss Rachel before they went home. It had been a wonderful moment for both of them, and she'd made sure to kiss him on the cheek when their dance had ended.

Rachel sighed in contentment as she watched Michelle in Nick's arms.

It had been a memorable night for everyone.

Chapter Ten

Late Monday afternoon Rachel was returning to town in the family's buggy. She had driven her mother to the Franklin ranch earlier that day after getting a desperate request for help from Ron Franklin. He'd sent a note to her father telling him that his wife, Mary, had just given birth to twins, and it had been a difficult delivery. The babies were sickly, and Mary was weak and not doing well. The doctor had been out to the ranch but had said there was little he could do.

From the sound of the missive, Rachel's parents had had no doubt that Ron was frantic, trying to tend to his wife and their four other children along with the sick babies. Anne had decided to go out to the ranch and help him, and Rachel had gone along. They'd reached the ranch and learned, happily, that Mary seemed to be improving. Even so, Anne had decided to stay on for a day or two to take care of the newborns.

Rachel had started the long drive home to let

her father know that her mother would be staying on at the Franklin ranch for a while. She hadn't been worried about making the return trip by herself. It was still daylight, and she did have the gun with her.

Rachel had been enjoying the drive through the quiet countryside until she noticed black clouds starting to build in the western sky. For a while, she'd believed she could outrun the storm, but then the wind picked up in near violent gusts, and she knew it was going to get ugly. As the distant, ominous rumble of thunder echoed around her, she realized she was in trouble. Slapping the reins on Buster's back, she urged him to an even faster pace. Fast as Buster was, though, he wasn't fast enough. The black clouds began to roil overhead, and crashing lightning split the storm-darkened sky.

Rachel grew more nervous as they raced toward town. When a jagged lightning bolt crashed earthward and struck a nearby tree with fiery fury, Buster panicked. He had been hard to manage before the lightning strike, and now he was completely out of control. He reared up in absolute terror as the deafening roar of thunder echoed around them.

Rachel almost lost her seat in the buggy, but somehow she managed to hang on as Buster charged off the road and raced wildly across the uneven ground. She worked at the reins, fighting to bring the terrified horse under control, but he was out of his mind with fear. He raced over the rocky terrain and didn't even pause when the buggy tipped over.

Thrown from her seat, Rachel landed hard on the unforgiving ground. She lay winded, struggling to catch her breath. Realizing how dangerous the storm might be, she knew she had to find some kind of shelter fast. Shaken and still a bit dazed, she managed to get up and start after her runaway horse and buggy.

Buster had continued his panicked flight, dragging the buggy behind him. When the buggy got hung up on some rocks, it brought him to a halt. As the lightning and thunder continued, he grew even more wildly desperate. He twisted and bucked, trying to break free of the restraining harness and buggy, but his struggle was to no avail. He was trapped.

Rachel finally managed to reach the top of the hill. It was then that she saw Buster caught among the rocks down below. She was thankful he'd gotten trapped that way, for it gave her the chance to catch up with him.

Even so, Rachel knew there was no way she would ever be able to right the buggy by herself. The only way she could get out of the storm would be to unhitch Buster and ride him into town. True, she was wearing a dress and it wouldn't be very ladylike, but with the bad weather almost upon her, she didn't care much about how she looked. She'd seen some bad storms in her time, but this one was one of the most intense she'd ever been in.

Knowing she had to act fast, Rachel ran down to Buster and began to talk to him in low, calming tones. He stilled and stood shaking as she set to work unhitching him from the buggy. Just as she finished and was holding him by the reins, there was a violent gust and another frightening bolt of lightning split the sky. The thunder echoed violently around them.

Buster reared frantically. Rachel tried to hang on to him, but he was too powerful for her. He tore free of her grip and galloped off, leaving her stranded with only the broken remains of the buggy for shelter as the torrential downpour began.

Rachel knew she was in serious trouble. It was almost dark, and there was no way she could get to safety on foot in this kind of thunderstorm. She offered up a quick prayer for help and sought what shelter she could find from the buggy.

Clint had hoped to make it into Dry Springs before the bad weather broke, but the storm front moved in faster than he'd expected. The lightning was powerful, and the rain was harsh. He'd managed to get his slicker on before the downpour started, but as powerful as the winds were, it offered little protection.

His mood was black as he spurred his horse to an even faster pace. He looked around for some kind of shelter, but saw nothing that would offer a haven from what he was sure was going to be a gully washer.

Another bolt of lightning lit up the heavens, and it was then that Clint topped the hill and saw the wrecked carriage below and what looked like a woman huddled against it. He had no idea how the woman had come to be out in the middle of nowhere, alone in the midst of a bad lightning storm, but he couldn't just ride off and leave a helpless female alone in the wilds. From the looks of things, he realized she might have been injured in the accident. Clint rode down to the overturned vehicle, hoping the woman was all right.

Rachel was drenched and more than a little shaken by the accident and the fierce weather. She'd crouched down as low as she could under what little shelter the buggy offered, but it wasn't doing much good. Rachel told herself that she was brave enough to wait out the storm and then walk to town on her own, if she had to. It might take her a while, but she kept telling herself she could do it. She was more afraid of the storm than of anything else, for she did have the gun with her. The thought made her smile, for even though the gun might help to keep her safe, it offered absolutely no protection from the wrath of Mother Nature.

"Are you all right?"

The sound of a man's call so close by shocked Rachel. With the storm raging, she hadn't heard anyone approach. Still, she was thrilled that someone had come upon her so soon.

"Yes! But I'm stranded!" she called over the roar of the wind.

Rachel peeked out from her partial haven to try to get a look at the man who'd come upon her. All she could make out in the downpour was a dark, cloaked figure on horseback, silhouetted against the storm-ravaged sky. At another time, she might have thought him ominous-looking, but at that moment he seemed a knight in shining armor.

"Come on!" the man offered. "Let me help you!"

Rachel didn't need to be asked twice. Leaving what meager protection she had, she grabbed up the small bag she'd carried with her and ran toward her rescuer.

"Rachel?"

When she heard her name, she recognized Kane's voice and looked up at him in amazement. "Kane? What are you doing out here?"

"Rescuing you, I think," he told her as he reached down and held out his hand to her.

Rachel took it without hesitation and was amazed when, in one easy swing, he pulled her up behind him on the horse.

She couldn't believe how strong he was to lift her up so easily. "I was glad to see you Saturday night, but I'm even more glad to see you now."

"Hold on tight," he directed.

"Don't worry. I will," she promised, linking her arms around his lean waist. Then she offered, "In case you didn't know, there's an abandoned shack about a mile to the north."

"We'll take shelter there until it lets up. There's

no way we can make it to town right now. This is one ugly storm."

Clint followed her directions, and they rode quickly through the pouring rain to the dilapidated building. He reined in and handed Rachel down before dismounting himself.

"This isn't much," he said. It was obvious the place hadn't been lived in for a long time.

"It's better than nothing."

"You're right about that," he agreed.

Rachel ran up the broken-down steps to the cover of the small porch. She shoved open the rotting front door and went inside.

Clint spotted a decrepit lean-to around back and took his horse there so the animal could have some shelter from the storm. Carrying his rifle, bedroll, and saddlebags with him, he joined Rachel inside and closed the door behind him.

Clint set his belongings down on the floor before looking around. He hadn't expected much more than a roof over their heads, so he wasn't disappointed. The abandoned one-room house was dirty, and the roof was leaking in several places. Still, it could have been a lot worse. They could have still been outside.

A flash of lightning lit up the place, and it was then that Clint got his first good look at Rachel. She was standing across the small room from him, drenched and visibly shaking. Her dark hair was half unbound and hanging loose and wet about her shoulders, and her shirtwaist gown was soaked. It was a modest garment, but now that it was soaking wet, it clung to her slender figure, outlining her very feminine curves. For a moment, he couldn't look away, and then he forced himself to lower his eyes.

"Are you sure you're all right?" he asked again, going to her.

"I—I think so."

"What were you doing out here in the middle of this storm all by yourself?" He was surprised that her father would let her ride out alone.

She quickly told him about the trip to the Franklin ranch and her mother's decision to stay on. "I was on my way home to let my father know when the storm came up real fast. The lightning spooked my horse. He bolted and wrecked the buggy. I unhitched him, because I thought I could ride him back to town, but then the lightning started up again and he got away from me."

"You sure you're not hurt?" His expression was concerned as he looked her over again.

"No, I'm just wet," she said, finally relaxing a bit and managing a smile at him.

"There's no way to avoid getting soaked in weather like this. It's blowing so hard out there right now, I wouldn't be surprised to see a twister come through."

Worried by the prospect, Rachel went to look out one of the windows at the still raging storm. "It is nasty out there. Thank heaven you came along when you did. I don't know what I would have done without you."

"It was pure luck that I came across you."

"It wasn't luck." She turned away from the window to look up at him. "You were the answer to my prayer."

"I don't think so."

"I do. You rode up just when I had finished praying to be rescued."

"I've never been the answer to anybody's prayers before," he said with a wry grin.

"Well, you were tonight. Your timing was perfect, and I'm almost beginning to think you might be my guardian angel, the way you keep showing up to help me whenever I'm in trouble."

Rachel heard a terrible roaring sound outside and quickly looked out the window again. The wind was so fierce, the rain appeared to be blowing sideways.

"Why don't you get over here away from that window? I don't like the way that sounds," Clint warned. He'd never been caught in a tornado, but he'd seen the damage they could do and knew they were deadly.

Rachel did as he suggested, coming back to stand in the middle of the darkened room. "I wonder how long this is going to last. My father will be getting worried. He's expecting Mother and I to be home tonight."

"The moment it lets up, we can head into town, but from the way things are looking right now, I don't think that's going to be anytime soon."

"We might as well try to get comfortable while we wait it out," Rachel suggested.

They took another look around the place. The only furnishings that had been left behind when the family moved on were two ramshackle straight-backed chairs and a broken-down bed frame with no mattress.

"I think it must have been a while since anyone lived here," Clint said.

"Over two years," she told him. "The family that owned the place belonged to our church. They fell on some real hard times and had to move on."

"Too bad, but at least they left us something to sit on." Clint dragged the chairs to a place in the room where there were no leaks.

Lightning lit up the room for a moment, and Rachel spotted a lamp on the floor near the foot of the bed. She hurried over to check it out.

"We've got a lamp!" she told Kane excitedly, but her mood quickly sobered. "Not that it's going to do us any good. I don't have any matches."

"I do." He went to his saddlebags and dug them out. "But does it have any oil?"

"A little. It should last us for a while."

There was no telling how long it had been since the lamp had been used, but they didn't care. What mattered was finally having some decent light in the cabin. They lit the lamp and put it on the shelf over the small fireplace. Knowing Clint had more matches, Rachel considered starting a fire, but after taking a look at the fireplace, she realized, that it had deteriorated too much to be of use.

She settled in, ready to wait out the storm. She had to admit to herself that if she had to be stranded with anyone, she was thrilled she was stranded with Kane. She studied him as he came to sit in the other chair.

"I told you my story. Now why were you out riding in weather like this?" Rachel asked.

"I had some business in Silver Pass I had to take care of, and I was on my way back to Dry Springs, too." As he spoke, another powerful, roaring gust of wind and rain battered the building. He tensed, almost believing the cabin was going to be leveled.

Rachel couldn't help herself. She started laughing as she listened to the driving rain. "I don't think it's very dry in Dry Springs right now."

"I think you're right," Clint agreed, actually laughing out loud at her jest.

It was the first time she'd ever heard him laugh. It was a deep, mellow sound, and as her gaze went over him, she realized again just how attracted she was to him.

"You should laugh more often," she said in a throaty voice.

Her words sobered him. "Sometimes there's not a lot to laugh about in life."

"But sometimes there is," she countered. "Like wondering what the odds were that we'd end up stranded in an abandoned shack together in the midst of this terrible storm."

The moment Rachel said she was wondering what the odds were, Clint found himself smiling at her. "You know, your father is a preacher. He wouldn't approve of any kind of gambling, now would he?"

At that, Rachel grinned back at him. "You're right, but if it meant he'd show up here right now to stage a protest, I'd be willing to risk it."

They both liked the idea of her father doing just that.

"I don't think he's going to show up, though," Clint said.

"I know. We'll just have to wait for the storm to pass before we can head home."

"And you don't want to make any bets on how long it's going to last?"

"No," she answered with a grin.

Clint was entranced by her smile. He'd always known she was lovely, but there in the flickering lamplight, Rachel was absolutely beautiful. A part of him silently hoped the storm would last all night so they would have this time together, but the serious side of him warned against allowing himself to care for her. He was in Dry Springs for one reason only, and it wasn't to court the preacher's daughter.

Chapter Eleven

Rachel was uncomfortable as she sat there in her wet clothes, but there was nothing she could do about it. She consoled herself with the thought that they were lucky this hadn't happened during the winter months. Just the thought of those cold temperatures made her shiver.

"Are you cold?" Clint asked, ready to offer her his slicker. It wasn't much, but he thought it might help a little.

"I'll be all right. I was just thinking about how bad this would be in the winter."

"The good news is it's not January. There's no way we could get a fire going in the fireplace." He could see the water dripping in the damaged chimney.

"Are you hungry?" Rachel asked, remembering the sweet roll her mother had given her for her trip. At the time, she'd thought she wouldn't eat it until she got home, but now she was grateful for the sustenance. Her mother had baked the rolls the night before and had taken them along as a treat for the Franklin family.

"I've got some hardtack," Clint offered. He was hungry, but he'd been looking forward to getting a decent meal in town, not eating hardtack.

"What about a sweet roll?"

"You've got a sweet roll and you're willing to share?"

"I'm my father's daughter," Rachel said. "And, yes, it's right here."

She got her bag, took out the sweet roll, and unwrapped it. She broke it in half, then handed him his portion. "Here."

"Thanks." He took a bite of the pastry, then said, "This is really good."

"My mother baked it."

"Tell her for me that it's delicious."

"One of these days you can tell her yourself."

"I'll do that."

Rachel took a bite of her half of the sweet roll. They both fell silent as they enjoyed their "meal."

"That was the best dinner I've had in a while. It was definitely better than my hardtack," Clint told her.

"My mother is a wonderful cook," Rachel agreed, getting up to take another look out the window.

It was almost completely dark outside now, and the roar of the storm continued unabated. She'd been concerned when they'd first taken refuge in the shack, but now that it was getting late, she feared they really might not make it back to town that night.

"You look worried," he said, watching her.

"What time do you think it is?"

"It's probably close to eight-thirty." Clint got up and went to stand by her side, where he gazed out at the sky. "The rain hasn't let up much, but if you want to, we can ride out. It won't be easy, but we can try to make it."

"I wish we could," Rachel told him, "but since it's getting dark, I don't think it's safe. The terrain is rugged, and I'm sure there's some flooding."

She was very aware of Kane's presence as he stood beside her. She looked up at him, taking in the broad, powerful width of his chest and shoulders, and the hard, lean line of his jaw, dark now with a day's growth of beard. She was surprised when she found herself wondering what it would be like to kiss him. As she imagined it, excitement tingled through her.

Clint happened to glance down at her just then, and he went still as he saw the desire in her eyes. A hunger stirred deep within him, and he didn't try to deny it. He reached out and drew her to him, then without saying a word, as a deep roll of thunder echoed across the countryside, he kissed her.

His kiss was tentative at first. He didn't want to frighten her with the power of the desire he felt for her, but when Rachel moaned softly in response and moved closer, he wrapped his arms around her and deepened the exchange.

Rachel's heartbeat quickened. She responded hungrily to his kiss. She clung to Kane, thrilled to be in his arms. It seemed to her she'd been waiting her whole life for this moment.

Clint crushed her to him as his lips moved possessively, hungrily over hers. The feel of her soft curves against him fed the fire of his need. There was no denying he wanted her. He had from the first moment he'd set eyes on her.

Rachel was in ecstasy.

This was Kane.

Just a short time ago, she'd feared she would never see him again, and now they were alone together. She wanted to stay in his arms. She wanted to be with him always.

Clint was savoring every moment of holding Rachel. He never wanted to let her go, but he knew he had to. Rachel was beauty and innocence and all woman, and because she was, he had to end the embrace before things got out of hand. As chaste as she was, he was certain she had no idea how much he wanted her, and since it looked as if they were going to end up spending the night alone together in the cabin, he didn't want to let his desire for her overrule his common sense.

With great reluctance, Clint ended the kiss. He gazed down at her and saw the bewilderment in her expression.

"You are a very tempting woman, Rachel Hammond," he told her, putting her from him.

She was puzzled. She didn't know why he'd stopped kissing her. She wanted to go back into his arms and stay there, but his next words stopped her.

"But you are the preacher's daughter."

His words jarred her back to reality.

"Oh—"

Conflicting feelings assailed Rachel as she stood there, momentarily lost in the confusion of the battle between her emotions and reason.

Clint knew they both needed a distraction, so he went to his saddlebags and rifled through them.

"Since we're going to be stuck here a while longer, you want to have a little fun?" he asked when he found what he'd been looking for.

"I thought we were having fun," she said, feeling a little wild.

Clint bit back a groan at her remark. In her innocence, she was the perfect, if unknowing, seductress. He could only imagine what she would have been like if she'd known what she was doing and the effect she had on him.

"That kind of fun will only get us in trouble. I've got something else we can do—if you feel like being a little daring tonight," he challenged her. He wanted to get both their minds off what had just transpired between them.

"All right—what did you have in mind?" She looked around the shambles of the damp and dirty room.

"Playing poker." He showed her the deck of cards he'd retrieved from his saddlebag.

"Poker?" Rachel was shocked. Her father believed gambling was bad.

"Poker is basically an easy game. It won't take you long to learn how to play."

"But my father—"

Clint understood her concern, and he had an answer ready for her.

"I'm not going to tell him—are you?"

"No," she answered with a grin.

"So your father will never know," he finished. "Sit down while I fix a place we can play."

Clint shoved the half-rotted bed slats together on the broken-down bed frame to create a makeshift table. Then he pushed their chairs in close and sat down.

"Are you ready?" he asked, glancing up at her as he began to shuffle the deck.

"I guess." Rachel still felt a bit wild as she went to sit down with him.

"If you're worried about your father's belief that gambling is wrong, we won't make any bets. That way our cardplaying won't really be gambling."

Rachel smiled at him, relieved that he'd found a way to ease the guilt she'd been feeling. "All right—how do we play?"

"Like this."

She watched as he expertly dealt them each five cards.

"Check your hand. Pairs are good, three of a kind are better. There are straights and flushes, too."

Clint explained the various combinations, and quickly discovered that Rachel was a very fast learner. After the first couple of practice hands, he knew she was ready.

"All right, this time we're serious," he said as he dealt the cards.

Rachel picked up her cards and immediately started to smile. She had a pair of kings.

"Serious gamblers don't let on if they've got a good hand," Clint advised as she looked up at him in obvious delight.

"Oh, sorry." She faked a frown.

He turned his attention to his own cards and found little to smile about. "I'm taking three. What about you?"

"Just two," she responded confidently.

He dealt her two cards, then picked up his three to see how his luck was holding up. He discovered that it wasn't. He threw his hand down in disgust.

"I'm out."

"That means I won, right?"

"Right. What have you got?"

"Two pair—kings and tens," Rachel stated proudly as she spread the cards out for him to see.

"All right, let's try it again."

Clint shuffled the deck and dealt another hand. The results proved much the same.

"This is fun!" Rachel proclaimed, winning for a second time.

"For you it is—you're winning," he remarked, slapping his losing hand down on the table. He was glad this wasn't a serious game. He didn't like being a loser.

"I'm only winning because I have such a good teacher," she complimented him.

"I'm sure that's it," Clint agreed sarcastically.

"It's too bad we're not betting."

"You'd be cleaning up, that's for sure."

"I know. Come on, deal again!" She realized he'd been right. Playing poker was fun—and distracting. Concentrating on the card game kept her from thinking too much about what had happened earlier between them and how hard it was still storming outside.

They continued to play, and Clint continued to lose. Every now and then he managed to win a hand, but it wasn't often.

Clint finally drew into a flush, and he was just about ready to show Rachel his winning hand when suddenly the lamp burned out and they were left in complete darkness.

"What happened?" she asked, looking around nervously.

"The lamp must have run out of oil," he answered, getting up to check.

Clint moved carefully across the room to the mantel and lit one of his matches so he could inspect the lamp.

"We've been left in the dark, and just when I had a winning hand, too," he told her.

"What are we going to do?"

"There's not a lot we can do except call it a night. You can use my bedroll. There's a place over here where you'll be dry." He blew out the match as it burned down low.

Rachel was tired, but she was unsure of the proper thing to do. There was no doubt it was inappropriate for them to spend the night together unchaperoned this way, but under these dire circumstances, they had no choice.

"If I use your bedroll, where will you sleep?"

"I'll sleep in the chair." Clint assured her. He got his bedroll and spread it out for her. "You're all set."

"Thanks." Rachel made her way over to him.

"Good night," Clint bade her. He was tempted to take her in his arms again, but he feared he would never let her go if he did. He started to move away.

But Rachel stopped him. She reached out and touched his arm, and when he turned back, she drew him down to her for a kiss.

Clint had been trying to deny himself, but her kiss was all the invitation he needed. His lips moved possessively over hers in a devouring exchange that left them both breathless and hungry for more—much more. Lifting her into his arms, he laid her upon the bedroll and then followed her down, covering her body with his. They kissed again and were caught up in the fire of their need. His lips left hers and trailed a fiery path down her neck.

Rachel arched instinctively against the lean, hard heat of him as desire coursed through her. She'd never known such intimacy or such passion.

"Kane—" she whispered as she caressed the powerful width of his back and shoulders.

Clint was caught up in the excitement of Rachel's kiss and touch. Only when she whispered "Kane" did reality return, and suddenly he realized how close he'd come to losing control. He kissed her one last time, deeply, hungrily, then moved away from her. He knew if he wanted to keep his sanity, he had to put distance between them.

"Good night," he said, his tone gruff as he fought down his desire for her. She was tempting, but he knew they could go no further. In fact, they had already gone too far for his peace of mind. He stood up and went over to the window to look out one last time.

Rachel stared after Kane, wanting to go to him, but knowing he'd done the right thing by moving away.

"Good night," she said softly. Covering herself with the blanket, she sought what little comfort she could find there on the floor. She closed her eyes and tried to sleep, but she knew it would be long in coming—if it came at all.

Clint stood at the window, watching the storm for a while longer, then went to sit down. He wanted to rest, but dark thoughts of his real reason for being there intruded. After the poker hands he'd dealt himself that night, he hoped his luck would change for the better before the Tucker Gang showed up.

Clint hoped, too, that Captain Meyers knew something about Sheriff Reynolds. He was going to ride back to the next town in a few days and see if there was any response to the telegram he'd sent his former captain. He had an uneasy feeling about the lawman and knew it was best to check him out. He didn't want anything or anybody to interfere with what he had to do.

Nothing was going to stop him.

Nothing.

Again the sound of distant thunder rumbled across the land. It sounded as if the storm was moving off now, and that was good. At first light they would head for town.

Clint wondered how Rachel's parents would react when they found out he'd been forced to spend the night with their daughter. He grimaced at the thought and put it from him. That was the least of his problems. He was closing in on Tuck and Ax. They should be showing up any day now, and once they did, it wouldn't be long before he found the real leader of the gang.

He was looking forward to that day.

It was what he was living for.

Nothing else mattered.

Clint closed his eyes, but sleep did not come.

Rachel lay staring up at the ceiling in the darkness. Until now, she hadn't realized how tired she was. It had been a long, eventful day. First the rushed trip to help the Franklins, then the storm and the wrecked buggy, and finally being rescued by Kane.

A feeling of warmth crept over her, and she turned on her side to study him where he sat in the chair across the room. In the darkness, silhouetted against what little light was coming through the window, Kane looked very much the loner. But, loner though he might be, he was still the man who'd saved her at the Last Chance and rescued her from the storm. Not to mention, he'd taught her how to play poker.

That thought alone left her smiling into the night. Rachel didn't know what the future held, but she would always have the memory of this night alone with him—and how she'd won almost every game.

Chapter Twelve

Martin Hammond spent a restless night. The storm that had passed through had been violent. He wouldn't be surprised if a twister or two had come out of it, and he had no doubt there was some wind damage around town.

Martin was up at first light. Though the storm had passed, he was still uneasy and on edge. He almost felt as if something was wrong, but he didn't know why. He believed Anne and Rachel had wisely chosen to stay at the Franklin ranch overnight rather than risk trying to make it back to town before the storm broke. He was certain they would be returning some time that morning with news of how Mrs. Franklin and the new-borns were doing.

After offering up his morning prayers in hopes they would calm his uneasiness, Martin set about making himself breakfast. He was just about to sit down at the table with his scrambled eggs and a cup of coffee when he heard someone come running up outside calling his name.

"Reverend Hammond!"

Martin hurried out on the porch to find it was Bill Clark, the owner of the stable in town.

"What is it, Bill? What's wrong?"

"Plenty!" the stable owner answered worriedly. "Your horse just came back—"

"My horse?" He frowned in confusion.

"The one I hitched up for Anne and Rachel yesterday."

"What!" Now Martin was shocked.

"I just found him. He came running into the yard down at the stable. He's real scared. He's still got the harness on, but there was no buggy!"

"No buggy—dear God! Rachel and Anne are in trouble!" Martin panicked. "Saddle me up a horse, Bill, and see if anyone else wants to ride with me. If there's been an accident, we might need a buckboard."

"I'll go with you," Bill offered. "I'll be waiting for you down at the stable."

"I'll be right there."

Bill hurried off.

Martin rushed to close up the house. All the uneasy feelings he'd been having now made sense. Anne and Rachel must have been in a wreck on the trip back home last night. They could both have been injured—or worse.

Martin refused to let his thoughts explore the terrible possibilities. He rushed through town to the stable, and on his way he saw the havoc the storm had wreaked on Dry Springs. Several trees were down, and some folks were already out, making repairs to roofs and shutters that had been damaged. When Martin reached the stable, he found Bill ready to ride out.

"Where's the horse?" he asked Bill.

"In the corral," Bill answered.

Martin went to check Buster over, and he could see by the animal's condition that he'd been out all night in the storm, for he was still spooked and edgy.

"I wonder what could have happened to them?" Martin worried as he mounted up.

"It's hard to say. Maybe they decided to wait it out somewhere along the way and the horse ran off." Bill tried to think positively as he took up the reins of the team hitched to the buckboard, but, in truth, a horse showing up this way usually meant trouble.

"I pray you're right," Martin said, silently offering up a prayer for his family's safety.

"So do I."

The two men said no more as they rode out of town.

Clint was awake as the eastern horizon grew lighter. The old wooden chair he'd passed the night in definitely hadn't been made for comfort, but even if he'd had a clean bed, he doubted he would have gotten any rest. His thoughts had been too troubled.

Looking over at where Rachel lay sleeping, he

felt a stirring of emotion deep within him. Last night in the storm, he'd found excitement and pleasure in her arms. She was beautiful and passionate and innocent—and she'd just spent the whole night alone with him in this cabin.

Clint knew they'd really had no choice. It was a new day now, and what was done was done, but the time they'd spent together unchaperoned didn't bode well for her reputation.

She was the preacher's daughter.

Clint frowned. He was troubled by the thought of what she might face back in town. He feared her reputation would be ruined even though nothing had really happened between them and he wondered how he could make amends. There was no doubt what his mother would have expected him to do.

With the thought of his mother, memories returned, and with the memories came the cold, driving fury that was his motivation now.

He had come to Dry Springs to find the Tucker Gang.

He was going to finish what he'd started.

Tearing his gaze away from Rachel, Clint got up and went outside to check on his horse. The sooner he got Rachel safely back to Dry Springs, the better—for both of them.

As he saddled Shadow, Clint found himself wondering if any of the Tucker Gang had shown up in town while he'd been away. He hoped they had, for the waiting was getting to him. Once they showed up, it would be just a matter of play-

ing his cards right to work his way into the gang
and learn who their real leader was.

When Clint realized he'd thought of dealing
with the outlaws in terms of gambling, he grimaced. After the luck he'd had last night playing
poker with Rachel, he knew he should probably
give up gambling on anything for a while.

Clint knew it was time to see if Rachel was stirring yet. With daylight upon them, there was not
a moment to lose.

Rachel had come awake to find it was morning
and she was alone in the cabin. She was surprised
that she'd actually fallen asleep. She'd been so excited by all that had happened, she hadn't expected to get any rest at all. She lay there quietly
for a moment, thinking of the night just past. The
memory of Kane's kiss and touch still had the
power to leave her breathless. It had been
thrilling to be in his embrace. She would have
been happy to stay in his arms forever. This
morning she understood far more clearly the
meaning of temptation.

Rachel smiled at the thought of the lessons
she'd learned the past night. She'd learned that
being in Kane's embrace was ecstasy, and she'd
learned how to play poker—and win. She would
always treasure the time they'd had together and
what they'd shared, but she understood just how
easily some people might be lured into a way of
life that would ultimately bring them nothing but
heartache and pain.

Getting up, she went to the window and saw Kane leading his horse around front. A tingle of excitement went through her at the sight of him—so tall and powerful. He moved with an easy male grace that left her mesmerized as she watched him. Rachel wanted to rush outside and throw herself in his arms and never let him go. She began to tremble in anticipation of being close to him again, and the thought came to her—

I love him.

Rachel was stunned by the revelation. Did she love him? She barely knew him, and yet there was no denying the power of her emotions. She did love him. She smiled and started toward the door as Kane came in.

Clint was surprised to find Rachel up when he walked in.

"Good morning," he greeted her with an easy smile. His gaze went over her, and he thought her even more lovely this morning, though he didn't know how that could be possible.

"Yes, it is," she agreed. "It isn't raining."

"The sky is clear, but there's been some storm damage. Several trees are down here, so I don't know what we'll find as we get closer to town. Are you about ready to ride out?" He wanted to get her back home as early as possible.

"Yes," she said as she crossed the room to stand before him. "But there is one thing—"

"What?"

Rachel reached up and linked her arms around his neck, drawing him down to her.

138

"Thank you," she whispered, and then she kissed him.

Clint allowed himself to enjoy the pleasure of her kiss for a moment, but as the heat stirred within him, he knew he had to break it off. They were going to be riding together on the same mount, and it wouldn't be easy to ignore her, pressed against him as she would be. With great regret, he ended the kiss and put some distance between them.

"Rachel, I don't know what you're thanking me for, but there's something I need to say, too."

"What?" She looked up at him, wondering what he meant.

"I'm sorry," he said simply.

"You're sorry for what?" Rachel was confused.

"We should have returned to town last night when the storm ended."

"But why? We talked about it. We both knew how dangerous it might be if there was flooding, and you just said there are trees down nearby. We did the right thing staying here," she insisted.

"I know, but I'm worried about your reputation. We did spend the night alone together."

"I'm the preacher's daughter. Nobody's going to think bad things about me. You saved me from the storm after my buggy was wrecked. That's what happened, and that's what matters."

"But what about your parents?"

"They'll believe me.

"Are you sure?"

"Yes. It'll be fine. Trust me."

"Then we'd better get going."

They gathered up their few possessions and rode out.

Martin and Bill were keeping careful watch as they traveled the road to the Franklin ranch. The storm's devastation on the countryside was evident, and with each passing mile Martin's concern for his family grew. In his heart, he prayed unceasingly that he would find his wife and daughter unharmed.

"What could have happened to them?" Martin worried aloud. "It just doesn't make sense for the horse to come back to town unhitched that way."

"I don't know, but we'll find them. Don't you worry about that."

They came around a curve in the road, and it was then that they spotted the wrecked buggy.

"Oh, my God!" Martin cried out as he spurred his horse to a run, leaving Bill to follow in the buckboard.

When he reached the wreck, he threw himself off his horse. Dread filled him as he ran toward the buggy. Were his wife and daughter there, injured or dead in the wreckage?

The relief that filled Martin was great as he reached the broken vehicle and discovered no sign of Anne or Rachel. He offered up a quick prayer of thanks to God that they weren't dead, and then immediately realized his worries weren't over.

"They're not here!" he shouted to Bill as the other man reined in nearby.

"Then where could they be?" Bill asked, coming to look things over with him.

Martin lifted his troubled gaze to stare around the landscape. A sick, worried feeling haunted him. "I wish I knew. As bad as the storm was, if they were abandoned out here all alone . . ."

"There are no homes nearby that they could have reached on foot in the midst of that storm."

"The nearest ranch is the Miller place, and that's at least three miles south of here."

"Isn't that old abandoned Harris place still standing?"

Martin was thoughtful. "I'm not sure, but it's worth taking a look. They might have been able to get there on foot."

Bill climbed back on the buckboard and Martin mounted up, ready to check out the abandoned cabin. They'd just started to ride when Bill noticed a horse with two riders coming over the hill.

"Martin! Look!"

Martin couldn't believe his eyes. Even from this distance, he recognized his daughter. "It's Rachel!"

Clint had just crested the hill when he spotted the horseman and a man driving a buckboard near the wrecked buggy.

"There's your father," he told her.

"It is!" She was delighted. She knew her father must have been worried sick about her, but the fact that they'd found each other now made everything all right.

Clint urged his horse on, and they rode down to meet her father and the buckboard.

Bobbi Smith

The minute Clint reined in, Rachel slipped down from where she'd been riding behind him and ran to her father, who'd also dismounted.

"Thank heaven, you're here and you're all right!" Martin said, hugging her to his heart. "I've been so worried about you. When Bill told me the horse had come back without you—"

"I know—it's been an ordeal. The weather was so terrible last night—"

"Where's your mother?" Martin asked, looking around but seeing only Kane McCullough with her.

"She's still out at the Franklin ranch. They needed her help, so she decided to stay a few extra days. I was on my way home last night to let you know when the storm came up and the horse panicked and took off."

"Were you thrown from the buggy?"

"Yes." She nodded. "It was scary, but I wasn't really hurt."

"Thank heaven."

"Kane showed up a short time later and rescued me just as the weather started to get really bad."

Martin looked up at the man who'd saved his daughter from almost certain harm. "Thank you, Mr. McCullough."

"I was glad to help—and you can call me Kane."

"All right, Kane. I appreciate everything you've done for my daughter."

Rachel asked, "How are things in town? We were afraid there might be a tornado last night."

Defiant

"I didn't see a tornado, but there might have been one," Bill put in. "Something bad hit Fred Garvey's place. I saw him in town real early this morning, and he said he'd lost the roof on his house, and his whole barn."

"It was a bad storm, that's for sure, but you're safe. That's all that matters." Martin was smiling at Rachel. "So how were things out at the Franklin place this morning? Is everyone all right? How'd they manage to weather the storm?"

Rachel realized at that moment that her father thought Kane had taken her back to the ranch after he'd found her, and she knew she had to tell him the truth. "I don't know how they are today. Kane and I couldn't get back there after the buggy was wrecked. The weather was too violent. We ended up spending the night at the old Harris place."

Bill looked shocked as he heard the news. He couldn't believe what he'd just heard.

Rachel had spent the night alone with this man—this stranger.

Bill said nothing, though, waiting to see how Martin would handle the news.

Martin was startled by her revelation, too.

"You two spent the night alone there?" he asked, an edge of caution in his voice.

"We had no choice, Papa," Rachel said simply. "Last night after the wreck, I was just grateful to be alive, and then when Kane appeared out of nowhere and helped me right in the middle of the downpour—well, thank goodness he showed up

143

when he did. I don't know what would have happened to me if he hadn't been riding by."

"I don't either," Martin agreed, dismissing any thoughts that anything untoward might have happened between them. They'd been caught in a difficult situation, and they'd made the best of it.

Martin walked over to where Kane was still sitting on his horse and extended his hand up to him. "I am grateful for your kindness to my daughter. Thank you." His words were heartfelt.

Kane shook his hand. "You're welcome."

"Martin, do you want to try to right the buggy now?" Bill asked. He was very uncomfortable with what he'd just heard. True, Rachel was the reverend's daughter and the storm had been a savage one, but a young, pretty, unmarried girl like her should never spend a whole night unchaperoned with a single man. He could imagine what the ladies in town were going to be thinking once the word got out.

"No. There's no need. I'll send some men out with an extra horse later on to bring it back in," he answered. "Right now, I just want to take my daughter home."

"And I just want to go home," Rachel agreed.

"Bill, why don't you ride my horse, and I'll drive the buckboard back with Rachel?" Martin suggested.

"Sure, we can do that," the other man said.

A short time later, they were on their way to Dry Springs.

Clint had been surprised by her father's easy

144

acceptance of her explanation of the night just past, but he'd been glad it had gone so smoothly for her. The last thing he wanted was for Rachel to end up in trouble because of him.

Chapter Thirteen

When Michelle heard about Rachel's accident later that morning, she was worried about her friend. She hurried over to the Hammonds' house to make sure Rachel was all right.

"What are you doing here?" Rachel asked, surprised by her friend's visit.

"Checking on you," she answered.

"I'm fine. Really."

"My mother heard that you'd been in some kind of accident coming back from the Franklin ranch yesterday," Michelle said as she came inside.

"Yes, but everything's fine."

"That's good to know."

"Can you stay for a while? Mother's still out with the Franklins, and Papa went over to the church for a while."

"Sure."

They went to sit in the parlor to talk, and Rachel told Michelle all that had happened.

"It's amazing you weren't seriously hurt."

"I know. It was scary. I was very lucky—or should I say blessed? And then, when Kane rode up out of nowhere in the middle of the storm, I was sure he was my guardian angel."

"Without the wings, of course," Michelle laughed.

"Of course."

"I wish Nick would come riding up and rescue me." Michelle sighed romantically, thinking of the handsome deputy and wishing she could see him more often.

"Just be glad you weren't stranded like I was. It was really frightening—until Kane showed up."

"I know you're right, but just think about it: You got to be alone with Kane all night."

"So everyone's talking about that, are they?" Rachel had expected the gossip to start, but not quite so soon.

Michelle looked a bit embarrassed for her friend. "There's talk going around, but anyone who lived through that storm last night knows you and Kane did what you had to do to survive. There's no scandal involved in that. It's called staying alive."

"I'm glad no one's trying to stir up any trouble about it. I was worried for a while last night about being unchaperoned with him, but we really had no choice."

"Gee, it must have been hard for you to suffer through all that time alone together," Michelle teased in mock sympathy, wanting to lighten their mood.

Rachel smiled. "I can't say much for the accommodations, but Kane was wonderful."

"What did you do?"

Rachel looked guilty for a moment, then confided, "He taught me to play poker."

"He did?" Michelle was shocked and then started smiling. She asked, "Did you tell your father what you did to pass the time?"

"No, and I'm not going to, because there was no gambling involved. We didn't place any bets. We were just trying to amuse ourselves while we waited out the storm."

"Well, I'm just glad you're back safely. That's all that matters. Have you heard anything more from your mother?"

"Nothing yet, but I'm sure she'll either be back later today or send word."

"Let's hope Mrs. Franklin and her babies are doing all right."

Michelle got up to leave, and Rachel walked with her to the door.

"The next time you plan a big adventure like this, let me know. Then I can figure out a way to travel with you, and we can arrange to have Nick rescue us when we get in trouble." Michelle smiled at the thought, imagining how romantic it would be to be stranded that way together. Thinking of romance and knowing Rachel's feelings for Kane, she had to ask conspiratorially, "Rachel—"

Rachel heard the change in her friend's tone and wondered at it. "What?"

"Did Kane—? Did he kiss you?"

Rachel blushed at her friend's question, but confided, "Yes. He did."

Michelle was delighted for her friend and gave her a quick hug. "That is so-o-o romantic! Are you going to see him again soon?"

Rachel frowned at that question, for, when they'd reached town, her father had driven straight home and Kane hadn't followed. "I don't know—but I hope so."

"I hope you do, too! The sooner, the better."

"You come by the Silver Dollar for an early lunch any day, Sheriff—I'll be glad to wait on you—and serve you up something real special," Melody told Pete as she lay naked on the rumpled bed; she was covered only by a sheet. She was watching him get dressed with open interest.

"You did just that today, darlin'," Pete complimented her as he strapped on his gun belt.

"Are you sure you wouldn't like some dessert?" she asked in a husky voice.

Her tone was sensual and inviting, and Pete was tempted, but he'd already spent too much time with her. He had to get back to work. He gave Melody a lewd grin. "I know you're a sweet little thing, but if I stay here any longer, people are going to start wondering why I took such a long lunch hour."

"Because you were hungry?" she purred, letting the sheet drop away to bare her breasts.

Heat rose within Pete again, but he tried to ignore it.

Melody pouted when he seemed unaffected by her deliberately seductive move. Most of the men she served fell all over themselves in their rush to get back into her bed when she did that.

"Are you sure you wouldn't like a little something more?" She rose up on her knees before him and let the sheet fall completely away from her. She watched Pete closely, enjoying the struggle he was going through. Very few men had ever been able to just walk away from her when she began enticing them this way. "Dessert never takes very long—and you know I'm a real good cook. Wouldn't you like something—sweet?"

Pete considered how quiet it was outside and knew an extra few minutes wouldn't matter today. He walked over to the bed and took Melody up on her offer.

The dessert she offered was sweet, just as she'd said, and he did enjoy it.

He left her a big tip on the bedside table for the quick, satisfying service.

When Pete made his way downstairs, the bar was still mostly empty.

"Business pretty quiet so far today, Silas?" Pete asked, looking around.

"So far, but it's early yet. Not everybody can get away for lunch like you—if you know what I mean," he said with a conspiratorial smile. He made it a point to have his working girls give the sheriff anything he wanted, any time he wanted it. It kept the lawman happy and encouraged him to look the other way when there was any trouble at the Silver Dollar.

"I do enjoy your lunch hour. Your waitresses serve it up real good, Silas. I'll see you later."

Pete left the saloon and started back to the jail to see what Nick was up to.

"Did you have a good lunch?" Nick asked, looking up from the desk when Pete walked in the office.

"You know it," he said with a more than satisfied grin. "What's been happening here?"

"Nothing much, except for the talk I heard about Rachel Hammond's accident."

"Something happened to Rachel? What?"

"Evidently she was on her way back from the Franklin ranch yesterday when the storm hit. Her buggy was wrecked and her horse ran off. She was stuck out there all alone until Kane McCullough found her," Nick explained.

"McCullough? What was he doing out there?"

"He was just passing by, I guess. Who knows? But it was lucky he showed up when he did. Otherwise, Rachel would have been stuck out there all night."

"Where is she now?" Pete asked.

"I think she's probably back home."

"So she's all right?"

"As far as I know," Nick told him.

"I'm going to go pay her a visit and make sure. If you need me, that's where I'll be."

Nick wasn't surprised that Pete was going to see Rachel. He'd figured his boss would want to look in on her, being sweet on her as he was. But Nick had deliberately not told Pete everything he'd heard around town that morning. Pete would hear the rest of the gossip soon enough, but he wouldn't hear it from his deputy.

Pete wasted no time getting over to the Hammond house, and he was glad when Rachel answered his knock at her door.

"Why, Pete—this is a surprise," she told him. "Won't you come in?"

"Thanks, Rachel." He went inside and waited in the foyer, hat in hand, while she closed the front door.

"Who is it?" Martin called out from his study.

"It's Pete, Papa," she answered.

Martin came out to welcome him. "Good to see you, Pete. Come on in and sit down for a while."

They all went into the parlor and settled in.

"Nick told me you'd been in an accident, and I wanted to come by and make sure you were all right," Pete told Rachel. "What happened?"

She quickly told him of her adventurous trek home and how she'd been stranded in the storm. "It was amazing that Kane showed up the way he did."

Pete was struck that she was calling McCullough by his first name. A surge of jealousy went through him. "I'm glad he did. If you'd been left out there all night, you would have been in grave danger. What time did you finally make it back to town?" He wondered how they'd managed to travel during the storm.

It was then that both Rachel and Martin realized he hadn't heard the whole story of what had transpired. They shared a quick look of understanding, and then Rachel went ahead and told Pete the full truth of how they'd ended up in the abandoned homestead.

"We didn't get back to town until this morning. There was no way we could travel after dark when it was raining so hard."

"So you spent the night there alone with him?" Pete repeated, shocked.

She lifted her chin a little at his reaction. "Yes, and thank heaven Kane saved me. Without him, I might not have made it back at all."

"But your reputation—after spending the night with a man like McCullough. He's nothing but a fast gun—"

Martin had anticipated that Pete might react this way, and he was ready for him.

"My daughter's reputation is immaculate, Peter," Martin declared in a stern tone. He knew what a lot of the lower-minded folks around town would be thinking, and he wasn't going to abide it—not from them and certainly not from Pete. "Kane McCullough may be a fast gun, but he was a fast thinker yesterday. The man saved my daughter's life, and for that I will always be grateful."

"You're right, of course." Pete looked at Rachel, backing down a bit in the face of her father's righteous indignation. "I have to be getting back to work, but I just wanted to come by and let you know I'm glad you're all right."

"Thanks, Pete," Rachel said as she walked him back to the door to see him out.

Pete was a bit frustrated, and his mood was pensive as he returned to the office. He believed what Reverend Hammond had said about Rachel's reputation being unspoiled, but he couldn't help wondering how the gossips around town were going to handle the situation. Some of the ladies could get real ugly with their insinuations and small talk, and he hoped Rachel wouldn't suffer from their attacks.

"Why didn't you tell me everything that happened with Rachel?" Pete challenged Nick when he entered the office. "I don't like surprises."

Nick was working at his desk, and he looked up at Pete as he answered, "I hadn't heard that much, and what I had heard sounded mostly like idle gossip. I figured you'd get the true story from Rachel and her father."

"I did, and it isn't pretty."

"Why? What happened?"

"She spent the whole night—alone—with Mc-Cullough!" he snarled.

"But you know nothing happened, Pete," Nick assured him. "This is Rachel Hammond you're talking about. She's the preacher's daughter. She's a perfect lady. McCullough might have taken her someplace safe and dry for the duration of the storm, but there's no way anything else happened between them. Give the woman some credit."

Pete muttered angrily to himself.

Nick went on, challenging him, "Would you rather Rachel had been left alone in the storm last night and ended up hurt or even possibly dead?"

"Hell, no," he snarled, angry that Nick was being so blunt with him.

"That's right, and while you were gone, a couple of men brought her buggy in. I got a good look at it as it passed by the office. Considering the extent of the damage, I'd say she's lucky she's alive."

"Even so, the town gossips are going to have a lot to say about what happened." Pete could imagine how they would condemn Rachel's actions.

"There's no changing people like that. Since she's the preacher's daughter, they're going to try to make the situation seem worse than it is," Nick said.

Pete was tempted to go after McCullough but decided against it. He'd let his anger pass and hope that Rachel's ordeal didn't get blown out of proportion.

It was late, but Clint was still awake, lying on his hotel room bed, fully dressed. Unable to sleep and feeling on edge, he got up and went to stare out the window. The streets of Dry Springs were quiet. No one was stirring, and yet he felt decidedly restless.

Earlier he'd gone down to the Last Chance for a

drink and to take a look around. He'd found there was still no sign of Tucker and his gang. Nothing had changed while he'd been away. He'd returned to his room and had been there ever since.

Now as the night aged, Clint found himself thinking about what had happened the night before and almost wishing he could turn the clock back. The memory of having Rachel in his arms, of kissing her, haunted him. She was everything that was beautiful and good, and because of that, she couldn't be a part of his world.

Clint lifted his gaze and saw the church's steeple over the roofs of the other buildings. Rachel was that close, but she was also that far away. As much as he wanted her in his life, he could not involve her in his quest for vengeance. He could not put her at risk. The men who'd murdered his family wouldn't hesitate to kill anyone who got in their way. It was for that reason that he would have to keep his distance from her. He was saving her again, but she would never know it.

Only he would know, and that would be his solace.

Chapter Fourteen

Clint stepped out of the telegraph office in Silver Pass two days later holding the response he'd been expecting from Captain Meyers. It was quiet on the street, so he took the time to quickly read the message:

> *Have no information on the person you mentioned. Ed Riley was the sheriff in Dry Springs for years, and Ben Taggart was his deputy.*

Clint had been hoping for some solid background information on Pete Reynolds, and Captain Meyers's response was disappointing. He couldn't decide if the fact that there was nothing known about Reynolds allayed his fears or not.

Frustrated, he rode back toward Dry Springs.

And this time as he made the trek, he couldn't help wondering if it would storm.

* * *

Pete had been doing some checking of his own, and he didn't like what he'd found out about Kane McCullough. He'd sent telegrams to people he figured might have heard of the man and had learned that McCullough was known far and wide as a deadly fast gun—a gun for hire. Pete was suspicious of the gunman's reasons for being in Dry Springs, and he wondered why McCullough had stayed around so long. He knew he was going to start keeping an eye on him.

Anne had just stepped into the General Store when she saw three of the town's most upstanding ladies huddled together by the yard goods section. They were so caught up in their conversation that they didn't notice she'd come in. Anne wondered what could have them looking so intense, and then she heard what they were saying.

"I tell you, Catherine, it's the worst scandal to hit this town in years!" Mary Ann Forester declared.

"I know it's a difficult situation for them, and I just don't know what Reverend Hammond is going to do," the good-hearted Helen Slifer added. She was trying not to be as judgmental as her companions. She knew Rachel and truly cared about her.

"It must be terrible to be a minister and know your daughter has sinned this way—and so openly," the matronly Catherine Lawrence put in, her tone condemning. "I mean, Rachel spent the entire night alone with that man!"

"Reverend Hammond should have insisted Kane McCullough marry her that very day. It's only right, after what he's done to her reputation," Mary Ann insisted righteously.

"But Andrew says he heard from the sheriff that McCullough is a gunslinger with a terrible reputation!" Catherine confided, repeating what her husband had learned. "What father in his right mind would want his daughter to marry someone like him?"

"How did Sheriff Reynolds find that out about him?" Helen asked.

"Lawmen have ways," Mary Ann said with confidence, not doubting for a moment that it was true. "And Sheriff Reynolds has never given us any reason to doubt him."

"That's true enough," Catherine agreed. "But even if McCullough is a gunman, heaven only knows what went on between the two of them out there overnight."

"I doubt 'heaven' had anything to do with it, Catherine," Mary Ann said snidely.

"You know, it could be that everything happened just the way Rachel said it did," Helen said in defense of the young woman, tired of the other women's ugly insinuations. She'd known Rachel for most of her life and knew she was upstanding and kind. "That was a terrible storm."

"But they could have made it back," Catherine insisted. "They didn't have to stay in that cabin all night!"

"What's her mother have to say about what happened?" Mary Ann asked.

"I haven't spoken with Anne about it yet," Helen said.

"What could she say?" Catherine sneered. " 'My daughter's nothing but a—' "

"Catherine!" Helen cut her off.

Anne appreciated Helen's attempt to defend Rachel, but she had heard enough. She glanced toward the shopkeeper, who was standing behind the counter looking a bit ashamed, then turned and walked out without saying a word.

Anne was in shock and deeply hurt by the women's vicious comments. Rachel could have been injured or even killed in the storm, and yet the hateful gossips were only concerned with spreading stories that were blatantly cruel and untrue. Only Helen had defended Rachel. Only Helen had been a loving friend.

Anne fought back tears as she made her way toward church. She knew Martin was working in his office there, and she had to tell him what she'd just heard. She didn't know how much truth there was to the talk about Kane's reputation, but they had to find out—for Rachel's sake.

Martin was at his desk in his small office when Anne came in. He looked up in surprise to find her there.

"Anne—what's wrong?" He got up and went to her, noting her distress.

"I just heard some ladies talking in the General Store"—she paused and looked up at him, all the

162

pain she was feeling reflected in her eyes—"about Rachel."

Martin stiffened, sensing what was coming. He helped her to sit down in the chair in front of the desk. "What did they say?"

Anne repeated what she remembered about their conversation and then added, "Catherine said her husband had talked to Sheriff Reynolds and found out McCullough was a gunslinger with a really bad reputation."

Martin was scowling as he listened to her. He had never had any use or respect for gossips, and what Anne was telling him just conformed his opinion. He thought of Kane and realized he hadn't seen him for a few days. He hadn't thought anything of it. He'd believed Kane was a good man who'd had business of his own to take care of, but if he was a deadly gunfighter as they were saying . . . Where had he gone and what was he doing? Martin knew a horrible sinking feeling in the pit of his stomach.

"I'm going to speak with Sheriff Reynolds," Martin told Anne. "You go on home. I'll see you there later."

"You don't want me to go with you?" she offered.

"No." He was firm.

Once Anne had gone, Martin went straight to the sheriff's office. He was glad to find the lawman there.

"Reverend Hammond—" Pete sounded surprised when he saw him coming in the door.

"I have to talk to you, Sheriff."

Pete noted the preacher's serious demeanor and wondered at it. "Of course, have a seat. What can I do for you?"

"My wife has been hearing gossip around town about Rachel and Kane McCullough—and it's getting ugly."

"I'm sorry."

"There's no need for you to be sorry. It has nothing to do with you. I just need to know something."

"What?"

"Anne heard one of the ladies mention that Kane McCullough has a very bad reputation. Is that true?" He was tense as he awaited Pete's answer.

"I did some checking into his background, and what I found out wasn't good."

"What did you learn?"

"McCullough is a hired gun. His reputation is well known across the state, and it's a deadly one. He's a killer for hire," Pete told him.

Martin had never thought of Kane as a cold-blooded killer. "Are you certain?"

"Yes," he answered.

Martin's distress over the revelation was obvious. "Rachel insists that Kane saved her that night and that he was a gentleman during the time they spent together."

"I can only tell you what I know, Reverend. A man with a reputation like McCullough's can be trouble. The word is out on the street about him now, and, as you've found out, people are prone to talk."

"But this is Rachel they're talking about! This is my daughter!" he protested, confused by the narrow-minded opinions of some townsfolk.

"I know," Pete said, his tone sympathetic. "It's a difficult situation for you."

Martin drew upon his faith to respond. "Those who are saying these things should remember the admonition 'Let he who is without sin cast the first stone.'"

Pete said nothing more as he watched the reverend leave the office.

Martin stepped outside into the sunshine, but he didn't notice his surroundings. He was too troubled by what he'd learned. He knew in his heart that nothing indecent had happened between Rachel and Kane when they'd been alone, and he didn't understand why some people were being so critical of her. He would defend his daughter's innocence always, and he wondered why Pete hadn't been more outspoken in his support of Rachel and her reputation.

Martin considered the situation as he made his way back to the church. Faced with this savage gossip, should he seek McCullough out and insist he marry Rachel, or should he let her life be ruined by the hate-filled talk going around? The thought of Rachel being married to a man who was known as a deadly gunman tortured him, and he was at a loss.

When he reached the church, Martin didn't go

to his office. Instead, he went inside and sat down in a pew to pray for wisdom and guidance.

Right then, he needed all the help he could get.

Pete remained seated at his desk for a time after Reverend Hammond left. He was lost in thought as he considered the ugliness of Rachel's situation. Rachel was definitely one good-looking woman, and he did want her—there was no doubt about that. Just watching her dance with McCullough the other night had made him angry. He'd planned all along that she would ultimately be his. The prospect of marrying the preacher's daughter had been perfect, but now, Rachel had spent the night alone with another man.

For a fleeting moment, Pete considered stepping up and offering to marry Rachel to save her reputation, but he quickly dismissed the idea. The thought of her alone with the gunslinger, the image of the other man's hands upon her, disgusted him. Desire Rachel though he did, he knew that if he were to marry her, every time he looked at her he would be thinking of her with McCullough, and he didn't need that in his life.

Pete got up and left the office. He wanted to walk off some of his frustration and anger. He was just passing of the saloons when a drunk staggered out and ran into him. Pete reacted violently. He shoved the man to the ground and stood over him, his hand on his gun, glaring down at him threateningly.

"What the hell are you doing?" Pete demanded.

"I wasn't doing nothing, Sheriff—honest." the man said in a slurred voice.

"Get up and get out of here!" Pete ordered.

The drunk scrambled to get up, but just as he had almost regained his feet, Pete deliberately kicked him and knocked him back down. The man sprawled face first in the dirt.

Pete's anger eased a little as he turned and stalked away. He didn't pay any attention to those in the bar who'd been watching him. He didn't care what they thought. Dry Springs was his town, and he would run it his way.

Chapter Fifteen

It was late afternoon when Clint returned to Dry Springs. The trip had been long and uneventful. He was hot and tired, so he decided to have a drink before going to the hotel. After leaving his horse at the stable, he went to the Last Chance to relax for a while.

"McCullough, you're back," Trey greeted him as he walked in. "The usual?"

"That'll be fine."

The bartender poured him a whiskey and set it in front of him.

Clint paid him and took a drink.

"Didn't know if we'd be seeing you again or not," Trey said, noticing how some patrons were eyeing McCullough with open interest.

"I just couldn't stay away," Clint remarked.

"No wonder," a drunk seated at a nearby table muttered, loud enough for Clint to hear.

"What?" Clint looked over at him and noticed that Ed was seated with the man.

"It's no wonder you couldn't stay away, with that sweet piece you got waiting for you," the drunk chuckled.

"Yeah," Ed put in as he looked at Clint. "I only touched the preacher's daughter right here in front of everybody, but, damn, McCullough, you got to bang her for a whole night!"

Clint went rigid at Ed's words. He stalked over to the table to confront the two men. "What did you say?"

"You heard me," Ed sneered. "Everybody knows what you did to Rachel. Preacher's daughter or not, everybody knows she ain't nothing but your whore."

Clint reacted so quickly to the insult to Rachel that Ed had no chance to react. Dragging him up out of his chair, Clint hit him as hard as he could, and Ed collapsed unconscious on the floor.

The other drunk decided to join the fight. He threw a hard punch at him, but Clint was ready for him. They grappled savagely, both landing harsh blows.

"Somebody get the sheriff!" Trey yelled as he watched the fight. He had no doubt McCullough was going to win. The other man was no match for him, but he didn't want the Last Chance wrecked in the meantime.

Nick was just down the street making his rounds when he saw a man come running out of the Last Chance.

"Deputy Evans! We got trouble!"

Nick ran to the saloon, his gun drawn.

"We got a big fight going!"

Nick charged inside just as two more men in the bar decided to join in the melee. Chairs were being thrown, and the fighting was out of control.

Nick noticed right away that Kane was in the middle of it. He didn't know what had started the fight, but he was going to put an end to it.

"Stop right now!" Nick ordered, grabbing one of the drunks and shoving him out of the way.

The man fell, but staggered to his feet to rejoin the fight.

Clint was holding his own as he fought fiercely to defend Rachel's name.

Nick didn't know what had started the fight, and he realized he would not be able to break it up on his own. He fired one shot at the ceiling.

At the sound of the gunshot so close at hand, the drunks immediately froze.

Clint was surprised by the gunshot, and even more surprised when the fighting stopped. He was ready to keep at it. Tense and ready for more, he quickly looked around at the drunks cowering before the deputy.

"It's over!" Nick commanded, staring down the drunks.

"The preacher's daughter is nothing but a whore," one of the drunks muttered under his breath.

Clint heard the man's remark and was ready to go after him again.

Nick heard him, too, and anticipated what Mc-Cullough would do. Nick reacted quickly. He grabbed Kane forcefully by the shoulder and ordered, "Don't do it."

Nick had heard of Kane McCullough's reputation as a gunfighter from Pete, and he was afraid that this fight might turn into a bloodbath if he didn't get things under control. He knew he had to stop it now.

Clint was ready to throw off the deputy's restraint, but he backed down—for now. He had no argument with the lawman.

The drunks had been terrified that Kane would manage to get away from Deputy Evans, but once they were sure Nick had him under control, they turned away to nurse their own injuries.

"Who started this?" Nick demanded.

"He did!" one of the drunks shouted, pointing at Kane. "He hit Ed first!"

"Why? What did Ed do?"

"Ed didn't do nothing. He was just telling the truth about the preacher's daughter."

Clint glared at the man, more than ready to take up where he'd left off.

Nick immediately understood what had set Kane off.

"All right," Nick said, looking at Kane intensely, then nodding toward the door. "Let's go. Let's get out of here."

Clint bent down to pick up his hat, which had been lost during the fight, then cast one last look at Ed, who was just beginning to stir where he lay on the floor. Clint could see an ugly bruise already forming on the side of Ed's face, and he was satisfied that Ed would be reminded of their encounter every time he looked in a mirror for some time to come. Clint turned and walked out of the saloon ahead of the deputy.

Nick followed him outside. Only then did he feel comfortable enough to holster his gun.

"Just keep moving," he directed Kane, pointing down the street in the direction of the sheriff's office.

"Am I under arrest?" Clint challenged.

For a moment, the two men stared each other down.

Nick knew that at any time during the fight, Kane could have drawn his gun and shot up the place, but he hadn't. If Pete had been here, he probably would have arrested him, but Nick decided against it. He'd heard the drunk's last remark and had a good idea what had set the fight off.

"No. You're just going to go for a walk and cool down," Nick told him. "Let's go."

Clint did as he was told. It was still light out, and he knew some of the townspeople were watching. He was surprised when the deputy fell into step beside him.

"What started the fight?" Nick asked.

"Ed made a remark about Rachel."

Nick could only imagine what the fool had said. "Michelle told me that there's been talk going around town about you and Rachel and that night of the storm when you were stranded together. From what she tells me, the talk hasn't been pretty."

"I know," Clint ground out. "People shouldn't be saying these things about Rachel. She's done nothing to be ashamed of."

"They shouldn't be talking this way, but they are. The best thing you can do to help this all calm down, is stay out of trouble. Don't go starting any more fights. Just let the talk die down on its own," Nick told him.

"*If* it dies down," Clint said in disgust.

"It will, in time."

Clint doubted that would happen, but he didn't argue the point any further.

Nick went on, "There is one thing you should know."

"What's that?" Clint glanced over at him.

"Sheriff Reynolds did some checking on you. He knows who you are now."

Clint went still, worried that Pete had somehow found out the truth. "He does?"

"Yes, and he's going to be watching you even closer after he hears about the fight tonight. He likes things quiet in Dry Springs, and your reputation as a fast gun is only going to cause problems."

"I'll remember that," Clint said, pleased to learn that Captain Meyers had done such a good job in creating his new identity.

"Good. You know, Kane—" Nick stopped and looked hard at him. "Why are you here?"

"I'm just passing through."

"You've been taking your time just passing through," Nick said frowning. "Causing that ruckus at the Last Chance isn't a good way to make yourself welcome in town."

"I'm sorry, but, like I said, I was defending Rachel. I'm not going to stand around and let fools like Ed insult her."

"I understand completely, but Sheriff Reynolds may think differently about it, and he might be the one who shows up at the next fight. Try to stay out of trouble while you're here."

"I'll do what I can."

"Good." Nick found himself wondering about McCullough. Something didn't seem right about him. Fast guns were killers. They were generally amoral men who lived for the moment. He found it hard to believe McCullough was really that kind of man, especially since he'd gotten into the fight defending Rachel's reputation. "McCullough—"

Clint looked at Nick expectantly.

"If you find you need anything while you're here in town, just let me know."

Clint was surprised by his offer. "Thanks, Deputy."

"Call me Nick."

"Thanks, Nick."

They looked each other straight in the eye as they shook hands.

"Now go on," Nick said. "But remember what I told you."

"I will," Clint said as he walked away from the deputy.

Nick stood there watching him move off for a

moment, then turned away. He had to go back to work.

Clint's thoughts returned to Rachel; he couldn't believe what was happening to her. He understood why Nick had told him to let things die down, but there was no way he could stand by and do nothing when Rachel was being insulted. It was obvious to him now that her reputation was in ruins, and all because of him.

A sense of responsibility filled Clint. Deep in thought, he tried to decide what to do. He had come to Dry Springs to track down the Tucker Gang, not to get involved with Rachel, but it was too late to change what had happened.

They were involved.

Clint thought of the time he'd spent alone with the dark-haired beauty and the heat of her passionate embrace. He had been attracted to Rachel from the first moment he'd seen her that night at the Last Chance. Even now, the memory of her kiss and touch during the storm had the power to ignite the fire of his desire for her.

Try as he might to deny it, Clint knew he wanted her, but he was torn over what to do about it. Should he go to her and offer to marry her? Making her his wife would save her reputation, but he could offer her no security while he was after the Tucker Gang, and he was not going to stop until his family's killers had been brought to justice.

Clint realized there was always the possibility that Rachel might turn down his proposal. She believed he was Kane McCullough—a dangerous gunslinger. He didn't know that she would want anything to do with him, but a part of him needed to try to make things right for her.

Clint kept walking, his mood dark and troubled.

Rachel sat with Michelle on the swing in the garden behind her house. It was a lovely setting. There were trees and low-growing flowering shrubs and the flowers Rachel loved to tend. She enjoyed spending time in the garden and had been glad when Michelle had stopped by for a visit and found her there.

"It's good to see you," Rachel told her. "I've needed someone to talk to, and you're the only one who really understands."

Michelle had heard the gossip and knew how upset her friend must be. "How are your mother and father holding up with all that's going on?"

"Yesterday was really bad. When my mother went into the General Store, she overheard some ladies talking about me and saying my reputation was ruined. She even heard them say that Kane was a notoriously deadly gunfighter. She told my father, and he went to talk to Pete about it."

"What did he find out?"

"Pete told my father it was true. He said Kane is a gunman, but I still don't believe it. Kane's not like that. Kane's no killer," she insisted. "He couldn't be and treat me the way he did when we were together."

"What are you going to do?"

"I don't know. Things have gotten so ugly," Rachel said, tears welling in her eyes. "I've lived here my whole life. I can't believe anyone in town would think of me this way."

Michelle saw her friend's pain and hugged her. "Not everybody does, you know that. It's just a few stupid people who want to stir things up and make themselves feel important by acting like they're morally superior."

"Pride," Rachel said miserably. "It's one of the seven deadly sins Papa preaches about."

"Why don't we start praying that all the hateful gossips have a change of heart?" Michelle suggested. "The last time we prayed for something, it worked—remember the night of the dance?"

That got a small smile out of Rachel.

"Yes, I remember. Kane did show up and I got to dance with him." Her mood brightened a little at the memory.

"Everything will be all right. You'll see." Michelle sounded confident.

"But what if it doesn't get better?" Rachel worried. "I feel like I've humiliated my parents. We've got relatives back East. I guess I could leave Dry Springs and go live with them, but then I'd feel that I was admitting the gossips were right."

"You have done nothing to be ashamed of, so don't even think about running away," Michelle said, defending her and trying to bolster her spirits. "Where's the Rachel I know? The Rachel I know is a fighter. She never gives up."

"You're right." Rachel looked up at her friend,

feeling empowered by the confidence Michelle had in her. She was glad that they'd been able to talk this way. "I'm not going to let them hurt me or run me out of town."

Michelle heard the touch of fierceness in Rachel's voice and she was glad of it. "That's more like it. Now you're acting more like my Rachel."

"Thank you," Rachel said. "It's been so awkward. I haven't known what to do, and I've felt so bad for my parents, having to listen to all the lies."

"And they know they're just that—lies."

Rachel was feeling much better as she walked Michelle out of the garden a short time later. They were just starting up the path that led to the front walkway when she saw him.

Kane was standing across the street looking straight at her.

Chapter Sixteen

Clint's decision on whether he should try to see Rachel again was made for him as he stood there watching her walk up the path with Michelle. When she looked up and saw him, he crossed the street to join them.

"Evening, Michelle—Rachel," he greeted them. His gaze was hungry upon Rachel.

"Hello, Kane," she responded softly.

"It's nice to see you," Michelle said, and she meant it, for she knew how much his showing up meant to her friend.

"It's good to see you, too," he told them. "I was hoping to have the chance to talk with you."

"Michelle—" Rachel glanced at the house to see if her parents had noticed Kane's arrival. She didn't see them looking out any window, so she asked her friend, "Do me a favor, will you? Could you go up to the house and visit with my parents for a little while so Kane and I can talk privately?"

For a moment, Michelle remembered what Pete had said about Kane, and she was torn.

"Please?" Rachel asked again.

"My mother did want to know what your mother needed her to do at the church dinner in two weeks," Michelle said, giving Rachel a quick smile as she started up the walkway toward the house.

Clint stood silently with Rachel for a moment until Michelle had moved away.

"Let's go into the garden," Rachel said.

Clint followed her back to the swing, and they sat down on it together.

Rachel was very aware of the hard, lean strength of him beside her, and her heartbeat quickened. She looked over at Kane, studying his ruggedly handsome features, and believed with all her heart that he was no killer.

"I've been worrying about you," he told her.

"There's no need for you to worry."

"Yes, there is. Have you heard the talk that's been going around town about us?" he asked, and he knew immediately by the change in her expression that she was aware of it. "So, you have heard what they're saying."

"Yes. My parents heard it all, and they couldn't believe it. The things that are being said are so cruel." She'd been strong for so long, but now, here with Kane, tears welled up in her eyes.

The sight of her sadness tore at him. She was everything that was beautiful and innocent in life. She didn't deserve to be treated this way by any-

YES! ☐

Sign me up for the **Historical Romance Book Club** and send my TWO FREE BOOKS! If I choose to stay in the club, I will pay only $8.50* each month, a savings of $5.48!

YES! ☐

Sign me up for the **Love Spell Book Club** and send my TWO FREE BOOKS! If I choose to stay in the club, I will pay only $8.50* each month, a savings of $5.48!

NAME: _____

ADDRESS: _____

_____

TELEPHONE: _____

E-MAIL: _____

☐ **I WANT TO PAY BY CREDIT CARD.**

☐ _VISA_   ☐ MasterCard   ☐ DISCOVER

ACCOUNT #: _____

EXPIRATION DATE: _____

SIGNATURE: _____

Send this card along with $2.00 shipping & handling for each club you wish to join, to:

Romance Book Clubs
20 Academy Street
Norwalk, CT 06850-4032

Or fax (must include credit card information!) to: 610.995.9274.
You can also sign up online at www.dorchesterpub.com.

*Plus $2.00 for shipping. Offer open to residents of the U.S. and Canada only. Canadian residents please call 1.800.481.9191 for pricing information.

If under 18, a parent or guardian must sign. Terms, prices and conditions subject to change. Subscription subject to acceptance. Dorchester Publishing reserves the right to reject any order or cancel any subscription.

JOIN NOW!

one. Clint knew he was ultimately responsible for all that had happened, and it was up to him to make things right.

Clint knew then what he had to do.

He reached out to her to gently take her in his arms. He wasn't sure how she would react, and he was relieved when she came willingly into his embrace.

"I'm sorry, Rachel," he told her, holding her close.

She leaned back to look up at him. "None of this is your fault, Kane. You saved me that night."

Clint knew he had to save her this night, too. He lifted a hand to touch her cheek as he bent down to kiss her.

"Rachel, there's something I have to tell you," he began cautiously, unsure of how much to reveal. Most of all, he wanted her to be safe.

"I already know all about it, and I don't care," she said softly, thinking he was going to reveal what Pete had told her father about him.

"What do you know?"

"Pete told my father about your past—that you're a deadly gunfighter."

Clint almost breathed an open sigh of relief at her words. "Rachel, there's so much I want you to know, but—"

"It doesn't matter, Kane," she interrupted him. "All that matters is that I love you. I fell in love with you that first night we met at the saloon—"

I love you. Her profession forced Clint to admit the truth of his own feelings for her.

"I love you, too, Rachel," Clint murmured, drawing her back into his arms.

"You do?" His words surprised her and touched her deeply.

"Yes. I do."

They clung to each other as their lips met in a cherishing exchange that showed without words the depth of what they were feeling for one another.

When at last the kiss ended, Clint put her from him. As tempting as Rachel was, there was no way he could concentrate on what he needed to say with her in his arms.

Kane's kiss had been so wonderful that Rachel was confused when he ended the embrace and moved away from her. She stood up to go to him, but then saw the darkness of his expression and hesitated.

"What is it, Kane? What's wrong?"

Clint had been trying to decide how much to tell Rachel about his reason for coming to Dry Springs. Though he realized it was dangerous to tell her the full truth, he knew it would be even more dangerous to keep it from her.

"Rachel, there's something I have to tell you, but you've got to promise me—"

"What?" She waited, knowing this was serious.

"You can't reveal any of it. This has to stay between us—for now."

"All right," she agreed.

"There's more to my past than what you know," he began.

Defiant

She hastened to reassure him. "It doesn't matter."

"It does matter," Clint said firmly. "I'm in the middle of something very dangerous here, and I don't want to put you at risk."

He looked so deadly serious that Rachel knew something was very wrong. "Kane—what is it?"

"First, my name isn't Kane McCullough."

Rachel frowned in confusion. "I don't understand."

"My real name is Clint Williams, and up until a short time ago, I was a Texas Ranger."

"You were a Ranger?" She was shocked. "But Pete said you were a notorious gunfighter—"

"That's because Pete was told what I wanted people to believe about Kane McCullough. You see, very few people know that Clint Williams is still alive."

"I don't understand."

"My father was a Ranger, too, and he was on the trail of the Tucker Gang. He knew they were cold-blooded killers, and he was getting close. Evidently, the gang was worried about him, so they came after him. They murdered my entire family and left me for dead at our family's ranch some months back."

Rachel reached out to him, horrified by what he'd revealed. "I'm so sorry."

Clint went on to tell her everything that had happened on that fateful night. "It took a while for me to heal, but once I'd recovered from my wounds, I knew what I had to do. My father had

185

believed there was someone outside of the gang itself, running things and giving the orders. That was when I decided I'd have a better chance of tracking him down if I became known as a gun-fighter with a deadly reputation. This way I could try to work my way into the Tucker Gang, iden-tify their real leader, and bring them down. That's why I created Kane McCullough—and that's why I'm here."

"So you think the Tucker Gang is in Dry Springs?" She was aghast at all he had revealed.

"I'm reasonably sure they were the ones who tried to rob your stagecoach that day. It was real lucky you had your gun with you. There's no telling what might have happened if you'd been unarmed."

"But they're gone now, aren't they?"

"I don't know. That's why I've stayed around. I've been watching and waiting to see if they show up in town."

"So that's why you asked me if I remembered anything unusual about the outlaws—"

"That's right. I've studied their wanted posters, and I've been keeping a lookout for them. Glen Tucker and Ax Hansen are as cold-blooded as they come. They slaughtered my family, and I'm going to bring them to justice one way or another—dead or alive."

Rachel stared up at the man she'd known as Kane, seeing the fierce determination in his hard-ened expression. She could only imagine what he'd lived through, and her heart ached for him.

She went to him and put her arms around him. He had been holding himself rigid, but she felt him relax slightly at her touch. Rachel knew that words would hold little meaning for him right then, so instead she drew him down to her for a kiss, telling him with that embrace what was in her heart.

Clint gathered her to him, holding her close as they shared kiss after heated kiss.

In her arms he could forget the ugliness of the world—if only for a little while.

In her arms he could find peace.

"Rachel!"

The roar of Martin Hammond's outraged voice jarred them both and forced them apart.

"Papa." Rachel gasped at the sound of her father's voice so close by. Obviously, Michelle had failed in her effort to keep both her parents busy. Rachel moved away from Clint, feeling guilty as she faced her father.

"What are you doing?" Martin raged.

"I can explain." Rachel had never seen her father so angry before.

"Are you trying to prove all the gossips right?" he demanded.

Martin was still upset about all the hateful talk he'd heard, and now to find Rachel and Kane kissing right out there in the garden where anybody could have come upon them! He seared them both with a condemning glare. He had always considered himself a man of peace. He'd always preached God's love, but at that moment he was an angry father, and it was the closest he'd ever come in his life to wanting to hit someone.

"Papa—no! Listen to me," she insisted, stepping between the two men she loved. "There's more than you know going on here. You've got to listen."

"Listen to what?" he demanded, not taking his eyes off Kane. He had wanted to trust the man, in spite of what he'd heard, but now he had his doubts.

Rachel looked at Clint pleadingly. "You have to tell my parents, so they'll understand."

Clint had had misgivings about telling Rachel, but the idea of revealing the truth to her parents disturbed him deeply.

"They are my parents," Rachel repeated. "You can trust them."

"Why would he have to trust us?" her father asked, confused by her behavior.

"Papa, please, let's go inside and get Mother. Then he can tell you everything."

Clint faced the reverend. "Rachel's right. It would be best if we went inside."

Martin turned and led the way. He was not a happy man as he stalked back to the house.

"Anne!" he bellowed as he stood in the front hallway.

Anne heard her husband's shout and wondered why he sounded so angry. She rushed out of the kitchen to see what he wanted, leaving Michelle to follow.

Michelle had a sickening feeling that she

knew what had happened as she went after Mrs. Hammond.

"What is it, Martin?" Anne asked as she came into the foyer where her husband was standing with Rachel and Kane.

"I just found the two of them together in the garden. It seems Mr. McCullough wants to speak with us."

Anne moved forward.

"Should I leave?" Michelle asked, looking at Rachel. She regretted that she hadn't been able to do a better job of keeping the Hammonds distracted while Kane had been talking with Rachel.

Rachel looked up at Clint for a moment, then told her, "No. It's all right. I want you to hear this, too."

Clint wasn't comfortable revealing the truth to so many people, but there was really no way around it, considering what Michelle had already witnessed.

"I don't understand what's going on," Anne said as she went into the parlor with her husband and Michelle.

Rachel paused for a moment with Clint in the hall. "You can trust them—Clint." She said his name aloud for the first time.

He gazed down at her, trusting her, and nodded. He knew what he had to do, and he was ready to do it.

They walked into the parlor to find her mother and Michelle seated on the sofa and her father pacing in agitation.

Martin looked up when they entered the room. He'd been telling himself that, gunfighter or not, Kane had saved Rachel from harm at the Last Chance that first night and then again during the storm. He knew that nothing the gossips were saying about Rachel was true, but catching them kissing in the garden had shocked and troubled him.

"This had better be good," he stated, looking from his daughter to the man standing at her side.

Clint didn't wait for Rachel to speak. He wanted to put her father's fears to rest as quickly as possible.

"What I'm about to tell you needs to be held in strictest confidence," he began, looking from her father to her mother and then to Michelle.

"What are you talking about?" the reverend demanded.

"I'm talking about saving lives."

They looked stricken at his remark.

"We know you're a gunfighter, Kane, but—" Anne began worriedly.

"But you can always give up those evil ways and turn to the Lord," Martin said, struggling to find the peace he knew was his when he was doing the Lord's work. Whatever was troubling Kane, he could tell it was serious and it did involve his daughter.

"Clint is not a gunfighter, Papa," Rachel explained quickly, wanting the truth out.

"Clint?" Hammond said. They were all startled when she used the different name.

"His name is not Kane McCullough. He's Clint Williams, and he was a Texas Ranger."

Martin could only stare at the two of them as they stood together. This man had been a Ranger—

"You're not Kane McCullough?" Michelle asked first in open surprise, trying to make some sense out of what Rachel was telling them.

"There is no Kane McCullough," Clint answered. "I made up the alias to use as a cover while working to track down the Tucker Gang."

Rachel told them what had happened to his family, and both her mother and Michelle had tears in their eyes as they heard the terrible story of his loss. She went on to explain how he had tracked the gang to Dry Springs.

Clint spoke up, telling them, "I never wanted to involve Rachel in any of this. I came to town intending only to try to work my way into the gang as the gunfighter Kane McCullough, so I could identify their main leader and bring them down, but after the night of the storm, all that changed." Clint smiled down at Rachel as he told them, "I fell in love with your daughter that night." Clint paused and looked up at Reverend Hammond and his wife. "And I want to marry her."

Chapter Seventeen

"Rachel, will you marry me?" Clint asked, turning to Rachel.

"Yes." Rachel was breathless in her excitement. True, they'd said they loved each other, but she'd had no idea he was actually going to ask her to marry him. Her happiness was so great, she embraced Clint, unmindful that her father and mother were standing right there.

Martin and Anne were completely taken aback by all that had just happened. To learn that the man they'd believed to be a deadly gunfighter was, in truth, an ex-Texas Ranger was startling enough, but now, to find that he loved Rachel and wanted to marry her was the answer to all their prayers.

"Reverend Hammond, may I have your daughter's hand in marriage?" Clint asked.

Her parents shared a look before Martin answered Clint. "Yes."

"Oh, Papa." In her happiness, Rachel went to hug him and then her mother.

Michelle looked on, stunned by the revelation of Clint's true identity. She realized Rachel had been right when she'd sensed that he was not a cold-blooded gunman. When Rachel finished embracing her parents, Michelle gave her a hug, too. She was amazed that her prayers had been answered so quickly.

"But how are you going to be married if you're still looking for the Tucker Gang?" Martin asked.

"That's what I've been worried about. I don't want to put Rachel in any danger, and if the news of my true identity or our marriage gets out, whoever tried to kill me before might try to come after her, too."

"Can't you give up your desire for revenge and settle down here with us and be a part of our family?" Anne asked.

Clint's gaze was steely as he looked at her. "No. I'll never give up on bringing in the Tucker Gang. I'm going to see to it that they pay for what they've done."

"But what about Rachel? If you're married . . ." Martin broke off, worried about her future with Clint.

"That's why I thought it would be best if we kept the news of our marriage private. That way, Rachel can stay with you while I finish what I've started. It could be over real soon, if things work out the way I hope, or I could still be on their trail for months yet. One way or the other, nothing is going to stop me from seeing this through to the end, and that's why I need to know that Rachel is safe here with you."

Martin understood the seriousness of Clint's intent and knew there was no point in trying to dissuade him.

"Do you want me to marry you now—tonight?" Martin offered.

"Would you?" Rachel was breathless at the thought. True, her whole life she'd dreamed of a romantic church wedding—of a white wedding gown and a beautiful ceremony, but that was before Clint. Now all that mattered was that he loved her and wanted to marry her.

"Your mother and Michelle can be your witnesses, if this is what you want," Martin offered.

Rachel turned to Clint. "Are you sure about this?"

"I'm sure," he answered with no hesitation.

"I'll get my Bible," Martin said.

A short time later, Martin returned. He drew Clint aside to speak with him.

"This belonged to my mother," he said, handing Clint a simple gold wedding band. "I know that in the future you may want to get another ring, but I thought for today. . . ."

"Thank you," Clint said. He was truly grateful for the reverend's thoughtfulness.

Martin was ready then to begin the ceremony.

"Dearly beloved, we are gathered here to witness the joining in holy matrimony of Rachel Hammond and Clint Williams."

Rachel almost felt as if she were dreaming. Clint had saved her from the drunk and saved her from the storm. He had come to her and proclaimed his love. He was with her now, taking a vow that would bind them together forever.

"Do you, Rachel Hammond, take this man Clint Williams to be your lawfully wedded husband?"

"I do," she answered softly, thrilled at the thought of being in his arms forever.

"Do you, Clint Williams, take Rachel Hammond to be your lawfully wedded wife?"

"I do," Clint pledged.

"I now pronounce you man and wife," Martin proclaimed. "Do you have the ring?"

Clint took the ring out of his pocket and slipped it on Rachel's finger.

"What God has joined together, let no man put asunder," Martin added.

Clint didn't wait for the reverend to say anything more. He gathered Rachel in his arms and kissed her.

It was a tender moment that left them both breathless when they moved apart.

Clint went to her father and shook his hand. "Thank you, sir."

"God bless you, son," Martin said, looking Clint in the eye. "And take care of my daughter."

"I will," he told him.

When Martin turned to Rachel, she went straight into his arms. "I love you, Papa."

"I love you, too."

Anne was looking on, teary-eyed. This wasn't

quite what she had dreamed of for her only daughter's wedding, but it didn't matter as long as Rachel and Clint were in love. She embraced them both, and then said with a smile, "We won't be having a big reception tonight, but we can have cake. I baked one this morning. Shall we all go out to the kitchen?"

They laughed and started from the room.

Michelle gave Rachel a quick hug before following the others.

"Are you happy?" Michelle asked her.

"Oh, yes." Rachel smiled as she watched Clint walking away with her father. "I just can't believe everything happened so fast. I mean, it was such shock just finding out who Clint really is, and now we're married."

"See, your instincts were right about him. You believed all along he wasn't a gunfighter."

"Let's just pray that he's able to bring in the Tucker Gang fast. I'm worried about what might happen. He's only one man going after whole gang of killers—"

"He'll do it. You'll see."

They shared another quick hug. The men had already gone into the kitchen while the women lingered behind.

Martin and Clint sat down at the kitchen table together to eat their cake.

"Now that you're married, how do you want to handle this?" Martin asked.

"It's probably best if Rachel and I keep our distance. I know there's talk going around, but for now, there's not much we can do about that. When the time comes, the gossips are going to find out just how wrong they were."

"That's right. There is one thing, though, Clint." Martin looked up at his new son-in-law, wanting to counsel him.

"What?"

"Remember that the Lord said 'Vengeance is mine.' You weren't raised to be like those killers. You are not a cold-blooded murderer. You're a Texas Ranger. Arrest them and bring them to justice. Let the law handle them."

"They deserve to die," Clint ground out.

"And God will see that they are held accountable for their actions. Don't lower yourself to their level—for your own sake."

Clint looked at Martin and said slowly, "I have to bring them down."

"I understand, but remember, 'Thou shalt not kill.'"

Clint didn't respond. There was nothing he could say.

Martin spoke up to break the silent tension of the moment. "I think I already know what I'm going to preach about at the prayer service tomorrow night."

"What's that?"

"I think I'll try to reach our ladies who like to gossip so much. I think 'Judge not lest ye be judged' is appropriate. The only trouble is, those who need to hear it probably won't listen."

"You're right about that."

"What are you going to do about the outlaws if they don't show up in Dry Springs soon?"

"If they're not here within the next week, I'll have to ride out and start looking for them all over again." The prospect didn't sit well with Clint, and he hoped it wouldn't come to that. "That's why I need to know that Rachel is with you, because it could take a while to find them."

"Godspeed to you, Clint," Martin said, wanting him to find the peace he needed so desperately. He could only imagine the pain Clint had suffered in the loss of his family.

Anne, Rachel, and Michelle came into the kitchen then, and Martin looked up.

"I've never seen a more beautiful bride—except for my own, of course," Martin said.

Rachel sat beside Clint at the table, while Michelle took a seat next to Martin. Anne served them cake before joining them.

Clint listened to the easy conversation going on around him and realized again just how much he missed his family. He remembered the dinners his mother used to make when he was growing up and the closeness he and his brother had shared. It had been a wonderful time, and it was lost to him forever.

Rachel was watching him and sensed the darkening of his mood. She reached out to touch his arm. When he looked down at her, though, she saw only warmth in his gaze.

"You are one beautiful bride," he told her.

"And you're one handsome groom."

They had eyes only for each other.

Michelle was watching them together. She was saddened that their marriage had had to take place under circumstances like these. She knew the weeks ahead weren't going to be easy for them, but she was glad Rachel and Clint had found each other and professed their love. She just hoped the mission Clint was on would be over quickly so they could live happily ever after together.

Finishing her cake, Michelle rose from the table. "I'd better be going home. It's getting a little late."

"Thank you for being our witness," Rachel said as she got up to walk her out.

"I was honored," Michelle said, smiling. "I'll see you later."

Rachel accompanied her to the front door and saw her off. When she returned to the kitchen, her mother and father were also getting up from the table.

"We thought you newlyweds might like a little time alone," they said. "We'll be upstairs."

Martin went to Clint and shook his hand again. "Welcome to the family, son."

"Thank you."

Anne came up to him, but she didn't bother with small talk. She simply gave him a hug before leaving them alone.

"Do you want to go in the parlor?" Rachel offered.

Clint had other ideas. He took her arm and

Defiant

drew her to him. Wrapping his arms around her, he bent to her and claimed her lips in a passionate kiss.

Rachel gave a soft murmur of surprise that turned to a purr of delight as she nestled against him. Being in his embrace was ecstasy for her; she hadn't realized until that moment how much she'd missed being in his arms. When the kiss finally ended, Rachel was staring up at him in breathless wonder.

"I love you," she whispered.

Clint stared down at her and knew how blessed he was that she had come into his life. Rachel had proven to him that there was still beauty and innocence in the world.

"I love you, too."

He kissed her one more time. This time it was a cherishing kiss that spoke of tenderness and devotion, and then they moved into the parlor to sit on the sofa together.

"What's going to happen to us now?" Rachel wondered.

Clint had known they were going to have to talk about the future. There could be no avoiding it, and no matter how he tried to look at things, these next weeks weren't going to be easy.

"For right now," he began, "to the outside world, there is no 'us.' To everyone except your parents and Michelle, I'm still Kane McCullough and you're still Rachel Hammond."

"I understand, but it doesn't make it easy for me."

"There's nothing easy about this. The Tucker Gang is as cold-blooded as they come. The farther you stay away from me, the better—for now."

A flicker of wicked delight shone in Rachel's eyes as she leaned toward him for a kiss. "Do you really want me to stay away from you—'now'?"

"Well, not right now," he murmured, capturing her lips in a hungry kiss.

They embraced, clinging together as they shared kiss after passionate kiss.

Clint wanted to caress her. To strip away the barrier of their clothing and claim her for his own for all time, but it couldn't be. There was too much at stake. With the last thread of sanity that remained, he forced himself to put Rachel from him.

"Clint?" She breathed his name, wanting to go back into his arms, wanting to be near him, to hold him and never let him go.

"Rachel, we have to stop, because"—he paused and gave her a wry smile—"If I don't stop now, I don't know that I'll ever be able to stop."

"Good," she said seductively.

The husky sound of her voice sent a jolt of sensuality through Clint. He wanted Rachel more than he'd ever wanted another woman, but he couldn't allow himself to give in to his passion. He held himself rigid, struggling against his need to love her.

Rachel's sanity slowly returned. She wanted to go back into his embrace and stay there forever, but she knew this was not the time.

"This wasn't quite the wedding night I'd al-

ways envisioned—being at home with my parents." She tried to make light of the situation.

"I'll make it up to you," Clint said, drawing her
back to him for one last soft kiss. "I promise."

Rachel looked up at him as he rose to leave.
"I'm going to hold you to that promise."

"I'll be looking forward to it," he told her, and
then he forced himself to walk away—to walk out
of the room and out of her life, for now.

Chapter Eighteen

Clint left the Hammonds' house and started back toward the hotel. He intended to spend the night alone in his room, but after having held Rachel in his arms, he knew he wouldn't fall asleep anytime soon. He decided to stop at the Last Chance for a drink before calling it a night.

Clint wasn't quite sure what kind of greeting he was going to get when he went into the saloon. After the way he'd left there earlier that evening, he wasn't sure Trey would be too glad to see him again. Clint walked through the swinging doors and stood there for a minute, waiting to see what was going to happen.

Trey spotted him right away and called out, even as he set a glass on the counter and began pouring him a shot of whiskey, "Am I going to have to call the law out on you again tonight, McCullough?"

"No, Deputy Evans calmed things down," Clint replied, going to stand at the bar.

Trey handed him the drink and took the money he offered. "I don't think Ed will be giving you any more trouble about the preacher's daughter. The deputy came back in and had a long talk with him."

"Good."

Clint turned around and leaned back against the bar as he took a drink. He surveyed the room, checking to see who was there. He hadn't expected to find anything different tonight, and he wasn't surprised. The usual crowd was drinking and gambling, and, as he'd suspected, there was no sign of Glen Tucker or Ax Hansen.

"Things have been real quiet since you left."

"Just the way you like it, right, Trey?"

"That's right."

Clint drained his glass and put it back on the bar.

"You want another?"

"No. It's time to call it a night. Don't let things get too wild around here."

"I won't."

Clint left the saloon and made his way to the hotel. He went up to his room and let himself in. The room was dark, just like his mood.

Clint saw no reason to light the lamp. He didn't even bother to undress. He just put his gun belt within reach on the nightstand and then stretched out on his bed. He lay staring up at the ceiling, going over in his mind all that had happened that day, beginning with the fight in the saloon and his talk with Nick. He remembered his surprise at finding himself standing across the street from the Hammonds' house just as Rachel and Michelle came out of the garden.

He and Rachel were married now.

She was his wife.

Clint smiled into the darkness at the thought.

This was their wedding night.

And he was alone.

Clint realized he should have stayed at the saloon a little while longer and had a few more drinks; it was going to be a long, lonely night.

After Clint left, Rachel went upstairs. She sought out her parents to tell them good night, then went on to her own room to get ready for bed. She'd thought she was strong enough to handle everything that had happened that day, but as she sat alone in her bedroom, her tears started.

Rachel was crying for herself—and for Clint.

Their marriage was supposed to be the beautiful beginning of a new life together, but it was not the start she would have chosen.

This was their wedding night, but because of the vicious men who'd killed his family, they were forced to be apart.

Her heart ached for Clint and the suffering he'd endured. She could only imagine the horror he'd lived through, and she wanted to make his future one of joy. She wanted to be with him. She wanted to hold him and to love him, on this, their wedding night.

But it couldn't be.

Not yet.

Not until he'd brought the killers to justice.

Rachel tried to console herself with the knowledge that Clint had professed his love for her. She told herself he was staying away from her to protect her, but those reminders did little to ease the pain and loneliness that overwhelmed her.

"Rachel?" Anne whispered her daughter's name as she opened the door to her room. She had thought she'd heard Rachel crying. "Are you all right?"

Rachel looked up as her mother came in and closed the door behind her. "No," she managed.

"What's wrong, sweetheart?" Anne went to sit beside her on the bed, just as she'd done since she was a little girl.

"It's my wedding night," Rachel said in a tear-choked voice. "I should be with Clint. We should be together."

Anne embraced her.

"I know, love. I know." As Anne tried to soothe her, she remembered her own wedding night. It had been a night filled with great joy and love, with tenderness and passion. It had been a night she would never forget, and she knew that Rachel and Clint deserved no less.

"I love him," Rachel said miserably, "but I don't know when we'll ever get to be together again."

"You love him?" her mother repeated, drawing her attention.

"Yes." Rachel looked at her, a bit puzzled by her question.

"Then what are you doing here?" she challenged her daughter and gave her daughter a conspiratorial smile.

"What do you mean?"

"I mean—your husband is waiting for you," Anne said. She realized then how strange it was to speak of Rachel having a husband. "You should go to him."

Rachel brightened at her mother's daring suggestion. "Do you really think I should?"

"As long as you're very careful and make sure to get back here before sunup."

Rachel threw her arms around her mother and kissed her cheek. "Thank you!"

"Get Michelle to help you. She can sneak you into the hotel without anyone seeing you, can't she?"

"Oh, yes," Rachel breathed in pure excitement.

"Go on," Anne urged, knowing that the beautiful, loving memories Clint and Rachel created this night would last them a lifetime. "Your husband's waiting for you."

Michelle was still awake in her bedroom, sitting in bed reading an exciting dime novel when she heard someone tapping at her window. She put her book aside, went to the window, and was startled to find Rachel staring in at her. Michelle was afraid something was terribly wrong. Why else would her friend sneak over to her house? They hadn't acted like this since they were children. She immediately opened the window.

"What are you doing here?" Michelle whispered, looking nervously past Rachel to make sure she was alone.

"I need your help," Rachel said urgently.

"What do you need?"

"I need you to sneak me into Clint's room at the hotel."

Michelle's expression went from fearful concern to delight in an instant.

"What a wonderful idea! But we're going to have to be very quiet and very careful—for your sake," Michelle told her.

"I know."

"Are you sure you want to do this?" Michelle asked, thinking how terrible it would be if anyone spotted Rachel sneaking into Clint's room.

"Oh, yes. I'm sure."

"Well, give me a minute to get dressed, and I'll be right out."

Michelle was as good as her word. Within minutes, they were on their way to the hotel.

"How are we going to do this?" Rachel asked. She realized if they knocked on Clint's door, some people staying at the hotel might hear her.

"I've got the master key. I'll just let you into Clint's room," Michelle explained.

"I hope I don't scare him."

"He'll be surprised, but I don't think you're going to scare him. I'll bet you're going to be the best surprise Clint's ever had."

They moved quietly down the back alleyway. Fortunately, it was deserted. Michelle unlocked the back door of the hotel, and they slipped inside without anyone seeing them. There was no one stirring in the hotel either. Silently they crept up the rear staircase to the second floor, stopping outside Clint's room.

Clint had been lying in bed wide awake when he heard the sound of footsteps in the hallway. At first he thought nothing of it, but then he realized that whoever was out in the hall had stopped right at his door.

Without making a sound, Clint got up and retrieved his gun. He didn't know what was going on, but he had to be ready. It could be Ed coming after him for revenge. He backed into a corner of the darkened room and waited.

At the sound of a key in the lock, Clint tensed even more. Gun in hand, he was ready for whatever trouble was coming his way.

And then he heard Rachel's voice as she said softly, "Thanks, Michelle."

Clint watched as the door quietly opened and Rachel slipped inside the room.

Rachel closed the door behind her and tried to look around in the dark. She could see right away that the covers on the bed were thrown back and the bed was empty. For a moment, she was heartbroken, thinking Clint wasn't there.

"I must be dreaming," Clint said.

"Clint!" Rachel gasped as he emerged from the darkened corner holding his gun.

"I thought you might be trouble," he told her as he put his gun back in the holster.

"I am," she said with an enticing grin. She went straight into his arms.

"But I like your kind of trouble."

Clint kissed her hungrily, wanting to make sure he wasn't dreaming. He was thrilled to have her with him.

"Did anyone see you?" he asked, concerned when the kiss ended and they moved apart.

"No. Michelle let me in the back door."

"She is one special lady."

"Yes, she is," Rachel agreed. She owed her friend a lot for what she'd done tonight.

"Are you sure you want to be here?" Clint asked as what little self-control he had was rapidly slipping away.

He wanted Rachel.

He was hungry for her.

He loved her, but nothing was more important to him than her safety.

"Oh, yes. I'm sure. This is our wedding night," she whispered in a husky tone. "I couldn't stay away. I had to be with you tonight."

At her words, the last bit of restraint he'd had disappeared. Clint didn't waste any more time talking. He made sure the door was locked, so they would have the privacy they needed, and then turned to his bride and took her in his arms. He crushed her against him, his mouth covering hers in a devouring kiss that sparked the flames of their long-denied desire.

Rachel responded without reserve. There was

no need to deny herself the glory she found in his embrace.

This was Clint—

Her husband—

Her love.

Linking her arms around his neck, Rachel held Clint close and returned his kiss with abandon. When his lips left hers to press kisses down her neck, a shiver of sensual awareness trembled through her and she arched against the hard heat of him in an instinctive, age-old invitation.

Clint responded immediately to that unspoken enticement. He claimed her lips once more in a deep kiss as his hands traced a seductive path to the buttons at the back of her gown. He unbuttoned the dress with the utmost care and stripped it from her.

Standing before him clad only in her chemise, Rachel felt a bit nervous. She had never been so unclad with a man before, but when he came to her and took her back into his arms, all her concerns were instantly forgotten. Kiss after passionate kiss left her breathless and eager to know more of Clint's exciting lovemaking.

Clint felt her surrender and could no longer deny himself the perfection of her love. He lifted Rachel up in his arms and carried her to the bed to lay her upon its welcoming softness. He stretched out beside her, glorying in the intimacy of the moment. His hungry, heated gaze swept over her silken curves.

Rachel reached out to Clint and began to undo the buttons on his shirt, wanting to caress the broad, powerful width of his chest. She wanted no barrier between them.

Clint helped her with the buttons and quickly took off his shirt. Rachel reached out to sculpt the hard-muscled expanse of his shoulders and back.

The touch of her hands upon him aroused him to a fever pitch. He helped her take off the last of her undergarments and cast them aside to stare down at the perfection of her silken beauty. His gaze went over her slender curves in a heated caress, and he knew there would be no stopping now. He heard her gasp as his hands traced paths of fire over her shoulders and down to the fullness of her breasts.

Clint kissed Rachel passionately as he continued to caress her. His lips left hers to explore her lush curves.

Rachel moved restlessly against him as his every kiss and touch sent her senses spiraling out of control. She caressed his back and shoulders, thrilling to the strength of him, to the heat of him. Excitement pulsed deep within the womanly heart of her, and she knew she needed more.

"Please, Clint," she whispered, mindless in her passion. "I need you."

Her words broke the last thread of his self-control, and Clint could deny himself no longer. He drew away from her and shed the rest of his clothing.

Rachel watched him undress. She had always

known he was handsome, but seeing him this way only left her even more sure of just how perfect Clint was. His shoulders were broad and darkly tanned, his waist lean, his legs long and straight. He was powerfully built, and she wanted to be close to him—to be one with him.

Rachel lifted her arms to Clint in a loving invitation, and he came to her.

Clint moved over Rachel, his body a searing brand upon her silken flesh.

Rachel gazed up at him, all the love she felt for him shining in her eyes. "I love you."

"And I love you," he told her as he claimed her lips in a kiss of love and devotion that lifted their passion for one another to new heights.

They came together in a blaze of glory. Clint moved slowly as he claimed Rachel for his own. He knew she was an innocent, and he wanted only to give her pleasure. With utmost care, he kissed and caressed her, bringing her to the peak of love's desire before moving to make her his in all ways.

Rachel was on fire with her need to be one with Clint. She held him close as he moved over her. She opened to him as a flower to the sun.

Clint was the man she loved—her husband.

As he made her his own, she gasped and clung to him, delighting in his possession, thrilling at being one with him. When Clint began to move within her, she instinctively matched him in that sensual, loving rhythm.

They soared to the heights of passion, needing to be one, wanting to be one.

The ecstasy of Clint's kiss and touch swept Rachel away, and she cried out softly as they reached the peak of rapture together.

They were one.

Wrapped in each other's arms, they clung together in the glow of love's aftermath, treasuring the union they'd just shared.

Chapter Nineteen

"What the hell did you think you were doing?" the Boss demanded of Tuck as he met with him, alone, late that night on the outskirts of Dry Springs.

"We thought you'd be impressed if we pulled off a bonus job and brought in a little extra money. We were just having some fun, and we wanted to let you know we were here, that's all," Tuck told him.

"You call getting Holt killed fun? And you didn't even end up with the money!" he snarled. "You acted like a gang of incompetent fools!"

"It won't happen again," Tuck assured him. He knew how ugly the Boss could get if things didn't go his way, and he had no desire to challenge him.

"You're damned right it won't! If it does, you're dead. Do you understand me?" The Boss pinned Tuck with a lethal glare. He'd let it be known from the beginning that anyone who tried to cross him was a dead man.

"Yes."

"Good. Now here's your next job. There's an Army payroll shipment coming through the area in four days. It's a big one. Where do we stand?"

"Right now, it's tight."

"What do you mean, it's tight?"

"Rick's dead, and Sanders hasn't shown up."

The Boss cursed under his breath at the news. "Where the hell is Sanders?"

"I don't know. We haven't heard a word from him."

"So there's just the three of you?"

"So far."

"What do you think happened to him?"

"It's not like him to be late, so it must be serious—whatever it is."

"Then we can't count on him showing up at all," the Boss said in disgust, "and it won't be easy bringing in this payroll with only you, Ax, and Walt." He was angry over the complications. He'd wanted the robbery to go off without a hitch. "Wait a minute—I've got an idea."

"What?"

"Have you ever heard of Kane McCullough?"

"Yeah, there was talk about him in the last town we were in," Tuck told him. "From what was being said, McCullough sounds like a mean bastard. Why?"

"He's here in Dry Springs."

Tuck was surprised. "What's he doing here?"

"Who the hell cares? The point is, he's here, and he might be just the man you need to pull this job off. He's been spending a lot of time at the Last Chance, drinking and gambling, so he may be waiting for a job like this to come along. Go talk to him. If he's as fast with a gun as his reputation says, he should fit right in."

"I'll do it."

"I'll meet you back here in two days. We can make the final plans then."

Tuck watched the Boss ride away; then he mounted up and returned to the place where the going had made camp. As he rode in, he wasn't surprised to find that Ax and Walt were still up, sitting by the campfire waiting for him.

"How did it go?" Ax asked as Tuck sat down with them.

Tuck quickly told them about the next job coming up.

"That sounds damned good," Walt said with a big grin. He liked robbing payrolls. The Boss was always generous when they brought in a big haul.

"There's only one problem. He thinks we need another man with us, since Sanders hasn't shown up."

"Did he have any ideas?" Ax asked.

"Yeah. Evidently that gunfighter named Kane McCullough has been hanging around Dry Springs, and the Boss thinks he'd be a good one to use."

"But we don't know much about him," Walt pointed out.

"We know he's fast with a gun," Tuck said, "and that seems to be good enough for the Boss."

"How we gonna do it?"

"I thought we could ride into Dry Springs to-morrow and have ourselves a good old time at the Last Chance. From what I understand, they got some real fine lookers working there, and I could use a little loving right about now."

"It's a damned shame we ain't in town to-night," Ax said.

They all agreed with his sentiments and bed-ded down for the night. They had a lot to do the following day if they were going to try to recruit McCullough to ride with them on their next job. It had to be handled carefully. They couldn't re-veal too much to him without knowing he would be working with them and could be trusted.

Clint rose up on one elbow to stare down at Rachel as she lay nestled against him. His gaze went over her, taking in the tumble of her dark curls on the pillow and the classic elegance of her features as she lay with her eyes closed. His gaze moved lower, visually caressing her as he relived the glory of their lovemaking a short time before. Un-able to resist, he leaned over her to steal a soft kiss.

At the touch of Clint's lips, Rachel stirred and opened her eyes. She looped her arms around his neck and met him in that sweet exchange. She held him close as they deepened the kiss.

This time there was no holding back. They had only a few hours left to be together, and they wanted to share the beauty of their love for as long as they could.

They came together in a blaze of passion and desire. With heated caresses, they stoked the fire of their need until, caught up in the searing ecstasy of their embrace, they found love's glory.

"You are so wonderful—" Rachel breathed. She was in awe of the perfection of their loving. She had never known such ecstasy as she found in his arms.

"So are you," Clint murmured against her lips, kissing her again. "If I had my way, we'd stay here forever."

Rachel gave a throaty chuckle. "I like the way you think, but my parents might come looking for us."

"We're married," he told her in a husky voice as he rose up over her to look down at her.

She gave him a slow, sensuous smile as she lifted one hand to caress his cheek. "Yes, we are."

Clint pressed a cherishing kiss to the palm of her hand, thankful for the love and peace he found in her embrace. He hadn't believed he could ever be this happy again. He hadn't believed he would ever have a life after what had happened, but now, with Rachel, he knew there was a future for them—once he finished what he'd come there to do.

"I love you, Rachel."

"Show me," she whispered, reaching up to draw him down to her.

And Clint did show her.

It was much later when Rachel left Clint's embrace and began to dress. She looked over to where he still lay on the bed and marveled at how handsome he was. His lean jawline was shadowed now by a day's growth. The blanket covered him just to the waist, but the sight of his hard-muscled chest and powerful shoulders and arms left her breathless. She had just been in his arms, crushed against his chest, and it had been heavenly.

Rachel realized Clint was watching her, and she blushed at the direction of her thoughts. She was glad he couldn't see her face clearly in the darkness.

Clint had not wanted to let her leave his bed, let alone leave the room tonight, but they had no choice. There could be no denying the danger he faced, and he wanted her safe with her parents.

Rachel knew she had to leave the hotel and return home while it was still dark outside. The gossips would learn of her marriage to Clint soon enough, but there was no point in tempting fate by letting anyone see her leaving his room. Their relationship must remain a secret until Clint's work was done.

"I don't like you going home by yourself," he told her, getting up to help her button her dress.

"It will be bad enough if someone sees me alone, but if we were seen together—"

"I know," Clint said regretfully as he finished fastening the last button and turned her to face him. "But that doesn't mean I have to like it."

"Kiss me," she invited as she wrapped her arms around his lean waist and lifted her lips to his.

He obliged, cherishing the moment.

"I know you have to go after the Tucker Gang," Rachel whispered, "but hurry back to me. I'll be waiting for you—and praying for you."

She rose up on tiptoe to kiss him one last time, then moved to unlock the door. She opened it and peeked out into the hall. It was deserted, as she'd hoped it would be.

Rachel looked back at Clint one last time, and their gazes met across the room. Tearing herself away, she stepped out into the hall and closed the door silently behind her. She moved quickly and quietly from the hotel out into the alleyway. It took her only a few minutes to reach her home, and she crept inside without waking her parents.

Rachel quickly changed into her nightgown and lay in bed in her room. She longed to be back with Clint, in his arms, loving him, but it wasn't to be. Her heart ached as she thought of how long it might be before they could be together again.

Raising up her hand, she stared at the wedding ring she wore and knew she would have to take it off before she went out in public the next day. No one could know of her marriage yet, so she would wear the ring on the chain of her necklace. That way, it would at least be close to her heart until the time came when she and Clint could openly proclaim their love for one another.

Silently Rachel offered up a prayer that Clint would find the outlaws quickly and return to her, safe and sound. She wanted nothing more than to be in his arms forever.

* * *

When Rachel had gone, Clint returned to his lonely bed. He knew the night he'd just spent in her embrace had been a gift he would treasure always. He deeply regretted that their marriage must remain a secret for the time being, but there was no way he could change what he had to do.

It was the first week of the month. With any luck, the Tucker Gang would be showing up any day, and he had to be ready for them.

He didn't want to even consider the possibility that the gang might not show up. In that case, he would be forced to ride out and start tracking them down again. He would do it if he had to. Nothing was going to stop him from finding them.

It was time for justice.

Chapter Twenty

It was just getting dark when Clint left the hotel and headed for the Last Chance late the following day. He was passing by some horses tied up in front of the saloon when he stopped. There at the hitching rail was a roan with a starlike marking on its chest—matching Rachel's description of a horse one of the outlaws had been riding.

Clint looked over the horses in hopes of finding some other identifying features, but there was nothing. Ready to play out the role of Kane McCullough, he entered the saloon through the swinging doors and strode up to the bar.

"Where you been all day, McCullough? It's been awful quiet around here," Trey told him as Clint approached.

"I had some work to take care of," Clint answered without revealing any details. "But I'm here now. You think things will perk up?"

"I never know when you're around," Trey chuckled.

"I'm just ready to enjoy myself tonight—a little gambling and a little drinking. Give me a whiskey."

"Coming right up." Trey made short order of serving the liquor.

Clint paid him and turned to look around the saloon as he took a drink. It was more crowded than usual, and several poker games were going on in the back of the room. "Ed hasn't shown up tonight?"

"He ain't been back since your fight. I got a hunch he ain't feeling too good after the beating you gave him."

Clint shrugged. "A man ought to be smart enough to think before he speaks."

"Maybe you taught him that lesson."

"I suppose we might find out one of these days." Gesturing toward the tables in back, he said, "Looks like you've got some good poker games going tonight."

"Some new boys rode into town this afternoon. They've been spending real free and easy, so we're glad they're here."

"I think I'll go see what kind of stakes they're playing for," Clint said.

"Here—have a refill before you go," Trey offered, holding out the bottle to him.

"Thanks." Clint was obliged. His glass full, he walked to the back of the saloon.

Clint was careful to keep his manner relaxed as he approached the table, but it wasn't easy. He wasn't sure what he was going to discover, but he knew he had to be prepared for anything.

Even so, he felt like he'd been punched in the gut when he found himself face to face with the men who'd killed his family.

There at one of the poker tables sat Glen Tucker and Ax Hansen. The sketches on the wanted posters had been crude, but they'd done the two men justice. He recognized the cold-blooded killers immediately.

Rage unlike anything he'd ever experienced seared Clint's soul. He felt a burning desire to draw his gun and put an end to their miserable, rotten, no-good lives right then and there.

He wanted to do it.

He could have done it.

It was only by the sheer force of his willpower that he was able to maintain his self-control. Ultimately, the killers would pay for what they'd done, but not until he'd identified the real leader of their murderous gang.

"Got room for one more?" Clint asked casually as he came to stand near the table.

Tuck looked up at him, wondering how deep the man's pockets were. "It'll cost you."

"Good," Clint said, giving him a smile as he pulled out a chair to sit down at the table. "That means when I win, I'll be taking a lot of your money."

"We'll see about that," Tuck said, looking over at the man who was dealing. "Let's play."

The dealer shuffled the deck and began to deal the hand.

Tuck sat back, eyeing the new man with interest. He had spotted him the minute he'd come into the saloon. He could tell he was a force to be reckoned with. The way he carried himself and wore his gun all said "gunman," and Tuck wondered if this could be Kane McCullough, the gunfighter the Boss had been talking about. He was going to find out as fast as he could because they still had some planning to do before they could pull off their next job.

Kane felt good about the pair of aces he was holding and hoped it was a sign of things to come.

It was.

He won the hand and raked in a lucrative pot.

Tuck and Ax weren't happy about losing, but they sat tight.

A saloon girl named Suzie came to the table to see if anyone needed another drink.

After the other men had told her what they wanted, she looked at Kane. "What about you, Kane? Are you ready?"

"I'm fine," he declared, not wanting to risk drinking too much while he was with these men. He had to stay sharp and be ready, because anything could happen at any time with the Tucker Gang.

At the sound of Kane's name, Tuck and Ax exchanged knowing looks. They had their man. At the first opportunity, they would have to get Mc-

Cullough outside and make him an offer they hoped he wouldn't refuse.

"You boys are new in town, aren't you?" Clint asked, making conversation as they continued to play.

"We just rode in tonight." Tuck looked at him shrewdly and asked, "You're Kane McCullough, aren't you?"

"That's right." Clint purposely eyed Tuck with suspicion. All the while, though, he was silently offering up thanks that Captain Meyers had done such a good job in getting the word out about his bad reputation. Things just might work out the way he'd planned.

"What brings you to Dry Springs?" Ax asked.

"I heard it was a nice, quiet little town."

"From what I've heard about you, I wouldn't think you liked nice, quiet little towns," Tuck remarked.

Clint shrugged and looked him straight in the eye. "You never know who you might meet."

"You're right about that," Tuck agreed, throwing in his hand. "I'm out."

Clint dropped out, too, even though he had two pair. He wanted the chance to talk more with Tuck. "So, what about you? What are you doing here in Dry Springs?"

"Me and the boys—" He gestured toward Ax at their table and toward another man sitting at a secluded table being entertained by one of the saloon girls. "We got a new job coming up—a big one."

"What kind of work do you do?" Clint glanced toward the other man and assumed he was the outlaw named Walt, who'd been riding with the gang from the start.

"The kind that pays the best," Tuck answered elusively.

They shared a look of understanding.

"We need another hand for this new job, so—if you're interested . . ."

"I might be." Clint was deliberately evasive.

"Well, then, why don't we step outside for a few minutes and talk about it?" Tuck asked.

"Sure."

Tuck told the dealer to save their seats, then walked out of the Last Chance with Clint. They moved away from the main doors to stand near the alleyway for more privacy.

It was fully dark outside now, and Clint was glad. He liked being under the cover of darkness when dealing with Tuck's kind.

"What plans have you got for the near future, McCullough?" Tuck asked point-blank once he was sure they were alone.

"I was just planning on playing poker and winning all your money," Clint answered with a smile. "Why?"

Tuck wasn't amused. "I thought you might be interested in trying another kind of gambling— that is, if you're as good with a gun as your reputation says you are."

Clint looked him straight in the eye as he answered, "What do you think?"

"Good." Tuck smiled coldly at him, respecting his arrogance and his reputed ability.

"What've you got in mind?"

"The Boss says there's a shipment—"

"Wait a minute," Clint interrupted him. "What do you mean, 'the Boss says'? You mean you aren't running things?"

"No. The Boss calls the shots. He has from the very beginning when we first started riding together. We just do what he tells us to do."

"I don't work that way. Before I agree to be a part of anything, I have to meet with your boss face to face. I only deal with the top men."

Tuck was insulted by this refusal. "I already told you how things are with us."

"Then it looks like you're going to be short-handed on your next job."

"Don't be a fool, McCullough."

Clint stiffened at his insult. "I'm no fool, friend. I'm just careful."

"There's a lot of money to be made if you ride with us on this job. It's a big one," Tuck insisted.

"Good. Talk to your boss and tell him I want to meet him or there's no deal. You can send word to me at the hotel and let me know when he wants to get together."

Tuck was furious over McCullough's arrogant demands. He wondered who in hell this gunman thought he was. Unfortunately, he knew the gang would be shorthanded without him, and that could make things real tough.

"I'm due to hook up with the Boss again tomorrow. I'll talk to him then and let you know what he says about meeting with you."

"I'll be waiting." Clint said no more before walking off.

Tuck felt irritated as he watched him go. His mood was black when he rejoined Ax at the poker table.

"Where's McCullough?" Ax asked.

"I guess he's calling it a night."

Ax could tell by Tuck's terse tone that something wasn't right, but he didn't say anything at that moment. He would find out what had happened later, when no one else was around to listen in.

"Too bad he quit playing poker," Ax said, going along with Tuck. "I was hoping to win my money back."

"We'll be seeing him again, don't worry."

Ax thought that was good news. With the extra gun, they would definitely be able to take the payroll.

Satisfied for the time being, they went back to the serious pursuits of gambling and drinking.

Clint knew what he had to do. He got his horse and hid in one of the nearby alleys to wait for Tuck and the other gang members to leave the Last Chance. He planned to follow them when they headed out to their camp so he could keep Tuck under surveillance overnight. He planned to be watching when Tuck met with his boss the following day.

The news that the big boss was actually there in the area left Clint excited and on edge. Right now, he was closer than he'd ever been to bringing the gang down.

Tomorrow just might prove to be the day of final reckoning, and he was ready.

He'd been ready for a long time.

It was the night of the regular weekly prayer service. As Reverend Hammond made his way to the front of the church, he looked out over those who had gathered there. It was a good-sized crowd for the middle of the week, and he was glad. He wanted as many townsfolk as possible to hear what he had to say that night.

Martin's gaze fell upon Catherine Lawrence and Mary Ann Forester sitting near the front with their husbands, and he was hard put to control his temper. He reminded himself that he was a man of God, but that didn't stop him from having the normal feelings any father would have when bad rumors were being maliciously spread about his daughter.

Martin happened to still be looking their way when Anne and Rachel came into the church and sat down, and he noticed the almost smug look the two gossips gave each other when they his wife and daughter. He silently offered up a prayer that the two gossips would listen and understand the message he was about to deliver.

"Good evening, everyone," he welcomed them as he went to stand at the pulpit.

"Good evening, Reverend," they responded.

"It's wonderful to see all of you, and I thank you for coming. I've always believed it was an honor bestowed upon me to bring God's word to you. I believe I am blessed for having been given this calling," Martin began.

"We're blessed to have you, Reverend Hammond," one man called out from the back of church.

"That we are," another added.

Martin was humbled by their kind words. "Jesus told us to 'love one another as I have loved you.' The love we show to one another is truly a manifestation of our love for Christ. How we treat one another is how we live our religion." Martin paused for effect and looked out over the congregation. "Each and every one of us should remember that. It is important, if we are truly to call ourselves Christians, that we practice what we preach."

"Amen," another man said, affirming his words.

"But it is not enough just to come to church. It is not enough to just say we are Christians. We have to show our faith in our thoughts and in our words and in our deeds. It is our job to love and serve and spread the Good News." Again he stopped for dramatic emphasis. He deliberately looked down at Catherine and Mary Ann. "It is not for us to pass judgment on one another."

The two women realized their minister was staring straight at them. They shifted uneasily in the pew and dropped their gazes as they tried to avoid making eye contact with him.

"If you feel someone is in need of help or guidance in the Lord's ways, offer them that help and guidance. It would be wrong not to. We have been called to do God's work here on Earth, but we have been called upon to do it lovingly. We must do His work with compassion and with tenderness, and we must always do His work for His glory, not our own." Martin smiled as he lifted his gaze to look at the other members of the congregation, who were good-hearted and generous. "Our God is a loving, forgiving God. We should never take it upon ourselves to pass judgment on others. He alone has the right to judge us on that final day."

"Amen!"

Martin continued, "If we have fallen astray, it's never too late to come back into the fold. The Lord welcomes us with open arms—if we are truly sorry for our sins."

"Praise the Lord!" Helen Slifer exclaimed.

"Exactly," Martin affirmed her sentiment. "We must praise the Lord with our words and deeds. We must live our lives as examples of Christian love and charity. Remember that always. And I repeat"—he looked directly at the two women, his gaze piercing—"Judge not, lest ye be judged."

He encouraged those in attendance to offer prayers for others in need. It was some time later when the service ended with a blessing, after which the two gossips and their husbands made a quick exit.

Martin hoped his message of love and forgiveness had gotten through to them.

Only time would tell.

As Clint waited for the gang to come out of the saloon, his thoughts turned to Rachel, and he wondered what his beautiful bride was doing tonight. In a perfect world, they would have been together in a home of their own, celebrating their newfound love, but this was far from a perfect world they lived in. As he prepared to face down his family's killers, Clint just hoped that someday they would actually have a normal life together.

It was late when Tuck, Ax, and Walt finally left the Last Chance. Clint wondered if they'd had any luck recruiting more men to ride with them on their next job.

Clint watched as the three men mounted up and began to ride out of town. Then he got on his own horse and went after them.

It wasn't easy, tracking them in the dark. He had to be extra cautious and stay far enough back so they wouldn't be aware that he was on their trail. Clint was thankful the night was clear and the moon was close to full.

When Clint realized the gang had made camp near a stream about half a mile ahead of him, he found a secluded place to tie up his horse some distance away. Then, taking his rifle, he made his way on foot through the darkness to a good vantage point where he could keep watch on the camp.

Clint settled down, in tense anticipation of the day to come.

In just a few hours, he would learn the identity of the murderous leader of the deadly gang.

Chapter Twenty-one

"When is the Boss going to show up?" Walt complained as the gang bided their time at their campsite the following morning. "I was looking forward to spending the day in Dry Springs. I had a real good time with that girl Dixie last night, and I was wanting to look her up again today."

"Dixie ain't going nowhere," Tuck told him. "She'll be ready and waiting for you when you show up."

"I like the way you think, Tuck," Walt said with a grin as he imagined the voluptuous, redheaded saloon girl doing just that.

"What do you think the Boss will say about McCullough's demand to meet with him before the robbery?" Ax worried.

"It's gonna depend on how much he wants us to pull off this job. We need McCullough riding with us, so the Boss may agree to do it," Tuck answered.

"Do you think McCullough's as bad as his reputation says he is?" Walt asked.

"Why don't you call him out and find out?" Ax said, chuckling at the thought.

"One of these days I may just do that," Walt responded, imagining the glory that would be his if he could take down a fast gun like McCullough. He added quickly, "But not until after we take care of this next job."

"Good thinking," Tuck replied sarcastically as he looked over at the younger man. Walt had been riding with them for quite a while now. Tuck trusted him, but knew Walt had a wild streak. He hoped that wild streak didn't end up getting the younger man into trouble.

"Since you're looking for some action, come on," Ax challenged, pointing at a target he'd set up. "Let's see how good you are this morning."

"You're on," Walt said, ready to hone his skills.

The two moved away to practice for a while.

Tuck stayed at the campsite to wait for the Boss to show up. He knew it might be afternoon before he actually arrived, but it didn't matter.

He wasn't called the Boss for nothing.

As it happened, it was just past noon when they caught sight of the Boss riding in. Tuck was relieved to see him, for they still had a lot of planning to do for the robbery.

"It's about time you showed," Tuck said with a grin. He watched the Boss rein in and dismount.

"Sometimes a man has to work," he answered, looking at the three of them gathered there.

"We're just about set to go," Ax said.

"So McCullough's in?" the Boss asked, looking to Tuck for confirmation.

"He said he was interested, but he wouldn't agree to work with us until he'd met with you first."

"What?" the Boss exploded. "How did he even find out about me?"

"When I was talking to him, telling him how we worked, I mentioned our Boss, and he called me on it. He said he only deals with the Boss and nobody else. He wouldn't agree to ride with us until he'd talked to you."

The Boss swore vilely at Tuck. "You're an incompetent fool! Why didn't you tell him you were in charge? You know I don't want my connection to any of this revealed. That Ranger—Frank Williams—was the only one smart enough to figure it out, and that's why we killed him. No one outside of the three of you is supposed to even know I exist!"

"I know," Tuck replied, his tone apologetic.

"You know? That doesn't change what happened with McCullough, does it? What did you tell him?"

"I told him I was meeting with you today, and I'd let him know your answer this afternoon."

"Well, here's what you tell him," the Boss directed. "You tell him I only meet with men I trust, and he hasn't proven himself to me yet. If he works with you and the boys to pull off the job successfully, then I'll meet with him afterward when everything's calmed down—but not before."

"What if he refuses?" Tuck asked. He liked to be prepared for the worst.

"Then you'd better have another plan figured out on how to get this payroll with just the three of you. It's too big to let it go," he ordered harshly. "Do you understand me?"

"Yeah."

"Good. When are you going to talk to McCullough again?"

"He's waiting to hear from us now. I'm supposed to contact him when we get back to town."

"I'll find a way to meet up with you later tonight, so you can let me know what he says."

"I'll be looking for you."

In total disgust, the Boss mounted up. After giving Tuck one last cold-eyed look, he rode away and didn't look back.

From first light, Clint had been keeping watch over the outlaws' camp from his vantage point. When he'd first spotted the lone horseman coming, he'd grown excited. He'd known this had to be the Boss, for no one else would be meeting with the gang in this out-of-the-way location.

As the rider had closed in, Clint had been able to get a better look at him.

The man riding openly into the gang's campsite had been none other than Sheriff Pete Reynolds.

Clint had been shocked.

Was the lawman the secret leader of the Tucker Gang?

A wide range of tumultuous emotions had rocked him. Clint's first instinct had been to grab his rifle and shoot Pete down in cold blood. He'd wanted to see him die in the same way his family had been killed.

Clint had controlled the urge, though, and had waited to see if his suspicion might be proven wrong. He'd even hoped that the sheriff might have tracked Tuck, Ax, and Walt down for some trouble they'd caused in town after he'd parted company with them the night before. But the welcome the sheriff had received from Tuck and the others had disabused Clint of that notion.

After watching them together, he had had no doubt.

The gunmen had known who Pete was.

Pete was the Boss.

Rage unlike anything Clint had ever known had filled him. No wonder the posse had turned back after such a short time tracking the outlaws who'd tried to rob the stagecoach. It had been Pete's gang who'd attempted the robbery. It all made sense to Clint now.

Clint had wanted to take the gang out right then and there.

He'd lifted his rifle and taken careful aim.

He'd been smiling a cold, deadly smile when he centered Pete in his sights.

He had been all set to pull the trigger.

And then the memory of Martin's words from

the night of the wedding had come back to haunt him. *"Remember that the Lord said, 'Vengeance is mine.' You weren't raised to be like the killers. You're not a cold-blooded murderer. You're a Texas Ranger. Arrest them and bring them to justice. Let the law punish them."*

The words *"You weren't raised to be like the killers,"* had echoed in his mind and in his heart. He'd thought of his parents and of how his father had been working so hard to bring in the Tucker Gang. He'd recalled their last conversation: His father had told him that he'd never seen more cold blooded murderers than these men.

At this memory, Clint had realized that he wasn't like them—he wasn't a cold-blooded murderer—and he'd known what he had to do.

He had to bring them in.

Clint had lowered his rifle. He had continued his surveillance until their meeting had come to an end. When Pete had mounted up and ridden out of their camp, he was ready. He'd waited until Pete was far enough ahead of him, then mounted his own horse and ridden for town.

The gang would be contacting him later that day to let him know what the Boss had said about meeting with him. But before he ever heard from them, he intended to have already "met up" with the Boss.

Clint was going to take care of Pete right now.

Pete was angry with Tuck as he rode back toward Dry Springs. He'd never thought the man was particularly smart, but he'd believed Tuck had enough sense to keep the truth about his involvement with the gang quiet. He'd been wrong. The man was an idiot.

Pete swore under his breath as he thought about what might happen next. Kane McCullough was no ordinary fast gun. From what he'd learned, the man was smart and he was deadly, and that could prove dangerous. McCullough would be an asset to the gang, but only if he cooperated and did what he was told. They needed someone who would work with them and be happy with his share of the take. Judging from what he'd heard from Tuck, the gunslinger might not be their man. One way or the other, Pete knew he would find out later that day.

Pete liked being in control of things, and his mood grew even blacker as he neared town. He was seriously considering checking out the saloons, just to pick a fight or two and stir up some trouble. He'd be able to work off some of his anger and frustration on unsuspecting drunks. The idea had merit, and he made up his mind to do just that after checking in with Nick at the sheriff's office.

Pete reined in before the jail and dismounted. He headed inside to find that Nick was not there. In a way, Pete was glad. He wanted some time alone before he went out to make his rounds of the saloons.

* * *

Clint reached town and left his horse at the stable. Taking his rifle, with him, he started off toward the sheriff's office. He'd had plenty of time on the ride back to plan what he was going to do. By the time this day was over, he hoped justice would be served.

As Clint neared the jail, he didn't see anyone around. That was good. Things might turn ugly, and he didn't want any innocents getting hurt.

He strode to the door of the sheriff's office and walked in.

"McCullough—" Pete looked up from where he was sitting at the desk as Clint came through the door. "What are you doing here?"

Clint closed the door behind him and then turned to bring his rifle to bear on the sheriff. "I was looking for you."

"What the—" Pete was surprised by the other man's actions and started to reach for the gun he kept in his top desk drawer for moments like this.

"Don't even think about it," Clint ordered in a deadly tone, knowing exactly what Pete was trying to do.

"All right." Pete went still and remained unmoving, trying to figure out what was going on. If McCullough planned to join up with Tuck and the others, it made no sense to cause trouble in town like this. And if he was going to cause trouble in town, why would he go after the sheriff? Why hadn't he robbed the bank or one of the stagecoaches that had been passing through?

"Get up and move away from the desk. Keep

your hands where I can see them." Clint shifted his position to keep his back to the wall as he kept the rifle trained on the Boss. He didn't want anybody coming into the office behind him.

"What's this all about?" Pete demanded as he got to his feet and did as the gunman had directed.

"You can ask Tuck and Ax when you see them again. They can tell you."

"Who are Tuck and Ax?" Pete asked, playing dumb.

"I was at the campsite this morning. I saw everything. I know who you are, and I know what you do."

"Tuck is one dumb son of a bitch," Pete swore as he realized how Tuck's stupid remarks the night before had given everything away. McCullough had just proven he was every bit as smart as his reputation had claimed he was. Pete relaxed and grinned at the other man, believing he was just there trying to impress him with how clever he was. "I hadn't planned to meet with you ahead of time, but I'd say it looks like I don't have much choice, doesn't it?"

The fact that Pete was smiling at him only made Clint more furious.

"Wipe that smile off your face," he ordered in a cold, deadly voice. He motioned toward the back room where the jail cells were and directed, "Keep walking."

"Wait a minute—" Pete argued, believing this was some kind of game McCullough was playing and that he could still take control of the situation.

Clint quickly put an end to that belief as he said, "It wouldn't bother me at all to put a bullet in you right now, so don't try anything. Just turn around."

When Pete did as he'd ordered, Clint closed the distance between them and grabbed Pete's gun out of his gun belt. He shoved him in the direction of the back room.

"Move."

Clint didn't trust him for a minute. He was ready for anything Pete might try. It actually surprised him when he didn't put up a fight or try to get away.

"You know my deputy is due back here at any time," Pete said, hoping to make McCullough nervous.

"Good, then Nick will be the first to find out that the real leader of the Tucker Gang is behind bars," Clint told him as he shoved him forcefully into the empty cell and slammed the door shut, locking it and pocketing the key.

Pete turned and glared through the bars of the jail cell. He finally realized there was more going on here than just a gunfighter wanting to prove something to him. "Who are you?"

Clint looked him in the eye as he answered, "Does the name Frank Williams mean anything to you?"

Pete went still at the mention of the Ranger's name. Warily, he answered, "He's dead."

"I know. I was there when it happened," Clint

said quietly as he faced the sheriff down. A part of him still wanted to pull the trigger right then and there and claim his revenge. "He was my father."

"You're—" Shock radiated through Pete as he realized whom he was facing.

"That's right, I'm Clint Williams."

"But they said you were dead—"

Clint smiled coldly at him. "They were wrong."

Chapter Twenty-two

Pete was cursing Clint as he watched him turn and walk back into the front office. Clint closed the door to the cell area so he wouldn't have to listen to him.

A feeling of some satisfaction filled Clint.

He had Pete behind bars, and that was good.

But it wasn't over yet.

He still had to bring in Tuck, Ax, and Walt—the real killers—the men who'd actually done the shooting that fateful night. Clint was exhausted, but too tense to rest. He didn't know if they'd made it into town yet or not, but as soon as he could, he planned to head over to the Last Chance to look for them.

Pete had mentioned that Nick might show up at any time, so Clint sat down at the desk to wait for the deputy. He kept his rifle by his side, just in case there was any kind of trouble.

* * *

It had been a quiet day in Dry Springs, and Nick was in a good mood as he returned to the sheriff's office and saw Pete's horse tied up out front. He'd known Pete had had some personal business to take care of earlier that day, and he was glad the sheriff was back, for it was almost Nick's quitting time. He walked into the office.

"Kane—?" Nick stopped just inside the door to find himself staring at the gunslinger. Kane was seated at the sheriff's desk, holding a rifle.

"Hello, Nick," Clint said easily. His manner appeared relaxed, but in truth he was tense, worrying about the deputy's reaction to finding him there.

"What are you doing here? Where's Pete?" Nick looked around, confused.

"He's in back, but first we need to talk," Clint said, not shifting his position at all, still holding the weapon.

"What do you mean, Pete's in back?"

"Nick!"

Nick heard Pete's shout even through the closed door and thought it sounded like he was in trouble.

"What is going on around here?" He started to go for his sidearm as he headed for the closed door.

"Don't," Clint ordered in a steely tone as he got to his feet with the rifle in his hands.

Nick stopped and looked at him.

"There are a few things you need to know

about Pete," Clint began. Then, seeing Nick's wary expression, he added, "Hear me out."

"I'd say it looks like I don't have much choice," Nick returned, angry that he'd been caught off guard and was now cornered.

"You won't be sorry," Clint assured him.

"All right," Nick told him cautiously. "Talk."

"First off, my name's not Kane McCullough. I'm Clint Williams, and up until recently I was a Texas Ranger."

"What?" Nick exclaimed in surprise.

"That's right. The Tucker Gang attacked and killed my family. I was shot and left for dead, but I managed to recover. I turned in my badge and came after the gang on my own. I learned just today that Pete Reynolds was the leader of the gang."

"Pete's in with the Tucker Gang?" Nick repeated in shock.

"That's right. Why do you think the posse was so quick to give up on tracking down the outlaws who tried to rob the stage? It was because Pete realized the outlaws were his gang, and he didn't want to bring them in."

"Are you serious?"

"I'm deadly serious."

"So where's the gang?"

"They're still here in the area. I tracked them down last night and kept them under surveillance today. That's how I found out Pete was their leader. I saw him meeting with them earlier today, and then I followed him back to town from their camp. There are three gunmen in the gang, and they should be showing up here in town any time now. They're expecting me to join up with them and help them pull off the robbery of an Army payroll that's passing through the area. Pete's already got the whole robbery planned out."

"How do I know you're not lying?" Nick challenged. "Why should I believe any of what you're telling me?"

"You should believe me because it's the truth," Clint answered seriously. "If you need someone to confirm what I just told you, you can send a telegram to Ranger Captain Meyers. He'll back me up on everything."

Nick studied Clint. He remembered their earlier conversation and how he'd sensed the good in him. "I believe you."

Relief swept through Clint. "Thanks. I appreciate your trust, but if you want to send that wire to check on me, I understand."

They were so intent on their conversation that when the office door opened and Michelle walked in carrying a small basket, they were surprised.

"Michelle—" Nick said hesitantly, knowing she couldn't have picked a worse time to show up.

"Hello, Nick. I brought you some sweet rolls," she began, giving him an alluring smile before realizing Clint was with him. "Oh, hi, Cli—" Michelle cut herself off as she realized she'd almost called him by his real name.

"So you know who he really is, too?" Nick demanded, recognizing her mistake.

"Well—" she said hesitantly, uncomfortable that she might have ruined Clint's cover. She looked at Clint, trying to judge his reaction.

"It's all right, Michelle." Clint encouraged her. "You can tell him the truth."

Relieved, she looked back at Nick. "Yes, I know who he is, and I know the reason he's here. I was one of the witnesses when he and Rachel got married."

"You married Rachel?" Now Nick was truly shocked as he glanced over at Clint.

"Yes, I did," he answered simply. "The reverend married us the other night, but I can't risk being together openly with her until I've finished what I came here to do—and that's taking down the Tucker Gang."

"How can I help you?" Nick offered.

"You are so wonderful, Nick," Michelle sighed, gazing up at the deputy with obvious yearning. "Can you get Pete to help you, too? That would really make things easier if there were three of you going after them."

"I'm afraid not," Nick answered. "I just found out Pete is in with the Tucker Gang. He's the real leader."

"Oh, no! Pete?" she gasped.

"That's right. He's the man who calls the shots. He's the one responsible for the death and destruction they've been wreaking," Clint explained.

"What are you going to do about him? And what

about the other members of the gang? Do you know where they are?" Michelle asked worriedly.

"Pete will be standing trial for his crimes, and as for the other three—if they're not in town already, they soon will be. I'm supposed to meet with them at the Last Chance, and when I do, their days of murdering innocents will be over."

"Nick—what are you going to do?" Michelle was suddenly worried about the two of them facing down the group of deadly gunmen alone.

"I'm going to help Clint bring in the gang. That's what I'm going to do," Nick answered.

Uncaring that Clint was there, Michelle went straight to Nick and embraced him. "Be careful—please."

Nick put his arms around her and held her close for a moment. "Don't worry. Everything is going to be all right."

Michelle drew back to gaze at him. "It had better be."

Nick couldn't help himself. He bent down and kissed her, a quick kiss that he wished could have lasted longer. "You'd better go now."

Michelle moved away from him and looked at both men. "I will, but don't take any chances. Rachel and I want you both safe."

Neither Nick nor Clint said anything for a moment after she left them.

Finally Clint spoke up, "I need to go to the Last Chance and wait for the outlaws to show up. That's what they're expecting me to do."

"All right. Let me check on Pete, and I'll go with you."

Nick went into the cell area to make sure Pete was securely locked up.

"It's about time you showed up!" Pete snarled. "Get me out of here!"

"That's not going to happen. You're under arrest for murder and robbery. You're not going anywhere," Mick said.

"Let me out of here, now." There was a threat in Pete's tone.

"No. Your days of robbing and killing are over. The next time you get out of that cell, it's going to be to stand trial." Nick started to leave.

"You're going to regret this!"

Nick turned on him and pinned him with a cold-eyed glare. "No. I'm not."

Nick walked out. He locked the door to the cell area, then got several sets of handcuffs to take with them. He left the office with Clint, heading for the Last Chance.

Michelle rushed to Rachel's house, praying that her friend would be home so she could let her know what was going on. She knocked on the door loudly and waited in tense anticipation for someone to answer the summons. She was relieved when Mrs. Hammond finally came to the door.

"Why, Michelle, this is a pleasant surprise. Come in," Anne invited.

257

"Thanks, Mrs. Hammond. Is Rachel here? I have to talk to her. It's an emergency!"

Anne could tell this was serious. "Wait in the parlor. I'll go get her."

Anne hurried upstairs, calling out to her daughter as she went.

Rachel heard her mother's call and came out of her room. "What is it, Mother?"

"Michelle's here, and she says it's important."

Rachel wasted no time going downstairs with her mother.

"She's in the parlor waiting."

They went in to find Michelle anxiously pacing the room.

"Michelle? What's wrong?"

"Oh, Rachel—thank heaven you're here." Michelle hurried to give her a quick hug. "I just left the sheriff's office, and I'm so scared!"

"Why?"

Michelle quickly related what she'd learned. "Clint and Nick are on their way to arrest the gang right now at the Last Chance. But there are only the two of them against the three gunmen! They could be killed!"

As Rachel listened, her heart began to pound. She knew Clint would want her to stay out of it, but he had saved her twice, and if he was going to be in trouble, she had to help him in any way she could. "I've got to go there—"

"Not by yourself, you're not," Michelle said. "We have to help them. But how? What can we do?"

Defiant

Rachel looked over at her mother as an idea came to her.

"I know exactly what we can do," she said firmly. She asked her mother, "Can you get Papa? I think we need to go to the Last Chance again and pray for lost souls."

"Your father's at church. We can stop there on our way to the saloon," her mother told her.

"You're going, too?" Rachel was surprised.

"Clint's my son-in-law. Of course I'm going along."

"All right. Let's go." Rachel was ready to help Clint put an end to the days of terror caused by this murderous gang. "I only have to get one thing."

"What's that?" Michelle asked.

"My gun," Rachel answered.

Her mother didn't protest Rachel's decision. She and Michelle waited while Rachel got the gun from where it was kept locked up.

As they left the house, Anne felt armed, too. She had her Bible with her.

Within minutes, reached the church. Rachel hoped to find more people there who would be willing to march with them to the Last Chance.

Martin was in the meeting room talking with Eve and several other members of the congregation when they came in.

"Excuse me a moment," Martin told those he was meeting with. He could tell something was wrong, for his wife and daughter looked very serious. "What's happened?"

Rachel quickly told her father everything. "Can you come with us to the saloon? Just like we did the last time?"

"Rachel, considering the circumstances, the wise thing to do would be for you to stay right here in church and pray for Clint and Nick."

She met his gaze straight on. "We can pray on our way to the saloon and while we're there. Clint has saved me twice. I have to help him. Our showing up at the Last Chance would create a diversion, and that might be just what Clint and Nick need to make the arrests without putting anyone in danger."

Martin knew the situation was treacherous, but he also realized his daughter was right. "Let me talk to the others and see. Wait here. I'll be right back."

He returned to the meeting room to tell the people there what was happening. When he came back out, they all were following him, with Eve in the lead.

"Is it really true about Sheriff Reynolds?" Eve asked, stunned by the news that he was a part of the outlaw gang.

"Yes. Clint and Nick have him locked up at the jail, and they're going after the other members of the gang right now."

"Well, we want to help in any way we can," Eve told Rachel with a smile. After what Rachel had done to save her and Jacob when the stagecoach was attacked, this was the least she could do. "This is our town and we want to keep it safe."

"Thank you," Rachel responded with heartfelt emotion. "I think if we just do what we did the last time we went into the Last Chance, it should work."

Martin led the way with Rachel.

They were on a mission to save souls and lives.

Chapter Twenty-three

Clint and Nick made their plan to put an end to the Tucker Gang once and for all as they walked over to the Last Chance.

"Wait outside for me," Clint told him. "I'll tell them I want to talk to them privately, and when we come out of the saloon, we can make the arrests. That way nobody will get hurt if any shooting starts."

"I'll stay in the alley until I see you."

They shared a look of understanding, and then Clint entered the saloon.

"It's about time you got here," Trey said as Clint came up to the bar. "Couple of boys back there have been looking for you."

"I'll have to check that out," Clint answered.

He waited while the bartender poured him a drink. He paid him and then, with drink in hand, made his way to the back of the room where several poker games were going on. He spotted

Tuck and Ax at one of the tables but saw no sign of Walt.

"Evening, boys," he greeted them.

They acknowledged him but kept their concentration on their hands.

Clint relaxed and waited, keeping an eye out around the room for any surprises. Everything seemed normal. He turned his attention back to the poker game just as Tuck started to shout in excitement and rake in a huge pot.

"I won!"

"Damn!" Ax was snarling. His mood was ugly, for he'd lost a goodly sum to Tuck in spite of having three jacks.

"You ready to step outside and talk?" Clint asked them now that the hand was over.

Tuck looked up at him and sneered, "Hell, no. There ain't no way I'm quitting now. I'm winning, and winning big! Just sit yourself down and relax for a while. Lady Luck is on my side tonight, and I'm taking full advantage of it."

"But we need to talk. I want to know what you found out today," Clint insisted.

"I said I'm winning and I'm not leaving the game," Tuck told him angrily. "Ax is a loser. Talk to him."

"I'm not quitting either," Ax countered. "I want my money back."

"Good luck," Tuck taunted him.

"Where's Walt?" Clint asked, glancing around the saloon once more.

"He's playing another game," Ax chuckled as

he waited for the next hand to be dealt. "He disappeared upstairs with one of the girls a while ago, and I ain't heard from him since."

Clint was glad to learn there were only the two of them downstairs, but it still didn't help him get Tuck and Ax outside so he and Nick could make the arrests. He was tense as he sat down at a nearby table to watch them play out their new hands.

Martin was leading the group down the street toward the Last Chance. When they got within a block of the saloon, he stopped and said a short prayer for the protection and safety of everyone involved that evening. That done, they started off again for the bar.

Rachel and Michelle stayed right up front with her father. Rachel was tense as she carried the gun hidden in the pocket of her skirt. She prayed she wouldn't have to use it, but it was good to know she had it with her—just like on the stagecoach trip.

As they neared the Last Chance, they could hear the rowdy music coming from inside. They reached the swinging doors, and Martin started to lead them in a song.

Nick had been keeping an eye on the saloon from the alleyway across the street when he caught sight of Reverend Hammond and his group walking up the sidewalk. Knowing there might be trouble, he came out just as the reverend led his followers into the Last Chance. And as they passed through the door, there was no mistaking Michelle and Rachel following Reverend Hammond inside.

If they hadn't been church folks, Nick would have been cussing them all for getting in the middle of a showdown with the Tucker Gang. Somehow he managed to control the urge. He waited for a few moments, trying to figure out the best way to handle the situation. When he heard Trey's shouts all the way across the street, he knew he had to take action. He started after them to try to get the church folks out of the saloon before things got dangerous.

Martin led the way inside the Last Chance and encouraged his followers to sing even louder.

"What the hell—?" Trey raged at the sight of them coming though the doors. He'd thought this was going to be an easy night. He'd thought things were going to be nice and quiet, but he'd been wrong. "Get out of here, preacher man! Get out now!"

"Peace be with you," Martin told him as he came to stand before him at the bar.

"The hell with your peace!"

Martin was shocked by his blasphemy but continued to try to preach to him. "We've come to help you," he said, looking around the crowded saloon.

"I don't want or need your help! I said get out

of here, and I mean it! I don't want you in here disrupting my business and causing trouble!"

"But we've come to save you," Martin went on, facing him down.

"I don't need no damned saving! My business needs saving from you! Now get the hell out of here!"

"We're not going anywhere."

Trey was ready to use force if necessary, but he thought better of it for the moment. As the reverend and his followers continued to sing their hymns, he went down to the end of the bar to speak with Chip, one of his regular customers.

"Go get the sheriff! And make it fast!" he ordered, swearing under his breath. "I want them arrested tonight, not just chased out of here! I want to make sure they leave and never come back!"

"I'll see what I can do, but it'll cost you," Chip said with a grin as he drained his drink.

Trey set a bottle of Chip's favorite whiskey in front of him. "It'll be waiting for you when you get back."

Chip headed out, intent on finding the lawman. He didn't see Nick coming across the street.

Clint was waiting for Tuck and Ax to finish playing their hands when he heard the ruckus in front. He looked up to see Reverend Hammond marching into the saloon followed by Rachel, her mother, Michelle, and several others who he guessed were members of the church.

Clint had a feeling he knew exactly what they were trying to do, and he was worried. Michelle must have told them what was going to happen, and they thought they could help. Prayers could be powerful, but at tense times like this, the presence of the church group was more of a hindrance than a help. The gunfire could start up at any time, and he didn't want Rachel and the others to be in harm's way.

"Hey, McCullough!" one of the drunks called out to him from another table. "Lookee there! Your little sweetie from the other night is back! She's looking your way, so she must be back to try to save your soul again."

Clint glanced toward Rachel, and across the room, their gazes met and locked. He had missed her desperately and wanted nothing more in that instant than to get up and go to her and take her in his arms, but he couldn't. What was going down tonight was deadly, and he wanted her to be safe.

The drunk went on, "Or maybe she came back looking for Ed again since she had such a good time with him the other night. What do you think?"

The men sitting with him were laughing loudly at his drunken humor.

Clint tore his gaze away from Rachel and turned his attention back to Tuck and Ax. "I think she's probably here with her father to try to save all of us."

"Pretty as she is, she can save me any old time," Ed said.

"Don't go getting any ideas," Clint warned him. "She is the preacher's daughter."

The others piped down and tried to ignore the disruption the church people were causing.

Clint took a drink of his whiskey and wondered how to handle the situation. He had to get Rachel out of the Last Chance as quickly as possible. But how?

Rachel's heartbeat had quickened when she'd seen Clint seated at a table in the back. She loved him so much and she ached to be with him. She was relieved to know she'd gotten there before any trouble had started.

Rachel had just begun to make her way to the back of the room to pretend to preach to the gamblers when Nick came through the swinging doors, looking very angry. Michelle reached out and grabbed Rachel's arm to stop her from going any farther.

"What's going on here?" Nick demanded, confronting Reverend Hammond.

"We're here praying for lost souls," he responded.

"Deputy—I want them out of here!" Trey yelled. "I'm trying to do business here, and all they're doing is causing trouble! We don't go in their church and gamble, so why are they coming here to pray?"

"I think we're in trouble," Michelle whispered to Rachel, seeing Nick's furious expression.

"No, we're not. We're helping," Rachel insisted quietly.

Nick was determined not to let the church folks get caught in the middle of what was about to happen. "I need you all to leave the Last Chance and go back to the church, right now."

"We can't do that, Deputy," Martin told him, gesturing for his followers to keep singing. "We're on a mission tonight."

"That wasn't a request," Nick countered. "It was an order."

Rachel and Michelle moved forward to speak with him as the others kept singing.

"Nick, we have to do this. We came here to help you and Clint. We thought this might work—" Michelle began to explain.

"If you want to help," he ground out in a low voice, "you'll leave right now and get as far away as you can. We need to know that you're someplace safe where we won't have to worry about you. Clint and I are lawmen. We can handle this," he stated. Then he looked at the preacher. "Reverend, get these ladies out of here."

"They are here of their own free will to try to save souls," Martin insisted.

"And I'm telling you that if you don't exit the saloon right now, you're all going to be under arrest. Do I make myself clear?" Nick demanded.

Rachel and Michelle had never seen Nick so adamant or so furious. He was definitely a man to be reckoned with. They realized he was probably right. In wanting to help him and Clint, they had only made things more difficult.

"We'll pray on it," Martin offered, wanting to ease the tension between them.

"You'd better do more than that, preacher man!" Trey shouted, picking up his shotgun.

Clint had been trying to ignore what was going on, but when he saw Trey take out his shotgun, he got up and strode to the front of the saloon. He wanted to defuse the situation if he could.

"Well, well, well, what do we have here tonight, another prayer meeting at the Last Chance?" he asked, looking at Rachel. "I would have thought you were smart enough to stay away from here after what happened the last time you stopped by to try to save souls."

Rachel met his gaze and could see the worry reflected in his eyes. "We have a calling to help those in need."

"You need to leave. From the looks of Trey over there, you might be safer finishing your praying and singing outside."

"He saved you the last time, and he's saving you again!" Trey shouted at her. "You'd better listen to the man!"

"Leave. Now," Nick commanded.

The church group looked at the reverend, who nodded in acquiescence. They stopped singing and started praying as they filed out of the Last Chance.

The customers were hooting and laughing at them.

Reverend Hammond heard their hateful, bawdy remarks and turned to address them. "The name of this sinful place is the Last Chance. Hear the Lord's call or you may be facing your last chance at spending eternity in heaven."

Martin followed the others from the den of iniquity, praying in his heart that Clint and Nick could make the arrests without violence.

"I'll make sure they move on," Nick called out to Trey, so the bartender would relax and put his gun away.

Clint stepped outside to watch Nick do his work. He stayed by the doors so he could see what was going on inside, and he was glad that Tuck and Ax were too busy gambling to be distracted by the church people trying to save them.

It took Nick only a moment to tell the reverend to move on; then he came back to speak with Clint.

"What do you want to do?"

"Let's take them down now."

The two men shared a determined look and walked back into the Last Chance together.

Chapter Twenty-four

Chip reached the sheriff's office and though he didn't see anyone around, he went in thinking the sheriff or his deputy might be in back.

"Sheriff Reynolds? Are you here?" Chip called out.

"I'm locked up! Get me out of here!" Pete shouted from his confinement, unable to believe his good luck.

Chip tried to get into the cell area, but found the door locked. "It's locked, Sheriff. Where's the key?"

"I don't know where it is! Break the damned door down if you have to!"

Chip did just that, kicking the door in violently. He rushed into the cell area to find the sheriff locked up like a common criminal.

"What are you doing in there?"

"That gunslinger Kane McCullough did this! I think he's trying to pull off a robbery tonight, and I'm pretty sure he's working with Deputy Evans," he lied. "I've got to get out of here and stop them! Go get the key and let me out!"

"Where is it?"

"It should be hanging on the wall by my desk," he directed.

Chip hurried off to look for the key. "McCullough is over at the Last Chance right now," he called back.

"At least we know where he is. What about Nick?"

"I haven't seen him around tonight," Chip said. He searched where the sheriff had told him but found no trace of the cell key.

"Any luck finding it?" Pete called out, figuring Nick or Clint might have taken the key with them.

"No. It's not here."

"All right, there's an extra key in the back of the bottom drawer in the desk. If you can't find that one, we'll have to break this damned cell door down, too!"

There was a moment of silence while Chip rustled through the drawer.

"I got it!"

Chip ran to let the sheriff out. "We'd better get over to the saloon fast. Trey sent me here to get you because the preacher man led another prayer group into the Last Chance. He wants you over there to help him keep order. But with McCullough being there, if what you said is true, there might be big trouble tonight."

"You go on back to the Last Chance and tell Trey

I'll be there shortly," Pete ordered as he stepped out of the jail cell and headed into his office.

"We'll be waiting for you!" Chip said. He rushed off to let Trey know help was on the way.

"You'll be waiting a long time," Pete muttered to himself after Chip had gone.

Pete got his gun out of the desk drawer where Nick and Clint had left it. He checked to make sure it was loaded, then slid it back in his holster. Next he went to the gun cabinet and got a rifle and extra ammunition. After taking one last look around the office, he walked outside.

Pete was relieved to find his horse still tied out front. Sliding the rifle in its sheath, he mounted up. He had one last stop to make before he left town, and that was at his house to get the money he kept hidden there.

Pete gave no thought to helping Tuck, Ax, and Walt. They were on their own. If Williams took them down tonight, too bad.

He still couldn't believe how stupid Tuck had been. First, not making sure Clint had been dead the night they'd attacked the Williams's ranch. When he'd sent the gang to do that job, he'd expected them to make sure it was done right. Then, the fact that the boys had made it so easy for Williams to track them down. And finally, the mistake that had led Williams to connect him with the gang. They were going to get exactly what they deserved, and he was going to be long gone. He was getting out of town as fast as he could.

* * *

Clint and Nick were men on a mission as they strode back inside the saloon.

Trey was relieved when he saw them. "Thanks for your help, Deputy. I owe you a drink." He took out a glass, ready to pour him a free shot.

"Later," Nick said tersely, keeping his gaze fixed on the back of the room.

Trey was puzzled by his demeanor but went on to tell him, "I'm glad Chip found you—"

"What are you talking about?" Nick stopped and looked quickly over at him.

"I sent Chip over to the sheriff's office to get you—"

"You sent Chip to the office?" Nick repeated, a feeling of dread coming over him.

"That's right."

Clint knew this meant trouble. "Let's take care of these three right now. We can check on the other one once we're done here."

Time was of the essence as they moved to the back of the room and drew their guns. They faced down Tuck and Ax where they were sitting at the poker table.

"Tuck—Ax—you're under arrest," Clint stated.

"Sit down and shut up. We've got to finish this hand," Tuck told him, thinking it was some kind of perverse joke he was playing with the deputy.

"You heard the man." Nick stepped up. "Keep your hands where we can see them and move away from the table—*now!*"

When they didn't move immediately, Nick kicked the table over, sending the cards and money flying.

"What the—?" Ax was totally confused as he looked up at the two men holding guns on them.

"I said, you're under arrest. For murder," Clint told the two men coldly. He was watching them carefully and could tell they were ready for a fight as they slowly stood up. "Don't get any ideas about trying to draw on us, unless you want to die right here."

"What's going on?" Trey demanded, coming out from behind the bar to see what the trouble was. With the preacher man gone, he'd expected things to quiet down, not get rowdier.

"These men are Glen Tucker and Ax Hansen of the Tucker Gang. They're wanted for robbery and murder, and we're taking them in," Clint said as he stripped the two outlaws of their sidearms.

"*We're?*" Trey was confused as he looked between the man he knew as a gunfighter and the deputy.

"Don't worry," Nick assured the bartender. "He's Clint Williams. He's a Ranger."

At the news, Trey and all the others in the saloon turned to stare in awe at Clint.

Tuck and Ax heard what the deputy had said and exchanged worried glances.

"Did he say McCullough's name was really Williams?" Tuck asked nervously.

"That's right," Clint said, hearing his comment.

"We've met before, boys. That night at my family's ranch. You remember that night, don't you?"

Neither man responded, but each realized they'd made a huge mistake at the Williams ranch. They'd thought this man was dead, and they'd been wrong. Tuck and Ax knew they were in deep trouble. Their only hope was Walt, but he was busy upstairs with a saloon girl and had no idea what was going on.

Nick and Clint directed the outlaws closer to the bar, and then Nick made short work of handcuffing them.

"I'll be right back," Clint told Nick. "Walt's upstairs."

"I'll wait here for you. If you need any help, yell."

Clint looked over at Trey. "Which room is he in?"

"He's with Honey tonight. Third door on the left," Trey told him.

"Thanks."

"Here, take these. You'll need them." Nick handed him the last set of handcuffs.

Gun in hand, Clint climbed the stairs and made his way cautiously down the hall. He wasn't about to let his guard down until the entire gang was safely locked up in the jail.

Walt was exhausted as he looked over at the buxom blonde nestled against him. He'd just spent the most exciting hour he could ever remember with this wild woman named Honey, and he knew he was going to leave her a real nice tip when they finally parted ways.

"You ready to have another go at it, big guy?" Honey asked in a sultry voice as she ran her hands daringly over him.

"Are you?" he returned, amazed to feel the heat burning within him again at her practiced touch.

"Any time I can be with a man like you, I'm ready," she told him, smiling as she moved to kiss him.

Caught up in pure animal desire, they went at it again. They were unaware of anything but the pure pleasure of the flesh, until the sound of the door crashing open jarred them back to reality.

Walt reacted instinctively. He shoved Honey aside and started to jump from the bed to go for his gun, where it was lying on the floor with his hastily discarded clothing.

"Don't even think about it!" Clint ordered as he came to stand near the foot of the bed, his gun aimed straight at the outlaw.

Walt froze, and Honey scrambled to get as far away as she could.

Clint reached down and grabbed the sheet. He tossed it to the girl.

"Cover yourself."

Honey wrapped the sheet around herself and darted out of the room to safety.

"All right, Walt. Get up real slow and don't make any fast moves."

"Why are you doing this, McCullough? I never

done nothing to you. I thought we were supposed to be working together." He was totally confused.

"You thought wrong," Clint said as he stared him down. "And my name's not McCullough."

"It's not?"

"No, it's not. My name's Williams. Clint Williams. Sound familiar?"

Walt actually paled at his words as he realized whom he was facing. Frank Williams's son—the Ranger they'd thought had been killed along with his parents in the raid.

Knowing he had no choice, Walt followed Clint's orders and slowly got up from the bed.

Clint walked over and picked up Walt's gun belt, then directed, "Get dressed."

Walt was tempted to try to make a break for it, but naked and unarmed, he didn't have a chance. He didn't doubt for a minute that Williams would shoot him down.

Clint kept a careful eye on Walt while he pulled on his clothes and boots. Then he ordered him downstairs.

Nick had been tense as he'd stood guard over Tuck and Ax, waiting for Clint's return. He'd seen the saloon girl come running out of the room upstairs and knew something was happening. No shots immediately followed her hasty exit, and he felt a little better. It was obvious Clint had the upper hand with the other outlaw. When he saw Clint emerge from the room a short time later with the gunman in handcuffs, he breathed easier.

"Let's go lock these boys up," Nick said.

They'd just turned to lead them from the Last Chance when there was another commotion.

"Trey!" Chip yelled as he charged through the door, his gun in hand. "Those men are wanted!"

He stopped dead just inside the door as he found the two men the sheriff had told him were outlaws aiming their guns straight at him.

"Put your gun down, Chip! What are you talking about?" Trey demanded, relieved that the two lawmen hadn't fired when Chip had come running in with his gun out.

Chip looked nervously around as he slowly lowered his sidearm. He saw the other three men in handcuffs and was totally perplexed.

"The sheriff was locked up in the jail," he stammered. "And he said these two did it! Sheriff Reynolds said these two are working together to pull off a robbery here in town!"

Nick spoke up. "Reynolds is a liar, Chip. He was locked up because he's the leader of the Tucker Gang, and we're working to bring them all in. Clint here is a Ranger."

"No—" Chip denied in confusion. "The sheriff said you were outlaws—"

"Don't believe anything he said to you. He was trying to save himself," Nick argued. "Is he still locked up?"

"No! I let him out so he could come after you!"

Nick and Clint shared an angry look, knowing Pete was no doubt already heading out of town.

"Then where is he?" Clint demanded. "He should have come with you."

"He said he'd be right along," Chip hedged, suddenly fearing he might have done the wrong thing.

Trey assured Chip, "Deputy Evans and Clint are not criminals, Chip. Put your gun away. Because of you, they've got another killer to hunt down."

Chip looked from Trey to the others and felt sickened to know that he'd let an outlaw go free. He lowered his gun. "What can I do to help?"

"Come with us," Nick told him.

They herded the three gunmen out of the saloon and cautiously made their way toward the sheriff's office.

Clint kept a close watch for trouble. He wouldn't have put it past Pete to try to ambush them.

"Nick," Clint called to him as they reached the jail.

"What?"

"Pete's horse is gone."

They both knew what that meant.

"We have to move fast," Nick said, grimly determined to catch him.

It was obvious to Chip now that the sheriff had been one of the outlaw gang, and he felt bad about what he'd done.

Nick made short order of getting Tuck, Ax, and Walt into the jail cell. He left the cuffs on them for the time being, for he knew how treacherous they could be.

"Chip, we need you to stay here and guard these men. No matter what they yell at you, don't go near them. Do you understand?" Nick demanded.

"Yes."

"Good. Did you happen to actually see the sheriff leave the office?"

"No. I didn't pay any attention. I was too busy trying to get back to the Last Chance to warn Trey about you."

"All right." Nick was thoughtful.

"Where does he live?" Clint asked.

"Across town. I know the house."

"Let's hope we're not too late to catch him before he rides out."

They headed toward Pete's house, ready for the final showdown.

Reverend Hammond walked up to the front of the church to address those who'd accompanied him to the saloon. They were seated in the pews, awaiting his words of wisdom and inspiration.

"Tonight we did our best to help our brethren bring peace and justice to our town. While we do not yet know the outcome of the activities our lawmen are involved in, let us offer up a prayer for their continued safety."

They bowed their heads as he led the prayer.

"Dear God, protect those who bring peace and justice to our town. Guide them and keep them safe from harm. Amen."

"Amen."

Rachel looked over at Michelle, and their gazes met in understanding. The men they loved were in grave danger. They clasped hands and whispered together another, "Amen."

Martin dismissed everyone with a blessing, and they filed quietly out of the church to return to the safety of their homes. Anne, Rachel, and Michelle remained in the pew.

"Are you ready to go home?" he asked them.

"If it's all right with you, I'd like to stay here for a while," Rachel told him.

"Me, too," Michelle added.

Anne and Martin completely understood. "We'll stay with you, then."

They sat down in a nearby pew and joined the girls in silently praying for Clint and Nick, and for their town.

Chapter Twenty-five

Pete wasted no time once he reached his house. He didn't light any lamps, for he didn't want anyone to suspect he was there. Quickly grabbing up his saddlebags, he began to stuff them full of the money he'd kept hidden. His share of the gang's loot had been considerable, and he'd been saving it up all this time.

Pete was angry as he got ready to leave town. He'd thought when he'd given the order to take out Frank Williams, the gang's problems would be over. He hadn't counted on Williams's son being at the ranch that night, or his surviving the ambush and then tracking them down this way.

It just went to show how stupid Tuck and Ax were. Pete grew angrier with himself for having trusted their judgment. He was definitely going to find a quiet place a long way away from Dry Springs to hide out for a while. If Tuck, Ax, and

Walt did somehow manage to get loose again, he didn't want them to be able to find him. He was done with them.

Grabbing up his saddlebags and extra ammunition, Pete started toward the rear of the house. He'd left his horse tied in some trees out back, just in case word of his escape had spread and someone decided to come looking for him. He wanted folks to think that he had already left town.

Clint and Nick silently and cautiously made their way to Pete's house. The house was a small one-storey building with a porch across the front. There were several neighboring houses, but none were really close, so they knew they wouldn't have to worry about harming innocent bystanders in case of a shootout.

They saw that it was dark inside the house, and they weren't surprised. Pete must have realized they would be on his trail the minute they found out he'd been released.

They weren't sure if Pete was still there or not, but they wouldn't take any chances. They both knew the confrontation with Pete could prove deadly, so they drew their guns as they split up. Nick went to look things over in front of the house, while Clint went around back.

Moving carefully, Nick silently made his way up onto the porch and looked in one of the front windows. From what little he could make out in the darkness, there was no one moving around.

He quietly shifted to the window on the other side of the front door and looked in there, but the results were the same. Deciding to help Clint, he made his way silently toward the back.

Clint had circled wide around the building, staying under the cover of the trees and shrubs and keeping a careful watch. From this distance, he could see no sign that anyone was inside, but that didn't mean much when an outlaw was as sharp and fast with a gun as Pete.

Clint was just about ready to move in closer to the building when he heard the soft whinny of a horse somewhere nearby. He paused, listening to see if Pete was already saddled up and riding out. When it became quiet again, Clint checked farther back among the trees and found Pete's horse tied there. Determination filled Clint, as well as excitement, at the thought that the outlaw hadn't gotten out of town yet. He and Nick were going to bring Pete in—right now.

Clint went over to the horse and untied it. He slapped the animal on the rump and watched in satisfaction as it ran off.

Knowing Pete was probably still inside the house, Clint positioned himself so he had an unimpeded view of the back door. When he saw Nick come around the side of the building, he went over to meet him, staying down low and moving silently.

"I didn't see anyone inside," Nick told him quietly.

"He's here somewhere. I found his horse tied up out back and I just ran him off."

"Good. That means the only place Pete's going to go tonight is to jail."

"Do you want to go in the house or wait outside for him to come out?"

"Let's stay out here. It'll be easier to confront him."

"Fine," Clint agreed. "We know he's on the run, so he should be coming out any minute. Why don't you keep watch from here and I'll wait where he had his horse tied."

"You're on," Nick agreed.

The two lawmen took cover.

They were ready to wait Pete out.

Pete moved silently through the dark house. He had everything he needed and was on his way out. An uneasy feeling came over him as he was about to leave the house, so he stopped at the back door. The uneasy feeling didn't surprise him, considering the way the rest of the day had gone, and he decided caution was in order tonight. Rather than just make his exit out the back door, he moved to take a look out one of the windows.

Staying close against the wall so no one could see him if anyone was watching, Pete carefully brushed the curtain back and checked out the yard. He noticed nothing unusual. All seemed quiet.

Still, Pete decided the safest thing to do would

be to sneak out of the house, rather than just leave by the back door. Williams was an experienced Ranger. He had had him under surveillance when he'd met with the gang, and none of them had realized it. Tonight, Pete had to be extra careful. Making a clean escape from town was essential. He had to put as many miles between himself and Dry Springs as he could before sunup.

Pete went to open the window on the side of the house that was most sheltered by close-growing trees and shrubs. He dropped his saddlebags to the ground, then climbed out. Pete waited to hear if anything stirred because of his actions, but all remained quiet. He grabbed up the saddlebags and carefully started around back to where he'd left his horse.

Nick saw him first. It was just a slight movement near some bushes on the side of the house, but with no breeze stirring, that meant trouble. He hoped Clint had noticed the motion, too. As he was watching, Pete came around the corner.

Clint caught sight of him at that moment.

Pete was moving stealthily, trying to stay in the shadows, but each lawman had him in his sight.

Clint had a feeling of great satisfaction. For the second time that day, he was going to bring Pete in—and this time he was going to make sure he didn't escape.

"Hold it right there, Pete!" Nick shouted.

Pete recognized his deputy's voice and knew that Nick was on to him and there would be no talking his way out of this. Without hesitation, Pete drew his gun and began firing in Nick's direction as he ran for his horse.

Nick returned fire, and Clint cocked the hammer of his Colt.

Pete was running toward him, firing at Nick, when Clint stood up and took careful aim. With perfect marksmanship, Clint fired at the leader of the Tucker Gang. A great sense of satisfaction filled him as the bullet slammed into the outlaw.

Pete screamed as he was hit in the arm. He lost his grip on his gun and it flew out of his hand. Dropping his saddlebags, he clutched at his arm as he tried to find his gun.

Knowing Pete was unarmed, Clint charged forward from his place of hiding to face the murderous outlaw.

"Hold it right there," Clint ordered in a cold, deadly voice as he went to stand before him, his gun aimed straight at his prisoner.

Pete was hunched over, clutching his wound. He swore vilely at Clint as he glared up at him in the darkness like a cornered rat. "Go to hell!"

"I've already been there," Clint ground out as Nick came running up to join them.

Nick made short work of grabbing up Pete's weapon from the ground.

"It's all over, Pete," Nick told him in disgust.

Pete knew he had one chance and one chance only to try to make his getaway, so he decided to take it.

"It's not over, Nick," he said, ignoring Clint. "You're my deputy. You can still work with me on this."

Nick frowned, not understanding what he was talking about.

"Get the saddlebags, Nick. There's more money in there than you could make in a lifetime. Shoot your Ranger friend there, let me go, and it's all yours," Pete tempted him. "I'll give you every penny."

Clint felt uneasy as he listened to Pete trying to lure Nick into helping him get away. Clint believed Nick was a good man. He hoped he was right as he waited to see what Nick would say to Pete's offer.

Nick stepped forward and picked up the saddlebags, weighing them thoughtfully as he stepped away from Pete.

"You're right," Nick said easily. "There is more here than I'll make in my lifetime. But it isn't my money. You're under arrest, Pete."

"You're stupider than the deputy I had before you," Pete sneered. "I should have shot you, like I shot Ben Taggart."

"You killed Deputy Taggart?" Nick was startled. He'd always heard the other deputy had just up and left Dry Springs one day without telling anyone.

Bobbi Smith

Pete smiled coldly at him. "Yeah, I shot him. Taggart was getting too damned nosy for his own good, so I replaced him with you."

Clint faced Pete, hating him even more than he had before. "You're under arrest. We're taking you in."

Pete reacted instantly at his words. Though he was wounded and bleeding, his fear of what would happen to him if they took him in empowered him. He charged Clint, wanting to knock him down and try to get his gun away from him, but it didn't work.

Clint sidestepped the assault and struck Pete's head with his pistol, knocking him to the ground. Pete started to get up and come after him again, but Clint had had enough. He shoved the outlaw leader down and stood over him, his gun pointed straight at him.

"Come on! Shoot me!" Pete taunted him, not wanting to hang. "Go ahead and shoot me! Get it over with! I'm the one who ordered your father killed! Don't you want to see me dead? Then shoot me! Shoot me now!"

Clint was tempted, very tempted, but he wasn't about to give Pete what he wanted. He smiled down coldly at the murderer. "I'm not going to shoot you. I'm not going to make this easy for you. I want to see you swing, along with the rest of your friends."

"You—"

"It takes longer to die when you hang," Clint

went on. "And I like the thought of you suffering." He holstered his gun as he looked over at the deputy. "Handcuff him, Nick. We're taking him back and locking him up."

Nick didn't care that it caused Pete pain when he fastened the cuffs on his injured arm. Pete had been the sheriff. He'd sworn to uphold the law, but he was nothing but a cold-blooded killer. Nick dragged Pete to his feet.

"Move," he directed, pointing in the direction of the jail. "You know where you're going."

Pete had no choice. He did as he was ordered.

Martin, Anne, Rachel, and Michelle were still in church praying when they heard gunfire echoing through the night. Rachel and Michelle were terrified that Clint and Nick might have been hurt. They got up, ready to leave the church and go see what had happened.

"You're not going anywhere," Martin said firmly.

"But Clint and Nick—" Rachel protested.

"Are lawmen," he insisted. "They're doing their jobs right now. You stay here with your mother."

Then he added, "I'll go see if I can help them."

Rachel went to him and hugged him. "Thank you, Papa."

Martin kissed her cheek, then hugged Anne before starting from the church.

"Papa—" Rachel stopped him at the door. "Do you want to take this with you, just in case?"

She took out the gun she'd been carrying with her all night and offered it to him.

He looked at her, his expression calm. "No. I don't need a weapon. The Lord is with me."

Rachel gave him one last hug. As she watched him leave the haven of the church, she knew her father was one of the bravest men she'd ever known. She returned to keep praying with her mother and friend.

Martin found he wasn't the only one who'd heard the gunfire. Once he headed across town, he met up with a crowd of other men being led by the mayor, Tim Parker. They were all carrying their guns; it was obvious they were hoping to put an end to whatever violence was going on.

"Where did the sound of the shooting come from?" Martin asked.

"Down at the far end of town," Mayor Parker answered. "Are you with us, Reverend?"

"Yes."

They moved off together.

When they reached the end of town, they saw Sheriff Reynolds come staggering out from behind his house. They could tell he'd been shot in his right arm, and he was handcuffed.

"Sheriff Reynolds! What's going on? We heard the shots!" the mayor demanded as he rushed toward him.

Before Pete could respond, Nick came forward. He looked over the group of men with the mayor and saw the reverend with them.

"Everything's all right," Nick assured them.

"It doesn't look like it to me, Deputy Evans," the mayor said worriedly. He tightened his grip on his gun as he looked at the man with Nick. "That's Kane McCullough. He's a gunfighter."

"No, Mayor. He's not. His name is Clint Williams," Nick explained. "He's a Texas Ranger, and he's been working undercover to bring down the Tucker Gang. Reverend Hammond can verify that for you if you don't believe me."

"You can?" The mayor and the other men looked at Martin.

"That's right. Clint is a Ranger."

"But what's that got to do with Sheriff Reynolds? Why is he wounded and in handcuffs?" another man asked.

"Because Pete Reynolds is the leader of the Tucker Gang," Clint said, stepping up to address them.

"What?" They were shocked by the news as they looked from the wounded lawman to Clint and Nick.

"It's true," Nick affirmed.

"And if you don't believe us, take a look in his saddlebags."

Clint opened them and showed the men Pete's money.

"He didn't earn all that on his sheriff's salary, that's for sure," Mayor Parker remarked.

"You're right about that," Nick agreed. "We've already got the rest of the gang locked up at the jail, and now, with Pete's arrest, this should mean the end of the Tucker Gang."

"Good job, Deputy. Good job, Ranger Williams."

"Thanks," Nick said. "And we appreciate your showing up to help out."

"Do you need any help getting him back to the jail?" the mayor offered, eyeing Pete in disgust.

"We should be all right."

"Deputy Evans—" Mayor Parker got his attention. "Would you be interested in taking over the position of sheriff?"

Nick was surprised by his offer, but also honored. "Yes, I would."

"Consider it done. You're the new sheriff of Dry Springs."

"Good choice, Mayor," the men in the crowd agreed.

"Will you need some extra help tonight down at the jail?" Mayor Parker offered.

"We could use another man or two," Nick told him, realizing he had four very dangerous prisoners to keep watch over.

Mayor Parker and Lew Sutter, a shop owner, decided to go along with them and help guard the prisoners.

Confident now that their town was safe and everything was back under control, the men began to disperse.

Martin Hammond approached Clint and Nick. "Are you both all right?"

"Yes," Clint assured him.

"Anne and I have been at the church with Rachel and Michelle praying for you," he confided.

"We appreciate it, Reverend," Clint said.

Martin smiled at his son-in-law, relieved to know the nightmare was over for him. "Hurry home."

Clint was struck by his words. Until that moment, he hadn't considered that he had a home, but the thought of Rachel waiting for him touched him deeply. "I will."

"Let's go." Nick jabbed Pete in the back with his gun.

Still clutching his injured, bleeding arm, Pete started off with the two lawmen following him.

It didn't take them long to reach the sheriff's office.

Chip jumped up nervously from the desk chair when they came through the door.

"You got him!"

"That's right. With Pete Reynolds behind bars, the Tucker Gang is finished," Clint told him.

Clint knew a sense of grim satisfaction as he watched Nick lock Pete in the cell with Tuck, Ax, and Walt. Their days of killing were over.

Returning to the office, Nick sent Chip to get the doctor to look at Pete's arm.

When he'd gone, Nick looked over at Clint with open admiration.

"I'm glad you came to town," he told him. "As good as Pete was at keeping his connection to the gang a secret, I don't know that I would have figured it out on my own. And especially the truth about Pete killing Deputy Taggart."

"He killed Deputy Taggart?" Mayor Parker was horrified by the revelation. He'd wondered why the popular lawman had quit his job and left town so quickly.

"Yes," Nick answered. "Taggart must have caught on to what Pete was doing, so the sheriff killed him."

"Well, they're not going to hurt anyone else—ever again," Clint said. Then he asked, "How soon will they be going on trial?"

"The circuit judge will be coming through in two weeks," Mayor Parker said. "And we're going to keep them locked up good and tight until then."

"That's right," Nick agreed.

"I'll send a wire to Captain Meyers of the Rangers and let him know."

"That'll be good." Nick paused, then looked at Clint and said, "It's over."

There was a moment of silence in the office as the two lawmen realized what they'd accomplished that night, and with very little bloodshed.

"Have you got things under control here?" Clint asked Nick.

"We're going to be fine with the three of us here keeping watch, so why don't you go on?"

Clint managed a real smile, thinking of his bride waiting for him. "I'll check in with you in the morning."

Nick walked Clint out of the office. "If you see

Michelle, tell her I'll try to get over to see her to-morrow."

"I'll let her know."

Clint started off into the night.

Nick watched him go with admiration. Clint had defied the odds by surviving the wounds he'd received during the massacre of his family and by bringing their murderers to justice. Clint Williams was a lawman to be reckoned with, and Nick was proud to claim him as a friend.

Nick went back inside the jail to take charge.

He was the sheriff now.

Chapter Twenty-six

"It's time to go home," Martin announced as he returned to the church to let Anne, Rachel, and Michelle know that the danger was over.

They'd looked up nervously when they'd heard him come in and had hurried from their pews to join him in the greeting area.

"Is Clint all right?" Rachel worried.

"He's fine," he told her and then looked at Michelle. "And so is Nick."

Relief filled Rachel and Michelle at the good news.

"Did they get Sheriff Reynolds?" Michelle asked.

"Yes, and they should be over at the jail locking him up right now."

"Was anyone injured?" Anne asked.

"Just the sheriff. He was shot in the arm, but the wound is not life-threatening. I'm sure he's going to stand trial with the rest of them."

"Our prayers have been answered." Anne was

truly thankful that the arrest had turned out so well. "Everyone is safe."

Martin looked at Rachel. "I managed to speak with Clint for a moment and told him to come home when he was finished at the jail."

Rachel gave her father a heartfelt smile. "Then we'd better go. I want to be there waiting for him when he shows up."

"You're right. Let's go home," Anne agreed.

"Here, Papa." Rachel handed over the gun she'd been carrying with her.

Martin took the gun, saddened that good folks had to be prepared to defend themselves that way. He couldn't wait to get back home and lock the weapon up again. Martin left them for a moment to put out the lights as Rachel led the way out of the church.

Rachel had just opened the door and stepped out into the cool, dark night when she caught sight of Clint coming up the street.

Her heartbeat quickened at the sight of him.

Clint was her love.

He was her life.

Clint had been a man on a mission as he'd headed to the Hammond house next to the church to get Rachel. As he neared the church, he saw Rachel standing in the glow of the open doorway.

They both went still, staring at each other across the distance, and then nothing mattered but their being together.

Rachel hurried down the steps, and they

Defiant

rushed toward each other in the night, desperate to be in one another's arms. She ran straight into Clint's embrace and tightly clung to him as he lifted her up in his arms and kissed her.

"You're all right," she breathed, gazing up at him adoringly when they finally broke apart.

Clint looked down at her and smiled tenderly. "Now that I'm with you, I am."

Rachel kissed him again, just to make sure he was really, truly there with her. When the kiss ended, she drew him back to where her parents and Michelle were standing, watching them.

"Martin told us what you did tonight, Clint. We're very proud of you," Anne said.

"Thank you." Looking at Michelle, he told her, "I've got a message for you from Sheriff Evans."

"'Sheriff' Evans?" Michelle repeated, wide-eyed.

"That's right." Clint grinned easily at her. "The mayor offered Nick the job, and he took it."

"That's wonderful." She was delighted at the news.

"Yes, it is. He's a good lawman. Anyway, Nick said to tell you he'll be by to see you tomorrow when things have calmed down."

"I'll be waiting for him!" Michelle was excited—Nick was safe and he wanted to see her!

"Would you like to come over to the house?" Anne invited.

"If you don't mind, I think I'll take my bride 'home' now," Clint said. He appreciated Anne's invitation, but wanted nothing more than to be alone with Rachel in the privacy of his hotel room—without any fears or worries.

Her parents completely understood.

"We'll see you tomorrow," Martin said.

"Good night," Rachel bade them. Then she turned to Michelle. "We'll walk you home, since I won't need you to sneak me into the hotel tonight."

They all chuckled at the memory.

"Do you think we should change Clint's registration to read 'Mr. and Mrs. Williams' instead of just 'Kane McCullough'?" Michelle asked with a grin.

"Absolutely," Clint agreed. "Kane McCullough's gone."

Rachel couldn't help herself. She looked up at Clint and said, "But I loved him, too."

He reached out and took her hand, and they started off with Michelle.

Martin and Anne watched them walk away and knew they were truly blessed.

After seeing Michelle home, Clint and Rachel wasted no time getting to the hotel. Mr. Lofton was working the desk that evening, so they went up to speak with him.

"I heard what happened tonight. Congratulations on bringing those outlaws in," he told Clint.

"I'm glad it's over."

"You did a fine job."

"Thanks."

"How can I help you?" he asked.

"We need to change my registration listing."

"To what?" He frowned.

"To 'Mr. and Mrs. Williams,'" Clint told him with a smile.

"That's right," Rachel said, reaching in her pocket to take out the wedding ring she'd been carrying. She slipped it on her finger and smiled up at her husband.

"Congratulations!" he said.

"Thanks."

They didn't bother to make any more small talk. They just hurried upstairs to be alone, finally.

As soon as they were in their room with the door locked safely behind them, Clint he lit the lamp and turned to his wife.

"Come here, woman," he growled, giving her a wicked smile.

Rachel all but threw herself into his arms. He kissed her hungrily, letting her know by that embrace how much he needed and wanted her.

When he drew back from the kiss, he gazed down at her and said, "I love you."

"Show me," she whispered.

With utmost care, Clint did just that. He swept her up into his arms and gently laid her on the bed. He joined her there, holding her close, fitting her perfectly against him as his lips found hers in a devouring exchange that left them both desperate for more.

Rachel reached up and began to unbutton Clint's shirt. She wanted to be close to him. She wanted to be one with him. When she'd freed the last button, he drew away from her just long enough to shrug the shirt off. Rachel reached out to touch his bare chest, sculpting that hard, muscular expanse with sensual caresses.

Clint gave a low groan as Rachel's hands trailed paths of fire over him. He decided to return the favor and quickly unfastened her dress and slipped it down off her shoulders. He pressed heated kisses to her throat, and then, unable to tolerate any barriers between them, he drew away from her and left the bed.

"Clint—?" Rachel wanted him in her arms, and she was confused as to why he'd left her.

He didn't speak. There was no need to. He just reached down and drew her up with him. They quickly stripped away the last of their clothing and went back into each other's arms on the bed.

They needed nothing more than to be as one.

There in the sweet heat of the night, they came together. In a blaze of passion and glory, with searing kisses and caresses they shared their love. They moved in a rapturous rhythm that stoked the flames of their burning need. The fire of their desire burned ever higher until, in a moment of pure ecstasy, fulfillment was theirs.

Still clinging to each other, Clint and Rachel collapsed back onto the bed, their passion spent—for the moment. Rachel nestled against him and rose up to press a sweet kiss to his lips.

"It's a good thing we didn't make love in the cabin that night," she whispered.

"Why's that?" Clint frowned, unsure of her meaning.

"Because if we had, we might still be there."
Rachel gave a throaty chuckle.

He felt the heat rise deep within him at her words. "We don't have to leave this room, you know."

"I know."

They smiled at the thought, and Rachel gave herself over to his loving.

Late that night Clint lay quietly beside Rachel, watching her sleep. He remembered the times when he'd saved Rachel from danger, and in that moment, he realized that she had saved him, too. Without her love, he would have still been lost. He would have still been dead inside. Her innocence and devotion had freed his soul and made him whole again.

Clint found himself thinking of the future, and he knew that with Rachel by his side, life would always be worth living. He closed his eyes and sought sleep, cherishing this time of peace and renewal.

It was in the predawn hours that Rachel slowly came awake. She opened her eyes and stared at her husband. Her gaze traced his lean, handsome features, relaxed now as he slept, and then moved down lower to visually caress his broad, powerful shoulders and hair-roughened chest. She was tempted to reach out and touch him, but she held back, knowing he needed his rest.

Rachel's heart swelled with love for him.

Whether he was Clint Williams or Kane McCullough, he was the man she had waited her whole life for. He was her love.

Rachel didn't know what the future held for them, but she knew it would be bright as long as they were together. Their days would be filled with love—and so would their nights.

At the last thought, she smiled to herself.

"What are you grinning about?" Clint asked, waking to find her watching him and smiling.

His question startled her, for she'd thought he was sound asleep. She gave a soft laugh and purred as she rose up over him and fit herself boldly against him. "I was thinking about how exciting our life together is going be if every night is like this one."

"So you've enjoyed yourself, have you?" he murmured, pressing heated kisses to her silken flesh.

Rachel didn't bother to answer with words. She showed him how much she was enjoying this blissful time of loving him.

It was much later when they collapsed together, sated for the moment. Clint held Rachel close, cherishing her nearness as they rested.

"Clint," she began slowly, not quite sure how to broach the subject. "Do you know what you want to do now that you're done tracking the Tucker Gang?"

Clint had been wondering the same thing. After what had happened that fateful night, there was no way he could go to live on his family's ranch. The memories were too painful. He considered leaving the Rangers and possibly finding some other kind of work, but he knew he couldn't.

Clint raised himself up on one elbow to look down at her as he answered, "I'm a Ranger, Rachel. It's my calling. It always has been."

"And you'll be happy staying with the Rangers?"

"Yes—as long as I know I have you to come home to."

Rachel looked up at him adoringly and lifted a hand to caress his cheek. She was proud of her Texas Ranger. A shiver went through her when he pressed a heated kiss to her palm. "Will Dry Springs be home?"

"Yes." He wanted to keep her close to her family, so she wouldn't be lonely during the times when he was away. "We can look for a place of our own in the morning. Although, we could stay here at the hotel and call this home—"

"But it's only a—"

"Bedroom," he said, and he bent down to kiss her once more.

Rachel giggled and returned his kiss. "I don't think Michelle's parents take on long-term boarders."

"Too bad." Clint was smiling.

"When will you contact your captain and let him know what happened here?"

"I'll send him a telegram tomorrow. He's waiting to hear from me, and I'm sure he'll want to meet with me sometime soon so I can fill him in."

"I hope it's not too soon." Rachel didn't even want to start thinking about the times when they'd be apart—when he'd have to ride out, and she wouldn't know where he was going or how long he'd be away.

"I'll see what I can do about convincing him to give me some time off, since I just got married."

"Ask him for a year or two," she teased, giving him a seductive look.

"Do you think that would be long enough?" he asked ready to take her up on her unspoken invitation.

"We could try it and find out—if he agrees. What do you think?" She linked her arms around his neck and drew him down for a kiss.

"Knowing my captain, I think we'd better take advantage of every moment we have together, right now," Clint murmured against her lips.

And they did.

Chapter Twenty-seven

One Month Later

Clint rode to the top of the hill and reined in to look down at the scene below. There before him lay the deserted ruins of his family's ranch. Since the night of the attack, he hadn't been able to think much about the Lazy W, but now it was time.

The Andersons had been good to him and his family over the years. While he'd been away, they'd been tending the stock and watching over things. Clint knew they'd be interested in buying the place, and he was ready to sell it to them for a fair price.

Clint planned to ride over and see them later that day after he'd met up with Captain Meyers at the Lazy W. It would be the first time they'd met face to face since he'd brought in the Tucker Gang.

Clint knew he was early for their meeting; he had planned it that way.

There was something he had to do while he was there at the ranch by himself.

Urging his horse on, Clint rode slowly down to the gravesite where his family and the ranch hands who'd been killed that night had been buried. He reined in nearby and dismounted, then walked slowly over to their graves. Deep, painful emotions filled him as he looked down at their markers.

Clint stopped before his father's grave. His heart ached as he bowed his head for a long moment. He finally looked up at the grave marker that read "Frank Williams" and nodded.

"I brought them in for you," he said aloud, wanting his father to know that he'd finished the job. "They went on trial, and the law took care of them. They've gone to meet their Maker."

Clint felt some satisfaction knowing the killers had paid the price for their deadly crimes, but even so, nothing was ever going to bring his family back.

He stood there for a moment longer, staring down at his father's marker, before moving on to stare down at his own.

Clint Williams
Born February 16, 1852
Died March 23, 1877

Clint knew that for all these months those words had been true. He had been dead inside—until Rachel had come to him and shown him that life was worth living again. By the grace of her presence, he had been able to go on. He was going to continue to follow his father's example and work hard to be the best Texas Ranger he could.

That was why he was there today.

Clint took down the marker that bore his name. He was back among the living.

"Clint?"

He turned to find Captain Meyers walking toward him. Clint went to greet him, and they shook hands.

"It's good to see you," the captain told Clint, looking him over.

"It's good to see you, too—especially under these circumstances."

"I'm sorry I couldn't meet with you sooner, but I was finishing up a case."

"That's all right," Clint said. "Everything has worked out just fine."

"I'll say. That was some good work you did, finding Pete Reynolds and bringing the whole Tucker Gang to justice." Captain Meyers reached in his pocket and took out Clint's Texas Ranger badge. He handed it to him. "It's time you started wearing this again. You should never have given it to me in the first place."

"It won't happen again."

"I'm counting on that," he told him. "By the way, congratulations on your marriage."

"Thanks. Rachel is the best thing that ever happened to me. She told me to thank you for the extra weeks I had off," Clint said.

"You're welcome. You earned it."

"I warned her not to get used to it, though."

"That's right. We need you. You're a good man, just like your father was."

"Thanks, Captain." Clint knew there was no higher compliment Meyers could have given him. Solemnly, Clint pinned his badge on his shirt.

Captain Meyers watched him and was glad to have him fully back with the Rangers.

"I see you took down the grave marker," he said, gesturing toward the place where Clint's false grave had been.

"Yes, I'm back among the living."

"Good, because I've got a new assignment for you."

The two Texas Rangers looked at each other and smiled as they started back to where they'd left their horses.

Epilogue

One Year Later

It was a beautiful day for a wedding. The church was crowded with guests. As the music began, the bride started down the aisle escorted by her father.

Nick stood with Reverend Hammond in front of the altar, watching Michelle make her way toward them. She was a vision of beauty in her white gown and veil, and Nick was thrilled that this day had finally come. Soon, very soon, she would be Mrs. Nick Evans.

Michelle's heart was racing as she clung to her father's supportive arm on their way up the aisle.

Today her dream was coming true.

Today she and Nick were getting married.

She looked up at Nick, standing so tall and handsome beside Reverend Hammond, and she knew he was the love of her life.

As she passed by the pew where Rachel was

sitting with Clint and her mother, she cast her friend a quick sidelong smile.

Rachel smiled back up at Michelle, truly thrilled for her friend on her wedding day. She had always expected to be Michelle's matron of honor, but her current delicate condition had kept that from happening. Rachel rested a loving hand on the mound of her stomach. It wouldn't be long now until her son or daughter was born. Rachel looked up at Clint and knew she loved him even more now than she had before—if that were possible.

Rachel turned her full attention back to the wedding. She watched with joy as Mr. Lofton lifted Michelle's veil and then kissed her on the cheek before handing her over into Nick's safekeeping.

"Take care of my daughter," he told Nick.

"I will, sir."

Mr. Lofton joined his wife in the first pew as the ceremony began.

Martin smiled down at the happy couple standing before him. "Dearly beloved, we are gathered here today to join in holy matrimony Michelle Lofton and Nicholas Evans."

Clint looked on as Nick and Michelle pledged their love and devotion to one another. He hoped their life together would be as wonderful as his own was with Rachel. At the thought, he took Rachel's hand in his. He would always be saddened that they hadn't been able to have a proper church wedding like this one. Still, he wouldn't have changed anything about their marriage. Everything had worked out just fine, and now

Defiant

with the baby due at any minute, he knew things would only get better.

"Do you, Michelle Lofton, take this man Nicholas Evans to be your lawfully wedded husband, to have and to hold from this day forward, for better or worse, in sickness and in health, for richer or poorer, until death do you part?"

"I do," Michelle answered with no hesitation.

"And do you, Nicholas Evans, take this woman Michelle Lofton to be your lawfully wedded wife, to have and to hold from this day forward, for better or worse, in sickness and in health, for richer or poorer, until death do you part?"

"I do," Nick answered him.

"You may place the ring on her finger," Reverend Hammond directed.

Nick did just that, marking Michelle as his own forever.

"I now pronounce you man and wife," the reverend concluded, giving them a warm smile. "You may kiss your bride."

Nick didn't need to be told twice. With everyone looking on, he took Michelle into his arms and kissed her.

"Ladies and Gentlemen, may I introduce to you—Mr. and Mrs. Nick Evans," the reverend announced.

Everyone was thrilled for them.

Michelle's mother was openly crying for joy in the front pew, knowing her daughter was going to live happily ever after with Nick, just as she had with her own beloved husband.

The music began again, and Nick and Michelle made their way down the aisle to start their life together as man and wife.

Clint and Rachel watched them pass, knowing they were perfect for each other.

"Have you ever regretted that we didn't have a big church wedding?" Clint asked as they slowly made their way out of the church.

Rachel looked up at him with a look of tenderness in her eyes. "It would have been nice, but, really, all that mattered was that we were together."

"So you don't think you missed out on anything, getting married the way we did?"

She gave him a teasing half smile as she answered for his ears only, "We had a wonderful wedding night—thanks to Michelle. What more did we need?"

At her words, Clint grinned down at her, remembering that exciting night. "You're right. It was wonderful."

They followed the crowd to the wedding reception in the church hall next door. The food was wonderful and the celebration was joyous.

When it came time for the bride and groom to dance together, Nick escorted his wife out to the center of the dance floor and took her in his arms.

"I love you," Michelle said breathlessly as she gazed up at her handsome husband.

Nick gave her a quick, soft kiss as they kept dancing. "I've been waiting for this moment for a long time."

"Me, too. This is my dream come true—being married to you."

Nick squired Michelle around the dance floor, thankful that he'd been blessed enough to have her come into his life.

When it was announced that other couples could join them on the dance floor, Clint looked over at Rachel.

"Shall we?" he invited, holding his hand out to her.

"I'd love to," she accepted. She wasn't about to miss out on the chance to dance at her best friend's wedding.

They had only been moving about the dance floor for a moment when Rachel felt the first pang. She frowned slightly, wondering at it. When it didn't happen again right away, she dismissed the feeling as just a normal ache or pain from her condition.

The dance ended, and they made their way back to the table to sit down. Clint left her there while he went to get them something to drink.

Rachel was talking with her mother when the pain returned, and her mother noticed the sudden change in her expression.

"Rachel, what is it?" Anne asked worriedly.

Rachel tried to smile, but it turned into more of a grimace as she put a hand on her stomach and answered, "I'm not sure, but I think it may be time."

"Oh, dear, we'd better get you home right away."

"I think you might be right."

Anne took charge. When Clint returned to the table with their drinks, she told him, "We need to leave."

"Why?"

"Your son or daughter is getting ready to make an appearance."

Clint had known the moment would come, but he was both shocked and delighted that it was going to be tonight. He took Rachel's arm. "Let me help you."

They exited the reception quietly, not wanting to detract from Michelle and Nick's big celebration.

Rachel was relieved when she was finally back home. Anne helped her into the bedroom and made sure she was comfortable before going to speak to her husband and Clint.

"Clint, you should go find the doctor and see how soon he can get here to help me. Martin, you just start praying that everything goes well."

The men did as they were ordered.

Clint returned with the doctor a short time later and then joined his father-in-law in the parlor to wait it out.

"I guess there's nothing we can do to help, is there?" he asked, pacing nervously around the room.

Martin smiled sympathetically. He remembered the night Rachel was born and understood his son-in-law's unease. "Sometimes waiting around is the hardest part, but what you're waiting for is more precious than any treasure you've ever known."

Clint knew Martin was right. He forced himself to stay calm and bide his time. He just hoped Rachel would be all right. Several times he heard her cry out in pain, and he started to go to her, only to be held back by his father-in-law.

Time passed slowly. It was in the late hours of the night that they finally heard the door open upstairs and footsteps coming down the hall.

Clint and Martin hurried to the door of the parlor to see the doctor descending the steps.

"How is Rachel?" Clint demanded.

"She's fine," the doctor answered, and then added, "And so is your son. Congratulations, Clint. It's a boy!"

"A boy—"

"That's right. Go on up. Rachel's asking for you."

Clint rushed upstairs.

Anne was just coming out of the bedroom as Clint reached the door. She didn't speak. She just smiled at him and held the door wide for him to go in. She closed it behind her as she left to give the new parents privacy.

Clint stood just inside the bedroom door, staring at Rachel as she lay in bed holding the baby.

"He's perfect, Clint," Rachel said, smiling up at him.

He moved to the bedside and knelt down to get his first look at his son. The chubby newborn with just a sprinkling of dark hair was resting quietly in his mother's arms.

"You're right. He is perfect," he said, awed by

the miracle before him. He lifted his gaze to look at Rachel. "And so are you. I love you."

Clint leaned over and kissed her.

"I love you, too." She smiled, then asked, "What are we going to name him?"

Not knowing if the baby was going to be a girl or a boy, they had never settled on a name ahead of time.

"I'd like to name him Frank, after my father," he answered solemnly. He could think of no better way to honor his father's memory.

Rachel gazed down at her son and said his name aloud for the first time. "Frank Williams."

At the sound of her voice, the infant opened his eyes to look up at her. Rachel bent down to press a gentle kiss on his cheek.

"Thank you for my son," she told Clint with heartfelt emotion.

Clint tenderly kissed Rachel. She was all that was beautiful in his life, and he was going to spend the rest of his days showing her and their son just how much he loved them.

BOBBI SMITH
HALFBREED WARRIOR

Hawk always knew he was different. Everywhere he went, people scorned him, feared him, hated him. He never expected to meet a woman like Randi. Her impulsive spirit and generous heart break through his reserve and make him want to love again. But he can't afford to get close to anyone. Not with the job he has to do.

Randi Stockton grew up around rough cowboys on her father's ranch. None have managed to win her love…until the mysterious stranger with the power to tame the legendary wild horse strode into her life. Randi knows he is a halfbreed, but something about him calls to her. The danger lurking in the shadows and canyons threatens to draw the two apart, but Randi knows in her heart that Hawk will always be her…*Halfbreed Warrior*.

- -

Dorchester Publishing Co., Inc.
P.O. Box 6640
Wayne, PA 19087-8640

_5396-9
$6.99 US/$8.99 CAN

Please add $2.50 for shipping and handling for the first book and $.75 for each additional book. NY and PA residents, add appropriate sales tax. No cash, stamps, or CODs. Canadian orders require an extra $2.00 for shipping and handling and must be paid in U.S. dollars. Prices and availability subject to change. **Payment must accompany all orders.**

Name: _____

Address: _____

City: _____ State: _____ Zip: _____

E-mail: _____

I have enclosed $_____ in payment for the checked book(s).

CHECK OUT OUR WEBSITE! www.dorchesterpub.com
____ *Please send me a free catalog.*

HAVEN
BOBBI SMITH
Writing as Julie Marshall

Darrell Miller is running from the ugliness his existence has become. He finds refuge from his terror in the last place he expected—a church. With the kind of people he's never known before, people whose lives will intertwine with his in a most unexpected way....

Jenny, a single mother determined to welcome her baby into the world with love and joy....

Dorothy, who counts desperately on faith to reshape her identity now that years of striving to be the perfect friend, wife and mother are made meaningless...

Joe, a friend to anyone in need, always ready to reach out a helping hand. If only he can find a way to share his belief that love and a faith in God can get anyone through the dark hours....

BRAZEN
BOBBI SMITH

Casey Turner can rope and ride like any man, but when she strides down the streets of Hard Luck, Texas, nobody takes her for anything but a beautiful woman. Working alongside her Pa to keep the bank from foreclosing on the Bar T, she has no time for romance. But all that is about to change....

Michael Donovan has had a burr under his saddle about Casey for years. The last thing he wants is to be forced into marrying the little hoyden, but it looks like he has no choice if he wants to safeguard the future of the Donovan ranch. He'll do his darndest, but he can never let on that underneath her pretty new dresses Casey is as wild as ever, and in his arms she is positively...*BRAZEN*.